7-28-17

Ruth -

Best Wishes

# If My People...

*Gary H. Baker*

*All characters in this book are fictitious.*
*Any resemblance to real persons,*
*living or dead is strictly coincidental.*

*Copyright © 2012 Gary H. Baker*
*All rights reserved.*

ISBN-10: 1478105348
EAN-13: 9781478105343

# Dedication

There are some men that defy an accurate description, classification, or maybe what might be called a metaphysical portrait – a study of their soul. Douglas Baker was not that kind of man. Douglas was my father's first cousin. To be sure, the two of them could spin some colorful and all too worldly stories about some of their escapades and adventures back in the day. But if you got Douglas talking about God… oh, you had better get your pen and notepad ready. He could take you places no ordained pulpit preacher could take you. His assertions about humankind and our relationship with The Father were always original and powerful; and he made authenticity and truth ripple through those assertions, sometimes thunder through them.

Before he passed away I told Douglas that wherever he was going, I'd be there, too. I wasn't really sure what I was trying to say, but he and I both knew what the words meant. That's the way things were when we talked together. I miss him a lot.

# Landstar

*About Landstar Independent Agent's Tony and Cayce Phillips (SFM)*

Tony joined Landstar in 1991 as an Independent Agent. Before becoming an agent he was an Over the Road owner operator for over 10 years. Tony left the road but not the industry. In his 20 years with Landstar, Tony has been recruiting owner operators, moving freight and building lasting relationships with his customers and owner ops.

His son Cayce joined him 9 years ago and now handles the day to day operations of the agency. Together Tony and Cayce work on recruiting new owner operators and sharing with them the Landstar Opportunity. Once an owner operator becomes a BCO leased on through their agency, Tony and Cayce work with them to ensure their success with Landstar as well as building lasting friendships between the BCO and their customers.

You can see Tony and Cayce most years at the Joplin 44 Petro Jamboree and can contact them by a phone call or email. Give Tony or Cayce a call if you want to see what makes Landstar one of the Best Owner Operator companies in the industry today.

Call  (800) 445-3638

Email  caycephillips@ymail.com

*Romans 10:9*
*If you confess with your mouth that Jesus is Lord*
*and believe in your heart that God raised him*
*from the dead, you will be saved.*

A special thanks to the good folks that made my Joplin book signing so enjoyable. Bob and Robin Johnson and Bob and Emma Slone.

# About Big Bubba Buck's Belly Busting BBQ Bliss

If you find yourself driving interstate 65 in Kentucky and you open your window and detect an irresistible barbeque aroma, you'll know you are close to Big Bubba's. And if you feel a sense of friendly southern hospitality magically tugging at you and leading you down the exit ramp at mile marker 65, Munfordville, and then pull you into Big Bubba's, don't panic. It happens to the JETS all the time. The JETS, you will learn, are a key component of the Truck Dreams story.

Come on in to Big Bubba's on your next trip through Kentucky, and like the JETS, say hello to Robert, April, Jordan, Marjorie, Amanda, and Cort. They will invite you to sign the JETS membership board. It might be the best feeling you've ever had while signing your name to something.

# About the North 40 Truck Stop

Eight miles west of the Tennessee River you'll see the big sign for it. Its exact location is Interstate 40 at mile marker 126 on the Music Highway between Nashville and Memphis. What will you find in this big southern truck stop? A warm welcome from the friendliest people I've ever met out on the road. You'll also find great food and a sense of peace and quiet that is sometimes hard to find around a truck stop. I write this in order to say thanks to the good folks that allow me to hang out at the North 40 and do an occasional book signing. So, the next time you're in the neighborhood, stop by and say hello to Kendra, Betty, Kayla, and myself, and if you think about it, check to see if Paul Remers or Rambo is there. If they are, tell them, "Welcome home and thanks for your service."

I'll see you somewhere out on that big road.

# Forward

In the hopes of providing an explanation for the unconventional format of the two books you are about to read, let me offer this: The first book, *If My People ...* is a work of fiction. The second book, *The 1986 Just Say No Marathon, Running and Walking with God* is nonfiction. It was written approximately seven years before *If My People ...* was written. As the title points out, *The 1986 Just Say No Marathon, Running and Walking with God* deals with actual events that occurred before and during the year 1986. I tried my very best to write the story exactly as it happened.

The fiction book , *If My People ...* was pure joy to write . Without a doubt, I had more fun in its inception and construction than anything I've done previously. On the other hand, writing *The 1986 Just Say No Marathon, Running and Walking with God*, was a difficult experience for me. I was forced to reexamine several painful chapters of my life, and that is never an easy thing to do.

Part of my thinking on putting the two books together is that it should enable the reader to enjoy the fiction from the unique vantage point of seeing how its birth might have come directly from the nonfiction event that unfolded about twenty years earlier. I'm not sure how many times writers have used such a tactic to tell their stories. Frankly, I'm not aware of any who have employed my exact model – placing both stories in the same book. I'll leave that for the literary historians to quibble over.

It has also occurred to me that certain readers might ask, "Well, which should I read first, the fiction or the nonfiction?" That's easy; read the fiction first, *If My People ...*

GHB June 2012

*If My people who are called by My name will humble themselves, and pray and seek My face, and turn from their wicked ways, then I will hear from heaven, and will forgive their sin and heal their land.*

*2 Chronicles 7:11*

# CHAPTER 1

Father C.J. didn't look like an addict, and he wasn't. His drug of choice didn't require him to steal and rip people off. But what he was about to do would prove he could be every bit as dangerous as the worst heroin addict in Chicago. He goosed the gas a little and watched the speedometer hit ninety. The traffic in the right lanes on the 294 toll-way looked to Father C. J. like they were sitting still. He'd get off 294 in about two miles and slow down enough to worm his way in through the side streets to the air cargo depots. There he'd gun it through the security gate which opened up to O'Hare's intricate complex of runways. Once out on a main runway, he'd see if he could scoot up under an unsuspecting airliner just touching down. Father C. J.'s drug of choice blocked his ability to discern right from wrong.

*This is it. Turn here. Follow the signs to air cargo. What if the pilot sees me and pulls up? He still might crash. Yes, he probably will. His air speed will be too low. I could kill two hundred people, maybe more if he hits another plane. Tantalizing! There it is, the row of air cargo termi-nals, trucks all backed up to their docks – United, American, Air France, China Air, Lufthansa,* and all the rest. *The security gate will be down at the end.* Father C. J.'s mind focused on an even deadlier scenario. *Divert a landing so it will hit a terminal. I could kill a thousand! Here's the gate. Only light weight wooden barrier arms. One guard in the shack controlling the arms up or down. Big sign says STOP – show two photo I D's. Sorry mister, I won't be able to stop and chat. I've got people to kill.*

Father C. J. approached the lowered wooden arm on the secu-rity gate slowly. At thirty-five feet away he stomped the accelerator. Crashing through the gate, he looked in the guard house and saw the guard just raising his head from a security screen.

*Get out on the runway! Can't waste time!*

No sooner had that thought careened through his mind than an airport security pick up truck turned on his flashers and siren and gave chase. Then an airport security van came out of nowhere. It was a hundred yards to his right. Father C. J.'s inability to discern right from wrong, this time, led him to another killing decision. He aimed his convertible right at the van. He was going 70. Time didn't exist anymore. Everything was slow, stop and go movie frame shots. There the van was – dead ahead. The last thing Father C. J. saw the driver do was rip the steering wheel hard left, just missing him, but exploding the van into the security pick up behind him.

*The runway, there, follow that taxi way on out.*

He could see a very low jet liner approaching from the west, maybe a mile out.

*That's the one! Twenty seconds, that's all I have. Twenty seconds to get out there!*

He stomped the gas again. This time there were no flashing light, siren screaming security vehicles chasing him or trying to cut him off.

*Five planes in the taxi-way, if I can ram the left wing landing gear of the bird coming in, I bet the plane will drop on that side, and the uncontrolled skid will aim it right at those five, all of them full of passengers, and full of fuel. Ten seconds, here it comes, almost down. The pilot will never see me. He'll be busy looking straight ahead.*

At five seconds the pilot did see something on the ground approaching his aircraft from the left. He didn't hesitate for an instant. His right hand rammed the throttle forward and simultaneously hit the TOGA button (the take-off and go around switch). Half a second later his left hand pulled the yoke toward his seat in order to orient the elevators to pull the nose up. But at about the time he wanted to see the nose coming up, instead he felt a solid jolt of vibration run through the left wing to the fuselage. Then the runway in front of him was veering off to the right and he already knew there was nothing he could do to avoid the line- up of passenger filled aircraft on the taxi-way. The last thing he heard was the co-pilot in the seat to the right calling out his wife's and children's names.

* * *

Monty Relinger was a highly intelligent thirty-five year old systems analyst. His wife Betsy and his eight year old daughter Kimberly depended on him to be a solid provider. Betsy's family life as a child hadn't been very good. Her father was as close to being an alcoholic as one could get and still not be considered an alcoholic by most of his friends, but not by all of them. Betsy remembered junior high and later in high school, she was always just a bit out of step with the popular girls, the cute girls who always seemed to be on top of their game.

That all changed when she met Monty in college. They had hit it off very nicely from the first date. Monty had such a protecting and mature personality – just what Betsy needed. And he was smart too. She really liked that. Yes, he experimented with marijuana a little and he liked to drink with some of his friends occasionally, but none of it was over the top.

After they married, three years after college, Monty grew comfortably into the role of protector and provider for Betsy, and a year later, for their daughter Kimberly. Monty was a thinker. He loved to pull Betsy or anyone else he could into discussions on philosophy. He could detail all of the Greek Classics, and on into modern philosophers as well. Monty had a keen interest in the morality of civilizations. Boiled down, he was always after what makes right "right", and what makes wrong "wrong." That was the way he always set it up. The truth is there were not a lot of people he could get hooked into such a conversation, but none of it affected Monty. He never wavered from his responsibility of being the bread winner, the solid rock for his young family. With a loving wife, a bright, loving eight year old daughter, a good job, life was worth living for systems analyst Monty Relinger.

Monty was out with the guys one afternoon drinking a couple of beers after a softball game.

One of Monty's ball playing buddies was reaching in his front pocket and  pulled out a small packet. "Hey guys, let's plant a seed. I've got six seeds."

"What are you talking about? Plant a seed? With that?" Monty was looking at the small packet in his friend's hand. The other four were looking also and seemed equally befuddled.

Finally Mike, the guy who produced the packet from his pocket, could plainly see that none of his friends knew what he was talking about – "plant a seed."

"Where have you guys been? None of you have planted a seed yet? Look, it's easy." Mike opened the packet and removed a tiny aspirin or something resembling an aspirin, only smaller.

"Just pop it in. It will dissolve in five seconds. They call it a seed." Mike placed the tiny aspirin looking seed in his mouth and smiled at them.

"Okay, we get it. You've just gone sixties on us. You just dropped a tab of acid."

"No, guess again." Mike was still smiling broadly.

"It's a placebo. We all take one and our cares will vanish."

"Nope, but you're getting closer."

Monty spoke up again, "You have obviously just taken some kind of a drug. Let's see, I bet some crazy Berkley professor has finally developed the perfect synthetic to marijuana. He's gone way past the R and D of the medical marijuana. The "seed", I'll bet, has been refined and perfected to the highest laboratory standards. It will produce the ultimate high but with none of the annoying side effects of old timey Mary Jane. No bloodshot, dilated eyes, no paranoia, no uncontrollable munchies, no lethargy, and no sleepiness. The seed, I'm sure you are about to tell us, is the ultimate in smooth and easy highs with absolutely no negative side effects."

"You got it dead on. Monty, you are a trip. You knew all along. Here, have a seed." Mike extended the packet toward Monty.

"No way Jose'. I don't know a thing. I was just putting you on."

"Well," Mike said seriously, "You couldn't have put it any better. They call the stuff seeds. It hit the streets maybe three months ago. By now you can get it just about anywhere."

"I guess the family life has sheltered me a bit from the latest druggie's fad on the street. No disrespect intended. I'll tell you what. If all these guys try this new seed, and give me a good report, then no problem, I'll try it too."

Mike gave the five remaining seeds to his pals, Monty included. The other four had taken their seed in the next week and each one dutifully reported to Monty that it had been the smoothest and best high they ever had. Two of the guys told Monty the same thing. "Now I know why they call it the ultimate high. I felt in total control. At the same time it was an incredible mind blowing experience."

At twelve noon on the next Saturday, Monty found himself home alone. Betsy and Kimberly were eighty miles away at Betsy's sister's house. Monty was just finishing up a little yard work. He went in the house and poured a huge glass of iced tea. He started to turn the T V on and sit down, but then he walked through the family room and on into the master bedroom. He looked for the seed where he thought he had placed it inside a coat pocket, and then he remembered he had left it in the glove compartment of his car. He went outside to get the seed, and when he found it, he placed it under his tongue.

Mike was right. In five seconds it had dissolved. By one o'clock Monty had driven his car sixteen miles across town where he knew there was a major gasoline distributor located. He waited outside the gate and watched as two tanker trucks were a hundred yards inside and topping off their 12,000 gallon tanks. The first tanker approached the outbound gate and the electronic gate opened to let him exit the terminal and start his run to eight local gas stations.

Monty waited for the second tanker to come out, and then he followed behind the tanker. Monty turned off right, then a quick left. He gunned it up the street three blocks, made a left, and then another quick left. The tanker was lumbering along, coming his way, two blocks ahead. Monty sped his car up again, and now waited for the tanker to stop at the intersection dead ahead. When the tanker stopped, Monty came across the intersection and rammed the tanker head on, but not going very fast. He fell out of the door and lay prostrate on the pavement.

The truck driver thought he had seen every kind of idiotic wreck that a drunk could cause. But he'd never seen a drunk ram a tanker, *his tanker*, head on. He climbed down to check on the poor fool. There the drunk lay, next to his open door, on the street. The tanker driver approached the heap of alcohol wasted bone and flesh and was bending over to raise the drunk's head to see if he was conscious.

Monty kicked hard, straight up into the driver's groin. He hit the driver solid, right between his legs. The driver toppled over and was making a good bit of noise.

Monty jumped up and ran to the gasoline tanker and climbed in. He backed it up, and then swung it around his car and the driver still suffering on the pavement.

In twenty minutes he was nearing the town's recreation complex. It was a state of the art complex that any town would be proud of – six little league baseball fields, three regulation baseball fields, soccer fields, large snack stands, volleyball, and a nice pool way down on the end.

The designers of the complex had placed the six little league baseball fields, which could be used for youth softball as well, twenty feet down below the parking areas. In fact, a rather steep bank with steps and wheelchair access was the only way to get down to the fields. The design was implemented with tournament play as the main objective – all the fields would be very close together. In fact that is exactly what was going on today – a national ten year old girls' softball tournament. Teams from twelve states were participating and at the moment there were six games in progress. Including players, officials, coaches, parents and other fans, there were probably eight or nine hundred human beings down in there, twenty feet below the parking lots.

Monty entered the crowded recreation complex and drove slowly toward the rim of the six sunken softball fields. Monty was thinking, *get right on the edge of the rim, jump out, open the valves, drive the perimeter of the rim, the gas will run down the hill and be all around them, light this cigarette lighter, toss it out the window, and get out of here.*

The organizers of the girls' softball tournament had hired two off-duty police officers as security for the event. Young traffic patrol officer Ken Marcum was down below, behind the fence behind home plate on field number two where the Tulsa Tornadoes were beating the Joliet Bombers six to four in the top of the 5th.

When Marcum looked up and saw the tanker, its tires slightly over the edge of the rim, he smelled the gasoline first, then he saw it flowing out rapidly down the hill toward the bleachers.

*Oh my God!* He started screaming, "Get outa' the stands! Get outa' the stands! Get on the field!" He began madly chasing everyone away from the hillside.

He was doing a good job of getting them out of the track of the gasoline which was flowing down onto field two. But by now the tanker had sped up and was halfway around the rim, gasoline drenching everything in its path all the way to the ball fields. By now everyone in the complex knew something was dreadfully wrong, even the little ten year old girls out on the playing fields. But no one knew what to do. Panic was spreading. Many people actually started running up the hill, through the cascading gasoline flowing down.

Now Monty was all the way around the rim. He lit the lighter and intended to toss it out the window, but when the spark first hit, that was the end of Monty's world, the end of his quest for what makes right "right", and what makes wrong "wrong". It was the end of the softball tournament and the end of the recreation complex.

# CHAPTER 2

*Somewhere in the Rocky Mountains in Colorado*

Thadeus Pender Wiggins placed a wad of Red Man chewing tobacco between his gums and upper lip back in the corner of his mouth. He looked around the big campfire and reflected on how good it felt to be out here on this night with his friends. They were all there, the nucleus of the JETS: Old Soft Shoe, Jabez, Toby, Windjammer, Big Montana, Whiplash, Dinky, Daffy, Doolittle, Lugnut, and Turbo. Thadeus could tell you some amazing stories about these Christian truck drivers. Their tightly knit brotherhood was a lot more about praying for each other and always searching for a way to do God's work than it was of seeking attention or making a lot of noise about religion. Whether they sought it or not, the activities they sometimes engaged in automatically brought them plenty of attention. As a JET, Jesus Express Trucker, they often times found themselves pitted against evil forces, and they weren't about to back away from it.

The JETS could also tell some pretty amazing stories about Thadeus Pender Wiggins. After all, he was one of them.

Oh, it was a fine night! Thadeus, whom everyone simply called T. P., felt like a tremendous link of camaraderie existed between all of the truckers out here around this campfire. And it did. There was Toby Etheridge, T. P.'s cousin, a man who nearly went off the deep end following that infamous day of 9-11-01. And there was Jabez. He was such an extraordinary mix of spiritual being and mortal man that none of the JETS, including T. P. himself, could actually decide which one Jabez was – angel or man? Jabez was responsible for leading Toby away from a plot that Toby had nearly carried out to mass murder seven hundred Muslims in Dearborn, Michigan. And of course, over there across the campfire, drinking a cup of coffee and sitting next to Old Soft Shoe, was Big Montana. The big ex-lumberjack turned trucker had served eight long years in a Montana prison for a series of rapes he had committed. The JETS helped him extricate himself from more evil doings in the form of Big Montana's involvement in an international sex slave ring. Big Montana was able to turn his life around. Some would have thought it impossible, but Big Montana proved them wrong.

Another trucker seemingly unfit for status as a JET was Windjammer, the ex-Marine, ex-big-wave surfer.  Windjammer spent twenty-five years running from a murder charge that he had nothing to do with. The likelihood of his becoming an over-the-road trucker who loved Jesus was not very strong;  however, like Big Montana, he proved everyone wrong.

As T. P. continued looking around the campfire, his gaze finally rested on Old Soft Shoe, reputedly the oldest active over-the-road truck driver in America. By Old Soft Shoe's estimate, he'd logged over eleven million miles, and he'd tell you in a New York minute, that he planned on logging a couple more million miles before he was put out to pasture.

*Yes,* T. P. was thinking, *what a crew of unlikely candidates to carry out God's will. All of them maybe, except Jabez. No way could anyone mistake the Godliness in our leader.*

*What about myself? Would people see in me the same fervor to do God's will they see in Jabez? I doubt it. It would be pretty hard explaining myself, my background, to anyone other than the JETS. No problem with them. They understand. But what about ordinary folks?*

T. P. was right.  Who would believe the bizarre, land mine riddled trail his life had taken? Born in the Deep South to a father who taught him from an early age how to survive off the land, he was a legend around Lake Thomas, Alabama. Hunting, fishing, and living in the woods all came as natural to him as breathing. Back then he was Ronnie "Coon Dog" Matlock. In Vietnam he was Navy SEAL, Petty Officer 1st Class, Ronnie Matlock. On his second tour in Nam, he was shot down forty miles north of the DMZ, captured and held prisoner in a bamboo cage for two weeks. He killed an NVA guard, escaped to the jungle and found his way back to friendly forces. The next fourteen years took him to all corners of the globe, usually performing super sensitive secret SEAL missions. Nineteen years into his military career, Ronnie "Coon Dog" Matlock asked the Navy to allow him to be stationed close to his home in Lake Thomas, Alabama. His father was dying and Coon Dog wanted to make sure he would be able to be at the funeral. When the Navy refused the reasonable request, he went AWOL knowing full well he would be forfeiting his government pension. The next twenty years as a civilian didn't get any easier. Ronnie became good friends with Mr. James Beam and Mr. Jack Daniels, and as a result left three ex-wives in the wake.

After that he followed his cousin Toby into over-the-road trucking and soon after became a JET. Coon Dog played a key role in Big Montana's escape from the international sex slave ring. The boss of the sex slave operation went to prison but was able to grease the hands of some lofty politicians and only serve a two year sentence. When he came out of prison he was determined to get even with Coon Dog.

The crime boss was Ted Sciafano, and his family ties with the Mafia were thick as knots. Sciafano set up a double rape-murder and framed Coon Dog by extracting DNA sperm from him and planting it on the two victims. When Coon Dog was convicted, he was sentenced to life on the banishment island off the coast of Mexico. The United States had recently enacted the banishment law. Its reason for existence was to provide a real deterrent for "would be" criminals. If you were found guilty of any number of heinous crimes, you were transported to Isla De Lejarnia in the Pacific Ocean. There you were put ashore by U. S. Marines, and there you would die. If you were going to eat and survive, you'd better be a skilled hunter and woodsman. The government provided no food, clothing, shelter, medicine, or access to the outside world. In effect you were dropped into a cro magnum world.

The few who lasted very long did so because they became cannibals. Coon Dog didn't plan on eating humans, but he did plan on escaping from the island. It took him two years to plan his escape and to build the raft he would use to execute the escape.

The sequence of events that led to his escape would seem unbelievable, and the escape itself even more unbelievable, but then again, Coon Dog *was* ex U. S. Navy SEAL.

When he finally got settled back into a new life in the continental United States with a new identity, his name was William for a short period of time. When he paid good money for a complete new legal identity with all the bells and whistles – birth certificate, social security number, family background, work history, and new finger prints, he told the broker he purchased his new life from that he wanted to be Thadeus Pender Wiggins.

"No problem. You can be Ghingis Khan if you want to," the broker had said.

*No, no ordinary people would believe my life story, or the fact that as a JET I am just like everyone else out here around this campfire – sold out to God The Father, Jesus The Christ, and The Holy Spirit.*

Jabez and Toby were watching the campfire from twenty feet away. Toby had sensed that Jabez was uneasy about something and followed the old Appalachian spiritual man away from the fire to a rock outcropping.

"What is it?" Toby asked.

"Can't say. I've been feeling it for a while now. It started before that plane crash in Chicago. Yesterday, before that gasoline burned up them little girls and all those others, it came on real strong."

Toby didn't say anything. They were both gazing at the twinkling canopy of stars in the Colorado night. They moved another hundred feet away from the campfire where the JETS were gathered, talking easily, drinking coffee, and seemingly content with the world.

But Toby and Jabez were not content. There was something stirring in them that didn't feel good at all.

Finally Toby said, "Yeah, I felt it too. I didn't know what it was at the time, but when that plane crashed, I was in Iowa. I pulled the truck over on the shoulder and just sat there for a half hour. Then I turned the radio on and the reports of the crash started coming in. Yesterday the same thing; I pulled over because I just *knew* something had happened. I turned the radio on and they were talking about that gasoline tanker at the softball fields."

Neither man said anything for a long time. They were still gazing above, the glare of the campfire not a factor so far away. They were trying to read the stars, read the message God had for them.

"Get the others. Bring them out here," Jabez said. Toby went back to the campfire and gathered the JETS and they all walked back to where Jabez was standing, his gaze still unwavering from the pallet of twinkling stars above. "Look at them," he said. "What do they remind you of?"

It was Daffy, in his slow Georgia mountain twang, who answered up. "Why Mr. Jabez, ah reckon they reminds me of a big ol' bucket of seeds that God done tossed out up yonder, and with just a wisp of His heavenly breathe …. why He scattered 'em all about. Yessir, that's what it looks like to me – seeds."

# CHAPTER 3

It was two weeks after a China Air 777 crashed at O'Hare killing a total of seven hundred eighty-five, and it was thirteen days after six hundred and forty-six died at the Naperville, Illinois recreation complex. The country was on threat level red status.

Two other attacks had been stopped by alert security personnel. The seventy-two story Bank of America Plaza in Dallas was the target of an arsonist. If he'd been successful, the arsonist might have killed eight or nine hundred or more. And in Palo Alto, California a lone attacker launched a mortar attack on a soccer tournament. If he'd know what he was doing, he might have killed a lot of people. He was stopped after two mortar rounds found open areas out on one of four soccer fields. Eight people were wounded, three of them seriously, but no one was killed.

FBI special agent Bart Duncan had been a tight end at Michigan twenty years ago. Undersized at six-three, two thirty-five, he managed to leave a playing legacy that fans wouldn't forget for a long time. The years had perhaps taken some of his speed but not his mental or physical toughness. He entered the room at an FAA building near O'Hare, and the buzz around the room subsided. He scanned the room as he walked to the front. He recognized many faces in the crowd of federal officials and investigators. "Thank you all for coming. I think most everyone knows each other. Let's get right to it. Two new attacks since O'Hare and Naperville - the bank building in Dallas, and the Briarcliff soccer complex in Palo Alto. The suspects in both of these attacks have cooperated fully. At this point we have no reason to believe they are aligned with any known domestic or foreign terrorist organizations. Dallas and Palo Alto appear to be two random cases of attempted mass murder. At this stage of our investigation we have failed to identify a motive in either of these two attacks. The suspects have convinced us, so far, they didn't know what they were doing, or why they were doing it."

"Obviously, we don't have the luxury of questioning the two suspects from the O'Hare and Naperville attacks. The license plate at O'Hare quickly led to Father C. J. O'Ryan, a Catholic Priest. DNA from his remains verifies his identity. The attacker at Naperville, likewise, made no attempts at hiding or confusing his identity. A bright young family man, Monty Relinger evidently commandeered a gasoline tanker and took it to the softball complex in order to burn to death six hundred forty-six people." Duncan stopped to sip from a water bottle.

"People, all four of these attacks have many clues that might lead us to put Robot Mass Murder – RMM as a leading candidate for motive. I know you are all familiar with the theory of what a RMM might look like. I want to have Dr. Kate Wenderson walk you through it, just to make sure we're on the same page."

Duncan glanced over at Wenderson and stepped aside as she came to the front of the room. An FBI profiler for nine years, Dr. Wenderson was well respected in the business and a renowned author of several criminal psychology text books. She, like Duncan, got right to the point. "Essentially, RMM requires two players. One is the controller, the entity that conceives the crime and plans it out but does not execute the crime. The second player is the drone. The drone, as the name would suggest, is the entity that will actually commit the crime, usually in a remote control mode. That is, the controller will manipulate the drone by any number of devices. Hypnosis is the device that we usually think about, but other devices could be utilized. Subconscious stimulation directive has been used successfully by controllers in several high exposure cases we all know about. This is not the same as hypnosis. Electro shock stimulus has been successful particularly in the old days with the KGB. Also, there are some researchers that think certain drugs might be effective devices to control a drone. Blackmail and various forms of extortion have been used effectively."

Dr. Wenderson looked to Duncan to see if he wanted more from her.

He said, "Thank you Kate. If you would stay for a while when we're done, I'm sure there will be some questions for you."

He was about to tell the group of assembled investigators the content of the wire from the White House he received just an hour ago, but another special agent hurried into the room and said, "Sir, I'm sorry to interrupt, but I think you'll want to see this." He went to a panel of switches and live news feeds began playing on three different TV monitors on the wall.

The news anchor , Diane Warner with Affiliated National News - AFN, was professional and composed, but you could tell that she was having a hard time keeping up with the flow of information that she was reporting.

"And now, this just in from our affiliate in Philadelphia: A commuter train has been deliberately derailed as it approached a major loading platform near downtown Philadelphia. Eyewitnesses say they saw a man, operating a backhoe, destroy a section of rails just seconds before the train would have passed. The resulting crash took out another commuter train and damaged the loading dock. Authorities in Philadelphia estimate more than a hundred injuries and have confirmed twenty-three fatalities. Our own Jacob Emsley is live in Philadelphia. Jacob, what can you tell us?"

"Diane, the scene here is a tangled wreckage of rail cars and a heart wrenching display of human carnage. Emergency crews are still putting out fires as they search the rubble for survivors and victims. Police tell me they have a man in custody who was operating a backhoe alongside the inbound track. He is the same man whom eyewitnesses saw destroying the track just seconds before the inbound commuter derailed. The man has been transported to Mt. Tabor Medical Center with serious but not life threatening injuries."

"Thank you Jacob, we will have to get back to you. We have ....
let's see, yes, we have another breaking story just coming in." She was
being cued by her producer on her earphone and the teleprompter.
The story she was being diverted to was the fourth implausible and
unexplainable disaster she had reported in just the last six minutes.
The first was a shooting at Glendale High School in Cleveland. A
math teacher had gunned down eighteen people in cold blood and
another thirty wounded. Then, thirty-seven business seminar attend-
ees in Boise, Idaho had been trapped in a meeting hall and subjected
to carbon monoxide poisoning. Half of them died.

The producer's voice was pounding her from the hidden earphone. "GO. GO, GO." It was her cue to pick up the pace with the
script on the teleprompter. Her professionalism and composure were
definitely under attack, and a thought raced through her mind – *this
is my Walter Cronkite moment. I will be remembered the rest of my life
for what I say and do in the next thirty seconds, just like Cronkite when
he reported, "President Kennedy died at 1 p.m. Central Standard Time."*

She focused her eyes on the teleprompter and began reading the
words, "From St. Louis, we have just learned that a large aircraft has
crashed into Busch Stadium. The St. Louis Cardinals were hosting
the Cincinnati Reds, and ...."

"No, No, No! Oh my God, No!" Diane fought to regain her
composure, but the tears had their own destiny and they began
flowing.

The producer had his fingers on the controls and could have
switched away from her at any time, but he knew he wouldn't.

She was now the focus. Worldwide, Diane Warner was now the
focus. The world held its breath. The TV screens were silent. The
whole world was watching her.

Ten seconds went by. Twenty seconds. Silence. Thirty seconds.
Then her eyes went straight at the camera and she began to speak,
simultaneously mopping at the cascading tears with the back of her
hand, smearing and streaking her eye liner all over her face.

"Ladies and gentlemen, my husband, Troy Warner, is the starting pitcher for the Reds in today's game."

After she said it, she paused a moment, and went back to the teleprompter. "The St. Louis Cardinals were hosting the Cincinnati Reds, and authorities in St. Louis estimate the crowd at Busch Stadium was …." She couldn't say *was*. "The crowd at Busch Stadium *is* twenty-nine thousand. At this point there has been no identification of the aircraft or speculation as to terrorist involvement in this tragedy." Now she looked away from the teleprompter and she could hear the producer in the earphone, "Keep reading, keep reading," he demanded.

She'd done all the teleprompter reading she was going to do for this day, but she wasn't going to stop talking. "Tragedy? No, I don't think so. Attacked? Yes. A tragedy is something that could have been prevented, isn't it? Let's look at this for what it is. We are under attack. Look at the events of the last two weeks. Random tragedy? No. It's impossible these things could be happening at random. We are coming undone. There is something wrong. There is something amiss in our society. There is an evil on the loose."

The producer heard enough. He did a voice over, "Now we take you back to Cleveland where our John Randleson is standing by with more information on the shootings at Glendale High School."

Diane Warner crumpled the notes and script on the desk she had been broadcasting from, and threw them on the floor. She marched into the control room and stomped right up in the producer's face and backhanded him across his mouth as hard as she could. "You no good slime ball. Find yourself a new anchor."

There were no more bizarre attacks that day. FBI Special Agent Bart Duncan and the rest of the assembled investigators were breaking up. He still had the wire from the White House and shared it with Dr. Kate Sanderson. It was addressed to Duncan. She unfolded it and read: "I want to thank you for the quick response you and your team are taking to get to the bottom of the two horrific attacks two weeks ago and the two more recent thwarted attacks. Everyone here in the Executive Branch expects your mission to be completed successfully and in a timely manner. Although we must recognize the possibility of similar attacks in the future, it is my personal belief that we have seen the last of them. "Copy Cat" is, in my opinion, written all over these events. Again, we expect your report on a final explanation as to the motive of these attacks to be forthcoming. God bless America!"

Dr. Wenderson looked up from the wire and offered Bart Duncan a look of incredulous disbelief, "What planet is this clown from? Diane Warner has it dead on. There is an evil that has been loosed upon us."

She was correct, but the problem was that none of them knew what the evil was.

# CHAPTER 4

*Near San Diego, California, three weeks after the initial attacks in*
*Chicago and Naperville:*

Three miles to go. How sweet it is! Endorphins kicked in four miles
ago. Running with no pain. Pain? What is that? Running as high as
*a kite is more like it. When the runner's high kicks in, it really kicks in!*

Chris Remington usually had a steady stream of positive mental
images flowing through his head when he was out on a ten miler.
Today was no different. The blue Pacific Ocean dwarfed his thin five
foot ten inch frame. If someone had been looking down at him from
the cliffs above, a half mile away, he was no more than a speck as he
ran smoothly and confidently with the endless blue behind him.

Days like this are what distance runners live for. Body and mind
in perfect tune, a rhythmic free flow of energy, movement, and
psyche. Many times Chris entered an almost trance-like state. Not
a trance of deadened sensory awareness, just the opposite. It was a
trance of heightened sensory awareness. Seeing, smelling, hearing,
and feeling all seemed to be elevated when on a good training run.
In fact, experienced long distance runners know that you have to
treat the "runner's high" carefully. You cannot let it take control. You
can't let its influence trick you into things you should be wary of,
like maybe stretching a great ten miler into a physically damaging
twenty miler.

In Chris Remington's case, he was pretty good at reading his
body. If something didn't feel right, he would stop running and
stretch the problem area thoroughly and give it a good massage
treatment.

Another thing he did while running was to recite certain man-
tras that brought his breathing, stride, and mind into a yoga-like
harmony. "I am a winner, I will not quit, I am with God" was one

he used when he faced difficult challenges. That particular mantra, repeated over and over again, had gotten him over many tough mountain climbs. Another mantra he used when he needed to back off mentally and give his brain some relaxation was "I am the wind". This always had an immediate calming effect. His stride smoothed out, and his breathing became almost effortless.

*Two miles to go. I'll bet Cindy's got a taco casserole for dinner tonight. Got to wash her car. I told her I'd do it this weekend. And Charly, he'll want to jog around the yard a couple of laps. He's a pretty good runner for four years old. Must have got it from Cindy. Ha!"*

And so Chris Remington, about to conclude another ten mile training run, his thoughts now turning to family, was about to receive a direct communication from God.

*A mile and a half to go. Start backing the pace down. Use the last mile as recovery. Whoooaa! What's that?"*

He was coming up on a two acre patch of wildflowers between the cliffs and himself. He'd seen them many times before, their tiny blue and honey golden petals creating a lagoon of color at about knee high.

SIT DOWN!

Chris obeyed the command. Where was it coming from? Himself? Inside himself? No, it was coming from the sea. Actually he wasn't sure where it was coming from, but he stopped running and at first went to his knees, then to a sitting position. He bent over and took his left foot in his hand pretending to stretch his left Achilles tendon. He knew there was nothing tightening up in his leg, but he was confused about the instructions to sit.

SIT STILL! BE QUIET!

Again he obeyed the command. This time, he knew for sure, it wasn't himself the command came from.

He sat still and was quiet. His breathing was slowing down, and he felt the sweat running off his body. A lively breeze picked up from the ocean and was getting stronger. A minute later it was a whirlwind, blowing sand and anything else around in an accelerated flurry. It didn't last long. When it subsided, Chris got to his feet and noticed that his sweat soaked skin was nearly covered with golden brown seeds from the wildflowers. Seeds.

*What just happened? What is going on? I didn't really hear the instructions to sit down. I felt them! Look at these seeds all over me. What's up with that?*

And then it hit him. He knew where the instructions came from. And he knew what the seed shower was about. Most importantly, he knew what he was supposed to do, how God wanted him to respond to these strange events.

# CHAPTER 5

Thadeus Pender Wiggins, T.P. to those who knew him, was pulling his eighteen wheeler off the interstate at the 65 yard sticker on Interstate 65 in the Bluegrass State. He turned right on 31 and drove the half mile to Big Bubba Buck's Belly Bustin' Barbecue Bliss. That's seven B's.

T.P. parked the truck and was entering the restaurant from the back door where all the truck drivers entered. Tourist and locals usually came in the front door.

"Hey T.P., how ya' doing?" The friendly waitress brought him a cup of coffee.

"Hangin' in there like a hair in a biscuit I reckon."

"Well I'm glad to hear it. What are you having?"

"Let me have the hickory smoked ribs, some fried green 'maters, corn on the cob, and maybe a little nanna nanna puddin'".

"Comin' right up."

T.P.'s phone went off, "Hello."

"T.P., this is Chris Reminton. Are you sitting down?"

"I sure am. How you doin' Chris?"

"Oh man, I've never been better, but I've got something to tell you!"

"You sound a little agitated, sort 'a like the long tailed cat in a room full of rocking chairs. Go ahead and let her roll. What'cha got?"

"It's big. It's real big. I was going to drive all the way back east to tell you, but I couldn't wait. I had to call."

"You got my undivided attention young feller. What's going on?"

"Okay, you know all of these recent attacks on totally innocent Americans; you know how everyone is at a loss to explain what's going on? The government doesn't have a clue. The only thing they do know is that Muslim terrorists don't seem to be behind the attacks. Random homegrown terrorist is the only theory they will even take a stab at. Am I right? Are you with me?"

T.P answered him, "Yeah, I'm with you. I agree. Go on."

"This is going to be hard to explain. Bear with me. I just got back home from a ten mile run. I was on an isolated beach. God talked to me out there. I know it was God. It was incredible. At first I didn't understand what was happening, but then it all came clear. The attacks, I know what's causing them. I don't know exactly how it works. I don't know the timing or understand the why, but I know for sure what causes the attacks." Chris stopped and waited for T.P.'s response.

T.P.'s mind was racing, but nothing he'd heard so far had surprised him. After all, when it came to far-out spiritual adventure, when it came to six-man shared dreams orchestrated by a dead American Indian shaman named Lonely Bear- Brave Bear, Chris Remington was right in the middle of it. It would be no trouble at all to now hear Chris say 'God told me what is causing the attacks', and no trouble at all to believe every word of it.

T.P. recalled his escape from the banishment island. Chris Remington was the then twenty-three year old sailor that made it possible. How T.P. (then Coon Dog) and Chris were pulled together in that unbelievable series of events is a mind bender for the ages. Yet, it happened. And in no small part did it happen by the dead shaman who befriended T.P. Lonely Bear-Brave Bear met his death early on in the tale, but would not go away. His leading T.P., Chris, and a handful of the JETS in shared dreams is what paved the way for T.P.'s escape.

T.P. had no illusions about the veracity of what Chris just told him. "I'm with you Chris. What is causing the attacks?"

"I knew you'd understand. I knew I could trust you. Okay, here's the deal. Are you familiar with a new street drug called the "seed"?"

"No, I've never heard of it."

"It's supposed to be the new, hip, party drug to end all party drugs. I don't know much about it, just a little I've heard from some old Navy buddies. None of my close friends have gotten involved with it. I certainly haven't. I can't explain how He did it, but God told me the "seed" is behind all of the attacks."

"Did He tell you anything else?"

"Yes, He told me what I need to do to stop the attacks. It's a little fuzzy here. Maybe He meant that what I need to do is to negate the effect the seed has, or maybe that I need to get people to stop using the seed. I think that's it right there. I think He wants me to get people to stop using the seed."

"Did God say how you are to go about it?"

"Yes, He did."

"And ….?"

"He said I will run across America in an effort to get people to stop using the seed."

"Run across America? What do you mean?"

"You know …. run, beat feet, lace them up and hit the road. Go through all the major cities, mount a national campaign."

"What about your wife, your little boy? How long would you be gone?"

"I don't know. You remember you told me that once you made your mind up about getting off the banishment island, that was it? There would be no going back. You'd get off or die trying. Remember?"

"I sure do."

"Well, I think I'm at the same place. It's not every day you get a direct message, a direct instruction from God."

T.P. couldn't argue with that. "Okay, I know you trust me. Let's take it slow. Let's pray on it, and if you don't mind, I'll call Jabez and get him and the JETS to pray on it."

"You know I don't mind. I was hoping that's what you would say. I knew you'd understand."

"I sure do Chris. I sure do."

# CHAPTER 6

Pete Thompson was wheeling his truck out of a big frozen food warehouse near Tulsa, Oklahoma. He turned onto an industrial access route that in a mile opened up to a state route. In two more miles it fed out onto Interstate 44. Pete would be eastbound, passing through Joplin and Springfield on his way to his destination in St. Louis.

When Pete turned onto the state route he checked his mirrors, and he picked up the two state highway patrol cruisers that slid in behind him. He was told at the shipper that he would have a police escort for at least ten miles out of Tulsa. The local authorities weren't taking any more chances after another big truck carrying over forty thousand pounds of food had been attacked by a riotous mob two weeks ago.

Pete sighed deeply and reluctantly keyed his CB microphone. He rarely talked to "full grown bears" whether it be on the CB or in any other mode. It was something most truck drivers tried to avoid doing – even Pete, the leader of the JETS. He switched the channel selector to ten where he knew bears sometimes would hang out. "Smoky, you gotta' copy?"

"We sure do trucker. We're going to be with you for about ten miles. It's Pete Thompson, correct? That's what it says on the shipping bills you signed."

"Ten-four, just call me Jabez. That's my handle."

"Roger that. Have you had any trouble with your loads since the attacks began?"

"No sir, can't say I have. I think I've been lucky so far."

"Probably so. Okay Jabez, we'll be here behind you for ten miles. Be careful the rest of your trip. Keep your eyes open."

"Sure will Smoky. Have yourself a big ol' safe day."

"Ten-four."

Jabez settled into the five and a half hour trip. After the state troopers dropped the escort, Jabez paid close attention to the country side. It still looked like the America he knew. The same scrub hills east of Tulsa. The same Post Oak, the same Blackjack Oak, the same Prickly Pear staking out the higher ground from the onslaught of the prairie; the same occasional Sycamore down low near the streams, and the same scrawny Cedars fighting for their rights on the fence lines. Ghosts of the Cherokee, Chickasaw, Choctaw, Seminole, and Creek still roaming the land even as Steinback's Joads do the same. And there were still plenty of evangelical hellfire and brimstone preachers working the backwoods, trying to find those who had the ears to hear.

Of course the country really was not the same as it was before the attacks began. The truth was the country really hadn't been the same since the sixties when so very much had changed. The more he thought about it, the more he realized he could keep the backward, negative digression going indefinitely. The country and the world really changed after Hiroshima and Nagasaki. And how about the four years between those bombs and what set them off – Pearl Harbor? How about a big skip back to the Civil War? Did that change the country very much, the world? Jabez knew you could take it all the way back to the Garden of Eden. Now that's where it really changed. He'd studied it all for a long, long time. Some say he'd been a part of it all for a long, long time.

He checked his dials and instruments, and his tires in the mirrors. He checked the traffic around him. No potential attackers that he could identify, but he certainly did notice the increased automobile traffic out on the interstates and everywhere else since the attacks had begun. He figured that was a result of the fear of public transportation.

He crossed the state line and rolled into Joplin, Missouri, where a school had been attacked a week ago. Fifteen children had been slaughtered in the parking lot. A banker had turned into the school property as children were being loaded onto buses at the end of the school day. He had torn through and around special security that the school had set up to thwart just such an attack.

Jabez was thinking it all through. His apprehension, his uneasiness, had actually started before the attacks began. He knew something was coming down, but he didn't know what, and he knew that he and the rest of the JETS would be called on. What was the assignment this time? What extra duties would they need to be available for? What would they be asked to do over and above the old school trucker duties they were all so very good at? Stopping to help a broken down four-wheeler, giving a lending hand to stranded travelers, feeding a drunken derelict, giving a Bible to a lonely man or woman – these were the things they did all the time – what old school truckers used to do; they still did. But what is it God was about to lay on them now that America and the world was coming apart?

Jabez had been thinking about it, thinking about it and praying about it. For Jabez, there was very little, if any, difference in the two activities. The western Missouri landscape continued to roll by. It couldn't make its mind up; arid windswept plains or the northern foothills of the Ozarks? Then he got a call from T.P., "Good evening Mr. Jabez."

"Good evening Mr. Coon Dog …. Oops, I mean Good evening T.P. I've got to quit doing that. What's going on?"

"Well sir, I just got a call from Chris Remington. He's had a special visit, you might say, from an even *more* special identity."

"Now T.P., I must stop you right there. You know good and well that our God is a whole lot more than a mere "special identity." He is the One and Only Sovereign Deity, The Holy Light of this Universe, The Awesome Creator of this humongous cosmos we call eternity, and He is a lot more than all of that."

"Oh Jabez, I'm sorry. I know you are right. I get all discombobulated sometimes. Hey ….!Wait a minute …. How did you know it was God who paid Chris a visit"? But he already knew that Jabez was very capable of doing it – getting on a cosmic wave link that enabled him to see and sense things that others were incapable of doing.

"Slow down." Jabez many times would have to remind T.P., Toby, and others that his special skills weren't unlimited. "No, I don't know all about it. I have had a feeling that Chris Remington would be playing a huge role in something about to happen, but I don't know what it is. It sounds like you do." Jabez was silent and waited for T.P. to spill the beans.

"Well, here's the story he told me. He said he'd been out on a ten mile run. You know, he's a serious distance runner – marathons, 10 K's, 20 K's, whatever. So, he's out on this training run and God in no uncertain manner gets his attention and tells him what is behind the attacks. He says that God told him a new drug called the "seed" is the thing that's causing the attacks. Chris doesn't understand *how* it causes people to mass murder, but it does. And get this, God wants Chris to run across America to warn people about the drug. Run across America! And Chris says that's exactly what he's going to do. He also said he wants us, all of the JETS, to pray on the whole thing. What do you reckon Mr. Jabez?"

"Well, I reckon we better start praying. You ready?"

"I sure am."

"Heavenly Father, what an awesome thing you've done. Showing Your will to young Chris, telling him what it is he should be doing for Your Kingdom. Heavenly Father, we pray for our young brother Chris. We lift him up to You. Fortify him with Your light and Your strength. His heart is pure. He wants to do Your will. You spoke to him and he had the ears to hear. And Father, now that we know You have chosen a brave young warrior to combat this new evil that our enemy from the old has cowardly unleashed on mankind, we also pray for the other warrior you will send along with Chris, the other brother in Christ that Chris will need to accompany him on his dangerous mission. Heavenly Father we give You all the praise and glory, and we thank You now for the power and strength and victory that You will put on these two warriors You will send on this extraordinary and singular mission. In Jesus name we pray. Amen."

"Amen", T.P. said, then, "Jabez, who is the other warrior God will be sending with Chris?"

"You are, T.P."

# CHAPTER 7

*The White House*

It had been nearly five weeks since Father C. J. O' Ryan drove his convertible onto a runway at Chicago O'Hare Field and snuffed out seven hundred eighty-five lives. FBI special agent Bart Duncan had been ushered into the Roosevelt Room in the West Wing. He knew the room well. He'd been there before. It wasn't the bunker type military situation room located in the basement under the White House, but he knew that it was as secure as modern technology and several million dollars of electronic and physical safeguards could make it.

President Whitley was flanked at the big table by the Director of Homeland Security, The Director of the CIA, the Director of the National Security Council, the Mayors of Chicago and St. Louis, The President's Chief of Staff, The Majority Leader in The House, and a handful of others, two of whom he knew very well – his boss FBI Director Stewart Menkoff and Dr. Kate Wenderson the renowned FBI profiler.

An aide pulled a chair away from the table for Duncan. As he sat he realized that the assembled officials had been waiting for him. He was sitting across from the President. The House Majority Leader was on his left and a man he did not know was on his right.

"Thank you for coming Agent Duncan. Everyone here was hustled to this meeting in the last four hours. Because you are the last to arrive, I don't want you to think you are about to be zeroed in on."

The President paused and looked around the room at each official who had been summoned to this urgent meeting.

"The first thing I intend to do here today is to impress upon you the degree to which American citizens have given up on their government. Any confidence they may have had in the government stopping the attacks is gone. Anarchy is at hand. The curfews in all major cities will break down soon. Law enforcement and our military are stretched beyond their capabilities already. The only thing preventing all out total collapse is that our citizens are not aware of that fact. As soon as people realize we do not have the manpower to police the nation, then the limited rioting and looting we've already seen will go beyond our ability to control it."

"I have no doubt that everyone in this room is aware of the unbelievable devastation the attacks have caused. However, in order to get us focused at the highest level, we are going to take another look at the raw numbers, an overview of the carnage of the last five weeks."

The President looked to one of the men special agent Duncan did not know. "William Spears has been on a keen vigil at Homeland Security since the attacks began. William ….."

William Spears rose and walked to the end of the room and opened a curtain that revealed a tally board. "Thank you, Mr. President. Nothing fancy here, but I will guarantee the accuracy."

He used a lengthy pointer with a rubber tip as he spoke, "Total number of successful attacks – 316."

"Total number of unsuccessful attacks – 81."

"Total number of attempted attacks, successful and unsuccessful – 397."

"Total dead – 39,447."

"Total non-fatal injuries – 102,851."

"Total dead and injured – 142,298."

"The number of major structures destroyed – 114 – this includes office buildings, civic centers, ballparks, airports, etc."

"The number of bridges, railways, highways, and bus stations that have been destroyed or seriously damaged – 96."

"The estimated amount of destruction and damage, seventy to eighty billion."

"Total number of attackers who died as a result of their attack – 137."

"Total number of attackers alive and we have behind bars – 141."

"Total number of attacks we cannot account for an attacker – 119."

Spears hit a switch and a wide screen TV lit most of the wall next to the tally board. For the next twenty minutes the officials in the meeting viewed video of America struggling to deal with the attacks. At first people were understandably reluctant to travel aboard common carriers, then they abandoned all forms of transportation other than private vehicles. Simultaneously, Americans refused to gather where large crowds were assembled. For four weeks, the food supply seemed safe, but then there came the death of three hundred in Houston traced back to poisoned food.

Footage of riots and looting was especially troubling, but perhaps the most bizarre and damaging video that William Spears had prepared showed excerpts of statements made by all major politicians. Each one seemed inept at offering a way to stop the attacks. All they could say was, "The government is on top of the attacks, all leads are being pursued, we are certain the attacks are not a result of international terrorists – Muslim or others, and we must not panic. Please be patient. Your government will protect you."

Next, the President had Andrew Mitchell, the Director of Homeland Security address the meeting.

"Thank you Mr. President. In short, we are not at the present time any closer to getting a handle on these despicable attacks than we were five weeks ago. The obvious question, I'm sure, is ringing out across the globe – how can that be? You've got one hundred forty-one perpetrators arrested and behind bars. Again, all I can offer is a short version of the futility all our investigative resources have come up against. Not a single one of the dead perps or of the one hundred forty-one perps in custody had a motive to execute the mass murder they were responsible for. They are as perplexed at their actions as we are. Indeed, the only common thread running through them is one that is the antithesis of what you would expect. These men and in a few cases women, every one of them, possesses the profile of a model citizen. No criminal record, no medical history of mental disease, no ties to extreme political factions, certainly no terrorist ties – nothing. We've explored the Random Mass Murder, RMM syndrome. Again, we've come to a dead end. We can't identify any device that a controller might employ that could manipulate an army of drones that these attacks would suggest.

As you know, every developed country around the world is fighting for its survival as well as the United States. We followed the progression of the attacks, first from Chicago and St. Louis, then spreading out across the country, and as we now see all around the world. There is one notable exception. Undeveloped third world countries have experienced almost no attacks – less than five percent of what a developed country has experienced. We are studying any possible explanation that might indicate."

"Mr. President, I hate to say these words. We have no idea what is going on." Andrew Mitchell sat down.

When Mitchell was finished, the President rose to his feet and began again. "Anarchy is where we are heading. The attacks are intensifying by a multiple of thirty percent a week. In six months the country will be gone." His voice was beginning to wobble a fraction off the confident chief executive octave from which it normally operated, and a noticeable twitch was evident in his left eyelid.

"My staff and I have gone over your latest reports of all your various investigations." He looked accusingly up and down the table, and then he really cut loose with it. His voice became an axe with a deadly sharpened and gleaming edge. It stung with fire and was aiming at heads to be severed.

"I can't believe that with the enormous resources each of you command, you have failed to even come close to a possible motive or explanation behind the attacks. Supposedly the brightest and the best investigators in the world are either in this room or work for you, and not a single one of you idiots can tell me why we are losing our country."

President Whitley was screaming now and began violently shaking and nearly lost his footing. The CIA director and the President's chief of staff grabbed him and helped him to his chair. An aide rushed out of the room and in a moment the White House on duty doctor was at the President's side.

After a brief examination, the doctor said, "I think the President is fine. He probably just lost his breath for a moment, but I would advise the meeting to button up as soon as possible so we can take a closer look."

"Okay doctor, no problem. We'll be finished here in a couple of minutes," the President said.

The aide walked the doctor out of the Roosevelt Room.

"Sorry about that ladies and gentlemen …. it's just …. well, we've all been under a great deal of pressure …. and …. here's the program. I actually *intended* to lay the wood to all of you. I don't deny it." His control was back. "I also intended to end the meeting with a good old fashioned brain storming session. So now is the time. If any of you have any ideas whatsoever that have yet to be aired, I want to hear them, right now."

The room was quiet. Then a senate committee chairman on internal affairs offered two separate theories, only to be told by the FBI Director that the Bureau had thoroughly tilled that ground three weeks ago but nothing had grown out of it.

Others made a couple of what they considered fresh and creative stabs at motive and explanations, but the same thing happened. Other agencies had already been there.

The President's eye lid began another twitch, and his voice began to crack. "Okay, this is my last request. I imagine they will get the doctor back in here. Can anyone of you go deep down into a fantasy world and offer up the craziest, the most implausible stretch of a motive or explanation?"

No one said anything.

Folks started shuffling in their seats and putting notes and briefs back in their brief cases. Despair, disappointment, and frustration were visceral things, and they marched through the room. The President was about to adjourn the meeting.

"I can, Mr. President." It was Dr. Kate Wenderson.

# CHAPTER 8

**B**art Duncan and Kate Wenderson were in a coffee shop not far from the White House an hour after the big security meeting had ended. The White House doctor finally had to use his medical prerogative and insisted on getting the President out of the meeting so he could give him a thorough exam. He was glad he did. The President's blood pressure read 265/150, and his eye twitch had gotten much worse.

"So, tell me again. How did you come across the runner, Chris Remington?" Duncan intended to go over Dr. Wenderson's story as many times as it took for him to get all the details down pat. A story like that could have a lot of holes in it. It might be a fairy tale. And if he were to devote valuable time to it, a disastrous diversion could rob them of crucial time spent on better leads. But there *were* no other leads or theories. As the President's security meeting just pointed out, they were at a dead end, and time was running out.

Wenderson put her coffee cup down and dabbed her napkin at the corners of her mouth. She looked cool and confident in the conservative pants suit she wore. Her auburn hair was stylishly cut medium length to accentuate her attractiveness. She wasn't into a lot of makeup. Her beauty was of the all American, girl next door variety, subdued, yet very appealing.

"The first thing I did was pray to God that He would put me on a good lead. You'll recall I didn't mention that to the President. I probably should have. The second thing I did was a Google search for ordinary citizen's responses to the attacks. I just had a feeling that there might be somebody out there who had a clue. You know, we at all levels of government and law enforcement sure don't. So anyway, the hits on Google led to several tweets and a

face page – Chris Remington's face page, which led to the web site -
SAVEAMERICADONTDOSEEDS.COM."

"Right," Duncan said, simultaneously tweaking his original
notes from the White House meeting. "And this was three days ago?"

"Yes."

"What did you do next?"

"I ran a background investigation on Chris Remington. As I
stated in the meeting, it didn't show Remington to be anything
other than a civic minded, ordinary, young American; wife, one
child, ex-Navy, avid distance runner. Obviously the thing that got
my attention was the statement he made on the web site about his
certainty that a new designer street drug called the 'seed' is behind
the attacks."

Duncan interrupted, "Okay, and just as you told the President,
you haven't done anything else because you first wanted to report to
the meeting today and see what instructions the President, the director, or I would give you. Is that right?"

"Actually no; I have done a little more research. The web site says
Remington plans to run across the country warning people about the
seed." She hesitated a moment and had a doubtful look on her face.
"That seems to me to be a bit off the deep end. My first thought was
maybe he's just in this for personal gratification, you know, wants
to be a star and all that. I debated whether I should go to California
immediately to check this guy out, or simply make some calls to see
what I could find out. I decided to make the calls."

"What did you find out?"

"Not much; the website is asking for financial support of
Remington's run and for citizens along the route he plans to run
to provide lodging and food. It sounds as if Remington is trying
to make this a grassroots populist kind of project. They don't have
corporate sponsorship." She paused again and drank some more
coffee.

"Did you make any other calls?"

"Yes, I talked to officials in some of the cities Remington plans to run through. None of them knows anything about a marathon warning people about the seed coming through their town."

Duncan fixed his eyes into Dr. Wenderson's eyes, "What do you make of Remington's certainty that the seed is somehow behind the attacks?"

"Well, it's strange. As I just said, at first I thought he might be a phony, just grandstanding for strokes and publicity, possibly looking for a lucrative financial bonanza from a sponsor or maybe a Hollywood movie. But then I started getting this feeling that maybe, just maybe, Remington is for real. I think it's worth a trip to California to meet Chris Remington."

"I agree. Get a bag. We'll be on a flight out of Andrews in forty minutes."

"Don't you think we should get some samples of the seed and get it in a lab asap? I saw something on it recently, but I think a thorough lab analysis is what we need."

"I started that ball rolling back in the White House as soon as you told the President about Chris Remington."

# CHAPTER 9

**"H**ow are you going to do thirty miles a day? Isn't your average training run seven or eight miles?" Cindy Remington was a runner herself, and although she supported her husband Chris, she wasn't sure he could do thirty miles a day.

It had been two weeks since Chris had told her about his encounter with God and the instructions he received to run across America to try to save the country. Cindy wasn't surprised at the news. Chris himself was much more shocked by the new status of his life than his wife. It was just an hour ago Chris and Cindy watched as a TV anchor reported that the President nearly had a nervous breakdown earlier in the day at a top level security meeting.

The young couple had just tucked in their four year old son, Charly, for the night and were sitting in the den talking, "Yes, I know. Thirty a day is going to be tough, but I think I can do it. I've bumped up my daily average to fifteen miles a day already." Chris got a little closer to Cindy and took one of her hands in his.

Cindy said, "I guess it's natural to worry. I'll try to be strong for you. It's just …. well, you know, it's all come up so quickly. The attacks, the country's falling apart, and now you, my own husband, you're going to be gone. Oh, listen to me. I'm sorry. I promised I wouldn't go there." She gave him a soft kiss on his cheek.

The last two weeks had been a real roller coaster ride for Chris. First he told Cindy as soon as he returned home from his amazing run on the beach. Then he called T.P. to tell him. Next he told his boss at the electric power company. His boss wasn't one bit happy, but after several days to think it over, the management of the company authorized a paid leave of absence for as long as Chris needed.

The head honcho had lost two children to a bombing at their elementary school only a week ago.

The web site took several days to set up. Chris had a couple of tech-savvy friends who helped him build SAVEAMERICADONTDOSEEDS.COM, and with their help the expenses were kept to a minimum. None of them was prepared for some of the email responses to the web site. Three death threats came back almost immediately. Chris remembered the contents of one of them: "So, you think the seeds are the cause of the attacks .... Get real!! Finally we have a safe psychedelic drug that can save mankind, and then you and your right wing whackos mount an anti-seed marathon. You have nothing to substantiate your insane claims that somehow the seed is responsible for the attacks. Wise up Mr. Remington. Wise up and back off your marathon, or .... DIE. Anonymous."

Chris also remembered his response to the threat – *Back off? I don't think so. You are just making a stronger case for me to run. I wonder if this guy is into the manufacturing and distribution of the seed?*

Cindy removed her hand from Chris's hand and reached for the remote TV control. Like all Americans, Chris and Cindy were glued to the endless news accounts of the latest attacks.

News anchor Tim Foster had just detailed the hijacking of a light aircraft in Milwaukee which was flown to the Great Lakes Naval Recruit Training Center north of Chicago and crashed into a three story barracks. Twenty-seven recruits died and another fourteen were seriously injured.

Another story was about a botched attempt to steal nuclear fuel out of Oak Ridge, Tennessee. The bad guy intended to contaminate the public drinking water in Knoxville.

After several other near miss attack stories, the serious faced anchor continued, "The Department of Homeland Security announced today that eight new cities have decided to increase curfew hours from the previous midnight until to dawn to six p.m. until dawn. All eight mayors said the same thing – they had no choice. The cities are Topeka, Bowling Green, Winston-Salem, Redding, Pensacola, Scranton, Montpelier, and Butte."

The anchor's earpiece was telling him to switch to a live feed from the White House, "And now we go to Monica Cartwright, with breaking news live outside the White House."

The camera centered Monica Cartwright in front of the White House amidst a throng of aggressive reporters, all trying to make certain the floodlit entrance to the White House behind them was centered in the frame. Cartwright looked up just as the camera was catching her, "Tim, we have just been told that President Whitley has in the last two hours suffered a massive stroke that has left him in a coma. The President's personal physician, Dr. Anthony Meyers, has confirmed the diagnosis and has described the President's condition as extremely serious. Just minutes ago the President was moved from the White House to Walter Reed Army Hospital. And Tim, we've just been informed that steps have already been taken to transfer the power of the executive office to Vice President Edgar Rawlings."

As more and more information poured through and was being reported instantly, it became clear that President Robert Eli Whitley's medical crisis had started earlier in the day at the big security meeting. Whether this information had been leaked or not was not on any of official Washington's radar screens. But another leak emanating from the same meeting was definitely on some very sensitive radar screens. Half an hour after the President's stroke and coma story broke, Monica Cartwright reported another story. "Tim, we have learned from several reliable sources that an unnamed FBI profiler, when prompted by the President to brainstorm even the wildest, most bizarre scenarios possible as to a motive or explanation behind the attacks, told the President she thinks there is just such a scenario that she's been researching for several days. The profiler has discovered a young distance runner in California who says he knows what is causing the attacks. Tim, when FBI officials were asked to confirm this story, they said, 'Yes, we are pursuing the lead aggressively.' Tim, we have also learned that the young runner in California is an electric power company worker named Chris Remington. A web site set up by Remington claims that a new designer drug dubbed the "seed" is responsible for the attacks. The web site also talks about a cross country marathon that Mr. Remington plans to launch soon. The purpose of the marathon is to warn the country about the dangers of the seed, which is causing the attacks."

Cindy dropped the remote, and it banged hard on the floor. She sat stunned, staring at the TV.

Chris said, "Well, it looks like a lot of the promotion, P.R., publicity, and media stuff that I figured we'd have to battle hard to get, has just been handed to us."

Then his phone started ringing and within thirty minutes his yard was filled with TV news crews.

# CHAPTER 10

The next morning at 6:45 AM, Chris and Cindy had two strangers pull into their driveway, park, and walk up to their door. Chris was up making coffee and taking care of the early riser in the family, young Charly. All the news crews had left before midnight when they concluded they weren't going to get anything more out of Chris Remington.

Chris had eagerly gone out into the yard last night to make a general statement and hold a lengthy question and answer session with the media. He hadn't prepared anything to say, so he did what he was best at; he winged it, talking honestly and straight from his heart. "Wow! This is a shock, but I'm glad you are all here. My wife will be out in a minute. I think she needed a couple of aspirin when she saw all of you pull into the yard. I'll get right to it. I'm a runner. Historically, runners carry an important message. God has given me a message to carry to as many cities as I possibly can, large and small, all across America. The message is this: The new drug called the seed is what is causing the attacks. It is the reason people are dying and suffering, and it is the reason our country will collapse if we don't stop it now. I have a web site called SAVEAMERICADONTDOSEEDS.COM. You will see on the web site that I intend to start a cross country marathon as soon as possible. I will talk to as many people as I can, and I hope that you, the media, will get the message out as well. We must stop the seed if we want to save America."

Several reporters at the edge of Chris's yard were snickering and talking after hearing Chris's opening statement, "You got to be kidding. Who does he think is going to believe this nonsense? Sure, right, God, that big white haired, friendly spirit in the sky talked to him. Why are we wasting our time out here? Half the people in this crowd have done the seed, and I bet not a one of them has plotted a random mass murder."

When the question and answer session got started, there was one question most of the reporters asked, "How did God give you the message, and how did you know it was God?"

All Chris could say was, "I'd rather not get into that. It was one of those very special, very real, and very seldom encountered events that God sometimes shares with us. You wouldn't believe me, even if I told you. I think He will show more signs. We have to be patient. I know personally that I have to run and warn the country about the seed."

Chris heard his doorbell ring at about the same time he saw Charly throw a glob of cereal at the wall. "Charly do you want to go running with me this morning?"

"Yes Daddy."

"Good, but you can't go if you throw food on the wall. Do you understand?"

"Yes."

"Good boy." Chris hated dangling the carrot of running to help discipline his son, but sometimes it was the only thing that worked. He walked to the front of his house and opened the door.

The first thing he saw were two Federal I. D.'s extended out in front of a man and a woman.

"Good morning Chris. I'm special agent Bart Duncan of the FBI, and this is one of our investigators, Dr. Kate Wenderson." Duncan waited to see the response Chris might have and to see if there was any telltale apprehension or 'Uh oh, I've really done it now', look in his eyes. He saw neither. Instead, he saw a clear-eyed, robust look of self-confidence and friendliness. Chris was a striking figure of health and fitness. Wearing only running shorts, his chiseled, thin, runner's body was dark golden tanned, not an ounce of fat.

"Hi, come on in. It's good to meet you." He opened the door wide and brought them inside. "Let me grab a shirt." He went into the bedroom where Cindy was rolling out of bed.

"Did I hear people out there?" She was stretching and rubbing the sleep out of her eyes.

"Yeah, come on out and meet them."

"Okay, I'll be out in a minute."

Chris slipped a t-shirt on and returned to Duncan and Wenderson. "Let's go back here. My son and I were just starting on breakfast."

He led them back through a large family room that led into the big kitchen with a small table his family used for breakfast. "Grab a chair. I'll get you some coffee. Say hello to Charly."

Kate Wenderson sat next to Charly who was up good and high on his booster chair. "Good morning Charly. My! Aren't you a big boy?"

Charly was all smiles but was a bit shy when it came to strangers. He just looked at the two of them.

Chris placed two steaming mugs of coffee in front of Duncan and Wenderson. When he saw Cindy coming into the room he fetched her a cup also. "Cindy, this is Agent Duncan; and this is Dr. Wenderson. They are from the FBI"

In a minute everyone was seated around the table. Charly was finished with his cereal and he continued to look at the FBI agents as if they might be fun to play with.

Chris said, "Where are you guys from, here in San Diego?"

"No, actually we flew in from Washington last night. We heard about the news hounds out in your yard last night and actually saw a few brief clips, so we thought our business could wait until early this morning." Again Duncan waited to see what he might read in Chris's eyes. Kate Wenderson and Cindy exchanged polite looks but not much more.

"So, how can we help you?"

"We don't know. That's why we are here, to see if you *can* help us. Dr. Wenderson has been looking into your, let's say, status, for a few days. Do you mind if she asks you a few questions?"

"Of course not; fire away." Chris seemed anxious to cooperate fully. It was as if he *needed* to tell his story to as many people as possible, even if they happened to be FBI

"Chris, I must tell you, I've got a lengthy list of questions I could ask you, but let's not start like that. Why don't you just tell us the story? Start at the beginning and try not to leave anything out. Believe me, we want to believe your story. Maybe it's the break we've all been waiting for, the whole world has been waiting for. How good of a salesman are you?" She stopped, and like Duncan, she felt like this is the way to check this guy out. They both fed him plenty of rope. *Now let's just see if he hangs himself.*

"Okay, really it's a very simple story. My wife and I are believers. That is, we are Christians. We believe every word of the Bible. I haven't always been a strong Christian, but I am now. When I met Cindy, she impressed me with her faith. One of the first things she told me was she was not interested in men who didn't put God first in their life. Well, I sure didn't. But as we dated I began to see the beauty of a relationship rooted in God. We were going to her church regularly, and one Sunday morning I answered the altar call. I asked Jesus to take me. That's all I said. Everything became balanced after that day. I believe that was my 'born-again' day."

Chris paused a moment and looked over at Cindy who was smiling, and who was so very proud of him, and so very much in love with him.

"Well, not long after that, we got married. Somewhere along the way I've learned to put my trust in God for everything. I mean everything."

He stopped again and looked like he might be reluctant to proceed, but proceed he did.

"Okay, here's the part you want to hear, the reason you came to see me. They asked me the same question last night, and I answered them honestly, but I didn't give them the details, you know, the magical stuff, the God stuff. You'll get it all. Two weeks ago I was down at the beach running. I was getting near the end of a ten-miler. I was approaching a patch of wildflowers, and I felt like someone or something was giving me instructions to sit down. I stopped running, and I sat down. Then I was instructed to sit still and be quiet. I did that too. The wind picked up, and then it got stronger and stronger. Sand and the wildflowers were blowing everywhere. It didn't last long, and then everything was still. I got to my feet and noticed these tiny golden-brown seeds covering most of my body. The seeds were from the wildflowers. I didn't sense anything unusual at first. My skin was wet with sweat, so all the dry seeds just stuck to me. The next thought that came into my mind was the attacks, and what's happening to the country. The attacks I'm thinking, and now these seeds all over me. The attacks, the seeds …. I felt something coming over me like a revelation or an incredible insight into something. It was a powerful thing. All I could see in my mind's eye were the attacks and those seeds. It was the strangest feeling. And it was then that I knew who had given me the instructions to sit still and be quiet. It was God. He told me that the drug called the 'seed' was the evil behind the attacks. And He told me I must run, I must warn everyone about the danger; I must implore people not to use the seeds. I never actually *heard* a voice. I *felt* it enter me somehow in an even more powerful way than sound."

Chris was trembling slightly and his eyes had been distant as he recounted the last part of his tale. Then he regained his focus and went on. "Ever since then I've been doing all I can to prepare for my across America marathon. I've accepted the whole thing as God's will. I think that must have been my calling from the day I was born, or even before. I may not understand everything about it – I don't – but I don't need to understand. I just have to follow the instructions He has given me."

Dr. Wenderson was thinking the story through. Evidently Chris had said all he felt like he needed to say. The look on her face was of deep fascination. She cleared her voice and began, "So, let me make sure I understand. You are convinced that God has given you instructions to run across America and warn people about the seed."

"Yes ma'am."

"Now, can you tell me if God gave you any insight into how the seed is responsible for the attacks?"

"I figured you'd want to know about that, but no, I'm sorry, I'm afraid He didn't."

"Your story is very compelling Chris, but I must tell you that we see many cases where people feel they are led by God to do certain things. Of course, there is nothing illegal, that I know of, about running across the country. Are you sure you don't recall anything God may have said to you about how the seed is responsible for the attacks? Take your time. Try to remember everything that took place."

After a moment of silence around the table Chris said, "No, Dr. Wenderson, I'm certain He didn't tell me why or how the seed does what it does. He just told me to run and to warn people. That's all I'm sure of."

"I see."

Before she could say anything else, Chris started again, and he had a certain edge in his voice this time, as if maybe he *had* forgotten something. "You know, last night I told those reporters that I think God will give us more signs. I really believe that. And there's something else Dr. Wenderson. I received death threats as soon as I put the web site up. It seems there are people out there who don't want me running. They actually think the seed is a good thing. I can't imagine why they feel that way, but they do."

Bart Duncan now had something he could get his teeth into. The instructions from God, and Chris's response to them, as fanciful as they were, he must admit, were very interesting, but death threats …. *Ah, now we're getting somewhere.*

"How did the death threats come to you?" Duncan asked.

"Emails."

"Would you mind if I looked at them, and also have my people monitor your web site and all your online activity?"

"No sir, I don't mind. That would be great."

"And tell me Chris, particularly in light of these death threats, what kind of security will you have on the marathon?"

"Security? Well, uh, I guess T. P. will be about It.

"T.P.?"

"Yeah, T. P. is a good friend of mine. He's going to make the trip with me."

"Just the two of you?"

"Yes sir. So far that's all we have."

Bart Duncan didn't want to rain on Chris's parade. On the other hand, he felt like he had the responsibility to at least point out a few red flags to Chris.

"Two guys, one of them running across America, nearly three thousand miles with death threats on them? I admire your spirit and determination, but you understand, this will be a huge risk, especially when you consider the condition the country is in right now." Duncan looked over at Cindy and then little Charly.

"Sir, if I knew of a better way to warn people, I would. But God has given me a job to do, and I'm going to do it."

On their drive back to the airport to get their flight back to Washington, Duncan asked Dr. Wenderson, "So, what do you make of Remington?"

"A very dedicated young man; a religious fanatic to be sure; but you know what?" She had an expectant look that hinted of the contemplation of trust and something bigger.

"What?"

"When a serious born-again Christian feels like God has spoken to him directly, you might as well get out of his way. There's a story about Billy Graham as a young evangelist back in the late forties. He wasn't sure of his calling. He was having some serious doubts about continuing to preach. He was in California preparing to preach to a huge crowd. A day or two before the event he went atop the San Bernardino  Mountains to meditate and pray. When he came down, he was ready. People who were close to him knew he had an encounter with God on that mountain, and they say that Mr. Graham was a changed man. And of course, history tells us what happened after that. Chris Remington is way beyond the doubting stage of whatever it was that happened to him on the beach that day. Why shouldn't we believe him? The world is coming apart before our very eyes. If he is right about God telling him the seeds are responsible, who are we to question God?"

"Good point," Marcum said, but he was already thinking ahead.

"I'm ready to throw a lot, all we've got, at opening up this seed theory. I've got a couple of ideas. There's nothing back yet from the lab work we started on yesterday. What would be your next steps if you were pulling the strings?" He got his ears ready to listen closely.

"Well, I doubt we'll find any answers in the lab analysis on the seed itself. I pulled up all the info, what little of it we have, on the seed a couple of days ago. Drug enforcement has known about its existence for a couple of weeks. They already had some lab results. There were no new psycho-active chemicals or compounds that haven't been seen somewhere in some kind of hallucinogen in the last fifty or so years. I believe where we need to look is at the people who are taking the seed. We need to set up blind studies with control populations. If Remington is right, and the seed is responsible for the attacks, it can only mean one thing – the seed acts on a unique personality trait. That is, when it triggers an individual to attempt a mass murder, it does so because that individual has a particular code etched in his psyche the seed turns on. I suppose it could be chromosomal or DNA, but possibly it's just a quirky personality trait. It must be something along these lines. Otherwise everyone who took the seed would be out there murdering and blowing things up."

"What would you need to get the blind studies started as soon as possible?"

"Your making a call to Professor Ing at the Department of Psychology at the University of Maryland. It's close to D.C. I've worked with him before, and he lost his wife to an attack at a theater in Silver Springs last week."

Duncan began punching in some numbers on his cell phone. In a few minutes he had Professor Ing on the line. Within ten minutes he had Ing's commitment to open up the psychology department's vast resources to any and all studies that Dr. Wenderson and Ing himself deemed necessary to either rule out or accept the responsibility that the seed may be playing in the attacks. Ing said he would have to get the approval of the President of the University and the Board of Regents, but he did not see any obstacles there. He asked to speak with Dr. Wenderson and told her that he was anxious to get started immediately and said he'd meet her at Andrews as soon as she arrived.

# CHAPTER 11

When he heard the exaggerated HSSSSS of the air brakes setting, Chris knew that T.P. had just pulled his big Peterbuilt up into his driveway. He was out the door in a flash, Charly tagging along behind him. They stood ten feet away, waiting for T.P. to climb down out of the cab.

The door cracked open and a worn, scuffed cowboy boot dropped down to the first safety step, then another to the lower safety step, and then T.P. was walking to meet Chris and Charly.

Chris grabbed him by the shoulders and slapped his back a couple of times. "It's really you! You look great! This is Charly."

T.P. smiled at Charly, "Hi Charly. Your dad tells me you're a good runner."

Charly just shook his head in the affirmative and smiled back up at T.P.

"Come on in. Cindy can't wait to see you. We've had a big morning. The FBI was here two hours ago." Chris noticed a look of distress settle into T.P.'s face. "Don't worry. There's not a soul on this planet that would take you for anything other than a truck driver. All that stuff from four years ago, it's history. Come on in, Cindy's getting ready to go to work."

Cindy was gathering some things to take to work with her when she saw the three of them coming into the kitchen. She dropped everything and ran to T.P. to put a bear hug on him he wouldn't forget for a while. "T.P.! I've wanted to see you so bad. You look terrific. Every time I think back, I remember how we almost lost you. But look at you! I'm so happy to see you."

"Hello Cindy. It's good to see you again. I don't know if I ever did thank you, proper-like, for saving my life. I pray for you and Chris and Charly all the time."

"As we pray for you T.P." She finally let him go. "I'll make you a dinner tonight to celebrate. I hate to run, but I know you two have a lot of catching up to do."

Cindy took Charly with her to drop off at day care. Chris made fresh coffee and both men settled down in the family room where the news on TV continued reporting on the latest attacks, the President's medical condition, and the new aggressive initiatives to stop the attacks that Acting President Edgar Rawlings had just announced.

Chris muted the volume on the television and turned to T.P, "We didn't expect you for a couple more days."

"Yeah, I know, but the way things are going, I figured I'd better step on it. When Jabez said I was going with you, well …. I knew right then your run is our last chance. I'd never even heard of a seed, but if Jabez agrees with you about the instructions you received, then …. I'm with you a hundred percent. What's the schedule, what's the timetable, when are we leaving?"

"There's nothing stopping us now that you're here. We'll leave tomorrow morning. Did you see the camper sitting out back?"

"No, what kind of rig you got?"

"A thirty footer with a fifth wheel, sleeps four, kitchen, bathroom, and a fancy diesel auxiliary power unit. I got a big Ford F-350 with a 7.5 diesel to haul it around. One of the board members at the electric company brought them over here three days ago and said he insisted on lending the rig to me. And we've been receiving cash from a lot of people for fuel and food."

"You've been busy."

"Sure have." Chris saw something on the TV screen that caught his eye. It was Diane Warner, the news anchor whose husband was killed at Busch Stadium in St. Louis along with three thousand two hundred and sixty-seven other innocent victims. Chris turned the volume back up.

Warner was approaching a lectern with several microphones. A large banner in the background read, "GLADDS" an acronym for God Loves America, Don't Do Seeds.

Chris turned the volume higher and said, "Wow, look at that!" T.P., likewise, focused on the TV screen and gave it all of his attention.

Diane Warner stepped behind the lectern and began to speak. "Ladies and gentlemen, fellow Americans, and all of those around the world who, like me, have lost loved ones to the attacks. Today I will make several announcements that I pray with all my strength will give us some hope. Our own President has said the world is on the verge of anarchy, and now he is struggling for his life. Our acting President, Edgar Rawlings, has announced a series of severe legal and military maneuvers which will be put in motion if the attacks are not stopped. Our government and top investigators from around the world have been useless in stopping the attacks, and today they are no closer to determining a motive for the attacks than they were five weeks ago when they began."

"As many of you know, I was on air, broadcasting the report of the very event which ruthlessly murdered over three thousand Americans in St. Louis. And yes, my dear, loving husband was one of them. At that moment my world came apart. I didn't know if I would make it through that night or any other night. My grief, I'm sure, has not exceeded many of yours. It is for that reason that I make the following announcements:

"One: My leave of absence from AFN is not a leave of absence. I severed all ties with AFN the day after the St. Louis attacks.

"Two: Shortly after the St. Louis attack I made a personal decision and solemn commitment to dedicate the rest of my life to investigating and reporting every story connected with the attacks. When I lost my husband, I asked myself what is it I can do, in some way, to help stop this evil massacre. The answer was do what I've always done. Be a reporter. Therefore, with help from friends and supporters, I am launching an independent news broadcast network whose single purpose for existence is to help stop these evil massacres from continuing.

"My third announcement is this: You noticed I have described these unprecedented attacks as evil. I did so the day my husband died, and I continue to do so. Many of you may also be aware of the breaking story out of Southern California. There is a young man in San Diego named Chris Remington who claims that God has told him a new designer drug called the seed is responsible for the attacks. Mr. Remington also says that God gave him instructions to run a marathon across the U.S.A. in order to warn people about the seed, and to urge them to never use it. Also, Mr. Remington tells us that he feels like God will give us more signs. Let's face it. That's a pretty incredible story that Mr. Remington tells; but if we were to take an objective look at the three key elements of this entire situation, 1) random mass murders, on a scale which if gone unchecked, will destroy society as we know it 2) all of our investigations futile to this point and 3) a young man who says God has identified a drug as the evil, then I think there is only one thing we can do. That is to follow and report on the third element – Chris Remington. My broadcast team and I intend to do just that. I have not even spoken to Mr. Remington, but I will, and if he will allow it, we will dedicate all our energies to reporting every step of his marathon.

"It's my opinion that he is our best hope. One man who claims God has spoken to him, I think, is a far brighter light to follow than an inept government and countless legions of hopeless investigators."

After Diane Warner had concluded her announcements and sewn up the press conference, T.P. looked over at Chris with a big grin. "Well, if it's attention you wanted to kick this thing off, you're getting plenty."

T.P. and Chris stayed busy all afternoon loading the camper with food and supplies, and checking routes and mileage. T.P. removed the CB in his tractor and installed it in the Ford F-350 pick up.

That night Cindy had a big meal with spaghetti and meat sauce as the main dish. Pasta is always the traditional food that distance runners partake of the night before a serious distance run. Three thousand miles is pretty serious.

After dinner T.P. headed outside to sleep in the camper. He knew Chris and Cindy and Charly deserved all the privacy they could get tonight. He also took their phones to the camper with him. There had been a steady stream of reporters and media calling all day. T.P. learned quickly that a lot of his job was going to be handling the press. Chris, T.P. thought, has got the hard part – running thirty miles a day and warning all the druggies in America not to do the seed.

Before midnight, after taking countless calls from the media, and to his shock, receiving more death threats against Chris, T.P. made a call of his own. Jabez hit the receive button on his cell phone. "And a pleasant howdy-do to you Mr. T.P."

"Good evening Mr. Jabez. I got here this morning, and I tell you what …. This thing is moving along lickity-split. Chris is starting his run at 7:30 in the morning. The press has been calling here all day, but Jabez, I've got bad news."

"What is it?"

"He got fifteen death threats on the phone and about as many on the internet. What do you make of that? I don't understand."

"Well, let's just think it through. We've got a young crusader trying to do God's will. Right?"

"Absolutely. Chris is the real deal. He's as serious as a heart attack."

"Yes he is. Now, as I understand it, particularly after watching and listening to Diane Warner today, Chris is quickly becoming the focus, not of the attacks of course, but of any meaningful efforts to stop the attacks. Right?"

"He shore' 'nough is!"

"Yes, then think about it. Who would want to see that the movement to support Chris, and what he is doing never gets rolling?"

"Uh …. I see, I see. Let me think about it a minute."

Nothing but silence on the phone line, but both men were letting the cognitive juices flow. After a moment or two went by, T.P said, "Who would want to stop him? Let's see .... maybe dope pushers, the scum who sell the seed to people."

"Yep, could be them. But who else?"

"Well, I don't rightly know, maybe the users themselves. Did I hear someone say on a news report today that there are several groups coming out in favor of the seed, saying it is the cure-all, fix-all for what ails mankind?"

"I think you probably did. *I* did."

T.P.'s response had a certain sense of astonishment in it, "Are we saying what I think we are saying? This marathon of Chris's could come down to a war of words on a national scale as to whether the seed is the evil behind the attacks or not?"

"It already has come down to that. And the war isn't just going to be fought with words."

"Then Jabez, my being here with Chris isn't going to be enough. We're going to need a thousand JETS to get involved if we are to provide a security escort for him all the way across the country. Jabez, we are starting tomorrow morning, just me and Chris. He's not going to stand a chance."

"Oh yes he is. He's going to stand a real good chance. Me and fifty other JETS will be all around you tomorrow. Some will be close, and others spread out looking for trouble."

# CHAPTER 12

Chris, Cindy, Charly, T.P., and most of the neighborhood that Chris lived in were up at 5:30 in the morning. Already there were six video news crews from local and national networks, and a dozen or more writers and reporters were on hand. Diane Warner and her crew arrived around 6:00 and as soon as Chris spotted her, he invited her in to meet Cindy, Charly, and T.P.

They were all at the kitchen table drinking coffee and nibbling on fruit and toast. Chris was devouring bananas and oranges.

After the introductions Chris said to Diane Warner, "Words can't describe the grief I felt when you lost your husband. You must be a very strong lady to come back from that the way you have. Cindy and I have been praying for you and all of the victims' families."

"Thank you, Chris. That really means a lot to me. But I'm not really back yet. I won't be back until we get to the bottom of this. I believe in what you are doing. There is just something so amazingly pure and selfless in what you are about to do. Some say you're grandstanding and the story is all a hoax. I don't believe them. If you allow us, my crew and I plan on following you as much as we possibly can. We will report on everything we see and just as important, on everything we feel. I'm sure you've got a million things to do before you start running. I just want to tell you, don't give up, and keep going no matter what. Deliver the warning God gave you."

At 7:00 Chris and T.P. went to the front yard where the media was gathered. The first thing Chris noticed was a group of non-media people barking out a chant at the top of their lungs: Do The Seed, Save Mankind, Do The Seed, Save Mankind. After a minute they switched to: Good For Me, Good For You, Do The Seed Two By Two. Over and over they blasted the chants out. Then Chris saw a rival group try to drown them out with: God Loves America, Don't Do Seeds, God Loves America, Don't Do Seeds, over and over.

T.P. was thinking about what Jabez said last night. He couldn't believe what he was seeing. The run hadn't even started yet. Could it get started with all of these pro-seed fanatics in Chris's yard? With all of this going on, Chris wouldn't be able to make a statement to start the marathon.

T.P. walked toward the back of Chris's house, climbed up in his tractor and fired up the 475 horses that wanted to run. With the four-way flashers going strong he aimed the nineteen thousand pound tractor right at the pro-seed protesters. He wasn't going fast, just crawling along at maybe two or three miles per hour, but when he got close to the fanatic chanters he let go the twin locomotive air horns he'd paid five hundred dollars for. If there were any eardrums in that group that were left undamaged, they were mighty powerful eardrums. The group dispersed from Chris's front yard and reformed across the street. T.P. sat menacingly at the edge of the street, still in Chris's driveway. He was just waiting for them to start chanting again. For the time being they decided to behave. T.P. signaled Chris to go ahead and make his statement. The other group of chanters stopped their own chants and cheered wildly as Chris picked up a bull horn.

"Hey, hey, what a day, stop the seeds all the way!" Chris was into the chanting spirit himself. "Hey, hey, what a day, stop the seeds all the way!" In a moment, Chris's allies were with him, "Hey, hey, what a day, stop the seeds all the way!" They were all roaring it now, louder and louder, the pace picking up. Finally, Chris raised his arms up high and became silent. The crowd reluctantly calmed down, and in twenty seconds all was peaceful and quiet.

"This is amazing. Finally we have some hope. God has told us what is causing the attacks. We must listen. We must heed our Father in Heaven. He has told me to run and to ask people not to do the seeds. The seeds are the evil. They are killing us. The Father has not told me how this happens, but there is no question, none whatsoever. The seeds are the evil behind the attacks. Who are we to question God? We can't; we must not question God. In ten minutes I'm going to start running and I'm not going to stop until God tells us how these seeds are causing all of this pain and death. This is not putting a hammer against God's head and challenging Him as if we somehow question Him. No, it is not that. He already has told us what the evil is and what I must do. I am ready to do it. He will give us the other answer, the *how* the seed does what it does. And when He does, we will finally be able to stop the killing. He will not fail us, and I will not fail Him. In ten minutes I will start running north toward Los Angeles. Then I will run on to San Francisco. Then I will turn east to Reno and Las Vegas. Then north to Salt Lake City, then east to Denver, Kansas City, St. Louis, Chicago, Detroit, Toledo, Cleveland, Columbus, Pittsburg, Harrisburg, Washington, Philadelphia, and then New York City. Everywhere along my route I'm going to ask people not to use the seed, and I'll be watching for the day that God shows us how to stop the killing. I know He will. Are you ready? Hey, hey, what a day, stop the seeds all the way!"

They all started the chant again while Chris went back into his house to kiss his wife and son goodbye. T.P. still sat in his tractor keeping an eye on the rowdy, pro-seed bunch across the street. He was wondering how close any of the JETS might be.

Chris wrapped Cindy up in his arms and didn't want to let her go. They didn't talk. They just held each other. Finally Chris let her go. He picked up Charly and said, "You be a good boy and take good care of mommy while I'm gone. Don't forget to run every day, and say your prayers every night. Wherever I am, I'll be praying with you."

"Daddy, what's a seed?"

"Something very bad."

"Are you going to stop the seed?"

"No son. God is going to stop it. I'm just going to help God a little."

"I love you Daddy."

"I love you too Charly."

Chris knew he had to put Charly down and get moving. When he turned to the door, he didn't look back.

T.P. saw Chris come out and he started backing the tractor all the way back behind the house. He locked it up and met Chris by the Ford pickup truck hooked to the thirty foot camper. Chris was doing some runner's stretches to loosen up his hamstrings and Achilles tendons.

In a couple of minutes he straightened up and smiled at T.P., "You ready?"

"Ready, willing, and able."

"Okay, let's do it. You've got the route for the first thirty miles. Get out front five miles and wait on me."

"Okay, Chris. Double check your cell phone. I want to make sure you can get me if you need me."

Chris removed his tiny phone from the fanny pack he had strapped around his waist and hit the pre-set for T.P.'s phone.

A rowdy instrumental version of *Dixie* rang out on T. P.'s phone and T.P. said, "Alright, good enough."

Chris said, "Let's pray."

They both took a knee and T.P. grabbed Chris's hand. Chris started, "Heavenly Father, thank You for this day. Lead us, guide us, teach us to follow You and do our best to complete this mission You've laid out in front of us. Please protect Cindy and Charly while I'm gone, and pilot us across this land. Thank You Father for my friend T.P. I pray this will be a safe journey for him and that all of Your strength, power, and wisdom will accompany both of us. In Jesus name I pray. Amen."

And T.P. added, "Father put Your Spirit all over this young brave lad. I know You'll do it and I thank You for it. And Father be with the JETS, each and every one of them. Now, show us the way Father. We put it all in Your hands. In Jesus name I pray. Amen."

T.P. climbed in the Ford, started it up, and eased the camper out of Chris's driveway. In five minutes he was out of the residential area, and he parked five miles away in a roomy lot next to a strip mall.

Both crowds were into the chants as Chris began his three thousand mile trek. The pro-seed group actually got into the street and tried to physically block Chris from running. He simply darted into a neighbor's yard and outran them all. In a quarter of a mile he left the street for a back trail he knew very well. None of the pro-seed crazies would follow him there.

Running! Chris was running! He was doing what God created him to do. His breathing and pulse rate were up. His blood was picking up oxygen in his lungs and transporting it to his muscles and his brain. He was beginning to produce the endorphins which would, on most running days, allow him to run with a comfortable feeling of ease and "all is well with the world" feeling even while his body dealt with pain. He would soon learn that the added emotional stress, and the pure enormity of his intended mileage on the *Stop The Seed Marathon*, would pretty much negate the "runner's high" which the endorphins produced.

For now, the running was good, and he was glad to get moving. He was thinking it through – the day on the beach when the wind stirred up the little flower seeds and deposited them on his sweaty skin; his understanding that God was somehow giving him instructions. And he was thinking about his response to all of that. And now that he was running, he felt as though God was talking to him again. What he heard was, *I'm proud of you. I am pleased you've had the ears to hear my plans for you.*

Two miles were behind him now. He checked his runner's watch and noticed he'd run at a seven minute per mile pace. He slowed down after telling himself he had to be careful about his pace; the slower the better. He didn't even know if he could do the thirty miles a day that he and T.P. had figured. He knew for sure he couldn't do them if he went too fast. *This is not a race* he kept telling himself. At the four mile mark his pace had slowed to about seven minutes and forty seconds per mile. He was happy with it.

He came out of the back trail and hit a major commercial corridor. Running on the shoulder and the sidewalks, he continued on northward. As he approached the five mile mark he saw the camper in a vacant lot, and he saw that Diane Warner was there with her news van and two technicians who doubled as camera men and van drivers. They were talking with T.P.

Chris jogged up to the group, "Hey Diane! I didn't expect to see you again today."

"Remember, I said we're going to be here as much as we can. Do you mind if we get a live interview going right now?"

"No, let's do it."

The techs got the camera going and the feed on up to the satellite. In a moment America was watching and listening to the interview. "This is Diane Warner, live with Chris Remington in San Diego ...."

Three blocks away Jabez the truck driver was on the CB with Wind Jammer the third original member of the JETS. "Give that to me again. Nicodemus was making a racket," Jabez said, as he petted the born-again wonder dog Nicodemus, trying to calm him down.

"I said that I had a bad feeling about one of those pro-seed fanatics after he left Chris's house. You know, the one making a lot of the noise."

"Okay, okay, so what's going on?"

"Well, I'm not sure. I think I saw him put something into his mouth. That was about a half hour ago. Now, he's coming hard down the road and I think he's got a 12 gauge hanging out the window. You'll be seeing him in a second. I'm behind him. He's in a little red SUV."

"Yeah, shore nuff, here he comes. He's definitely got something out that window!" Jabez dropped the mike and it coiled up over his head on the elastic retractor. He gunned his eighteen- wheeler from the shoulder he'd been parked on and got over in the left lane of the big, heavily trafficked northbound side of the street. He saw T.P., Chris, and Diane Warner with her news crew up ahead in the lot on the left, and he saw the red SUV passing him on the right. The SUV cut him off and started veering over to the left shoulder. He saw the driver slowing down and simultaneously aiming the scatter gun at T.P., Chris, and Diane Warner. About the time the first blast rang out from the 12 gauge, Jabez had his bumper smashing the red SUV from behind. T.P. knocked Chris and Diane Warner to the broken pavement as two more blasts rang out. T.P. caught some of the shot in his back, but nobody else was hit, and T.P. wasn't badly hurt .

That night the major networks and the twenty-four news outlets barely mentioned the shooting. Diane Warner's news service, on the other hand, had nonstop coverage of the first day of Chris Remington's *Stop The Seed Marathon.* Viewers actually saw the red SUV pull up close to the curb, aim the shotgun and fire just as a big semi-tractor trailer hit the SUV from behind. The cameraman was quick enough to swing his lens to the red SUV and then to follow an old timey looking truck driver out of his cab to the SUV and drag the stunned driver out, tie him up, and wait for the police to arrive.

Warner didn't miss any opportunities to interview anyone involved in the bizarre shooting attack, including Windjammer. He arrived just seconds after Jabez had hit and pushed the red SUV over the curb into a telephone pole.

"So, you suspected the shooter was up to no good at Chris Remington's house. Please tell us all that you saw." Warner placed the mike up close to Windjammer.

"Yes ma'am, I noticed the man earlier this morning as Chris was preparing to run. I had my truck parked down the street, but I was in the crowd that was chanting with Chris. The crazies, the pro-seed folks, were making plenty of noise also. This one guy, I noticed he went back to the rear of the crowd with a couple of other people. They put something tiny into their mouths. I couldn't say if it was seeds or not, but if I were a betting man, I'd bet they were. They went back and joined the crowd, but about ten minutes later the man I was watching went to a little red SUV and drove away. Well, when Chris started running, I pulled my truck out of there and waited right down the street." He was pointing southward down the big street. "I didn't expect anything like this to happen, but some of us truckers have made up our mind to keep an eye on Chris while he's running. Then I noticed the same red SUV come tearing down the street, and it looked to me like he had a shotgun out the window. I got on the CB and told the other truck driver, and you see what he did to the SUV."

Warner wanted to interview Jabez and T.P., but both declined. Jabez was busy talking with the police, and T.P. was off to the emergency room to have several pieces of shot removed from his back.

Later that afternoon Warner was able to talk with the investigating detective on the case. The detective confirmed that the shooter admitted to taking a seed at the protest in front of Chris's house and then proceeded directly to a friend's house where he picked up a 12 gauge shotgun and then started searching the boulevard for where Chris might be seen again. He stated to the detective that he had no reason why he tried to murder Chris and the others around him. The detective said the man was the owner of a small grocery chain, had been married for twenty-two years, and had three children, two of them in college, and that he had no previous criminal record. Weeks later, investigators would learn that the shooter had a keen interest in ethics and morality conflict. His personal library had several hundred books on those subjects.

# CHAPTER 13

It was a week after Chris escaped the shotgun attack just five miles into the marathon. He was now approaching Santa Barbara, some ninety-four miles north of Los Angeles. He was averaging just over thirty miles per day, and his body weight was down from one hundred seventy to one hundred fifty-eight. At five foot ten, he still looked like a very fit runner. It would take more than a loss of twelve pounds before he took on the appearance of a gaunt and malnourished crazy man.

The mainstream media in the media megalopolis of Los Angeles stayed away from Chris. Only Christian radio and TV came out to interview him as he slowly worked his way through the city. True to her word, Diane Warner was constantly with the anti-seed marathon. Her camera crew broadcast about half of the thirty miles Chris ran every day. Warner herself was beginning to show the strain of just trying to keep up with Chris.

One day as Chris ran on the beach past the Santa Monica pier, a large crowd of vocal pro-seed toughs was threatening Chris. Warner, who had donned running shoes and sweats, dropped her microphone and ran with Chris until the crowd of roughnecks dissipated.

In certain parts of the city there were small groups that came out to support Chris. They were always Christian church groups, and usually the running stopped while they all prayed with and for Chris and for the country.

The country was in dire need of prayer. Attacks were increasing. And the country's polarization of pro-seed citizens and anti-seed citizens had reached an absolute crux. It was all people talked about. Chris's marathon may not have stopped many people from using the seed, but it certainly was responsible for the unprecedented scope and nature of the debate. As ironic as it seemed, it was actually the

Chris Remington anti-seed marathon which was responsible for more and more people using the controversial drug. Most people never heard of it before the runner who received instructions from God had declared it "the evil responsible for the attacks."

Bart Duncan, Kate Wenderson, and Professor Donald Ing were ushered into the White house for a meeting with Vice President Edgar Rawlings. President Robert Eli Whitley's condition just in the last few days, had been upgraded to "guarded". Most of his doctors gave him no chance of ever regaining the Oval Office. Congress had voted to maintain V.P. Rawling's title of Acting President in order to avoid a quagmire of legal and constitutional issues should President Whitley ever be ready to reassume office.

Edgar Rawlings welcomed the three into the Oval Office. Thomas Kennison, President Whitley's chief of staff, was in the room also. The Acting President gave the three of them a very serious look, "The FBI Director called me this morning and said he was sending the three of you to report the findings of the seed investigation in which you've been involved. So, what do you have for me?"

Instead of receiving the report from behind the Presidential desk, Rawlings pulled up a chair up near the three visitors. Trumanesque would be a good way to describe Rawlings – tough minded, yet an agile enough thinker to consider all sides of an argument or problem. Physically he was cut much like Truman – short, wiry, and he had a square jawline that was immovable when he chose to set it tightly. Many in and around government had nicknamed him "stubby".

Bart Duncan set a two inch thick, hardcover, bound research project down on a table. They had all pulled their chairs around the table. The document had the title *Seed Analysis and Correlation to Study Group* . Duncan looked to the Acting President and said, "Sir, despite the fact that it has only been two weeks since we got started on this, I must say two things: First, if we had a year to work on it, I don't think the outcome would be any different. Second, every single researcher involved in this project agrees with the scientific methods the project utilized as well as the conclusions that were reached. We had one hundred sixty-two case study researchers, fifty-four psychoanalysts, two dozen lab scientists, and twenty six other various professionals from the University of Maryland psych department. Needless to say, the FBI's top people were involved in all aspects of the study. The study population numbered exactly one thousand individuals. Everyone involved worked around the clock because we all knew what the outcome of the study might mean for the country. I'm going to turn it over to Dr. Wenderson, and Professor Ing."

In the next thirty minutes Wenderson and Ing detailed every step of the two week project. First they talked about giving each and every one of the one thousand members of the test population a seed to take; then the monitoring of their activities; then the analysis of the cases in the test population that exhibited serious anti-social behavior. That percentage was two percent of the total population or in other words twenty out of the one thousand. Finally, they talked about the hard part – connecting those twenty cases with the seed. Blood work, DNA analysis, virtually every kind of biochemical test that scientist knew how to use were used.

Dr. Wenderson summed up the results to Edgar Rawlings. "What we discovered, Mr. President," she'd done away with the title of "Acting President" the moment she'd entered the Oval Office, "is that the twenty test subjects, each of them, have a unique enzyme which, if not triggered by the exact same enzyme contained in the seed, would normally be of no concern. In fact, laboratory researchers have known about this enzyme for probably thirty years. Some researchers call it the "God enzyme."

Rawlings had to break in, "Why do they call it the "God enzyme?"

"Well sir, because it is only found in people who have an extremely high propensity to examine, study, and try their best to live by super high moral and ethical principles. You remember Father C. J. O Ryan in the very first attack. We later learned that he was exactly that kind of person. Whoever developed the seed either knowingly or accidentally included in its chemical composition a trace of the God enzyme." She paused to slow down. "We know that some chemical compounds react in strange ways. It happens, and we can prove it over and over again, that when the God enzyme in the brain comes in contact with the exact same God enzyme from outside the body, i. e. from a seed, a funny thing happens. The very positive personality traits become, for a brief period of time, exactly the opposite. Those test subjects, the two percent who possess the God enzyme, almost immediately exhibit bizarre, murderous activity."

"So, you are saying that not everyone who takes the seed will initiate murderous plans, but that twenty out of every thousand will?"

"That's right, Mr. President."

"And isn't it true that the runner out in California has been saying that God told him the seed was the evil behind the attacks?"

"Yes sir. That's what he's been saying. And of course he's also been saying that God told him to run across the country and warn people not to use seeds."

"What do you make of his story, Dr. Wenderson?"

"Well sir, we went out there and checked him out. Personally I feel he's very credible. I believe he believes God is directing all of his activities. I know this .... Unless we had stumbled on Chris Remington, we would not know what is causing the attacks. But now we do."

That night an emergency session of congress was held and the new anti-seed bill was law before midnight. Possession of the seed carried an automatic lifetime sentence to the banishment island, Isla de la Legarnia, off the coast of Mexico, and trafficking in or production of the seed carried an automatic death sentence.

# CHAPTER 14

*A week later in King City, California, on Route 101*

It was a chilly night. A storm had blown in off the Pacific ushering in a mild cold front. Eerie black clouds leaked moonlight in silvery, gray shafts around their edges, but the wind was giving up its sting, and seven JETS and one cross country anti-seed marathon runner were enjoying the warmth of a big campfire.

Chris's weight was down to one fifty-two, but he still looked like he could run circles around most any weekend athlete. T. P. was in the circle around the campfire, and he couldn't erase the big smile he'd had on his face for several days now.

Everyone was happy. Toby, Jabez, and Windjammer were laughing at some tricks that Nicodemus the wonder dog was performing as a result of the encouragement and coaching of Whiplash, said to be one of the most skilled truck drivers in the world, also said to be a pretty good dog trainer.

Old Soft Shoe and Big Montana were roasting hot dogs on a stick and feeding them to Chris. "Just two more," Chris said. He'd already eaten three, plus a pint of potato salad, and three tomatoes that Jabez had fetched for him.

Old Soft Shoe walked up next to Chris and asked him a question, "How about some dessert after you polish off those dogs? I've got some banana pudding from a deli down the road. It's fresh, and mighty good."

"That sounds good." Chris got to his feet and found buns and condiments for his last two hot dogs, and then he addressed all seven of the JETS: "Don't forget guys, you promised me that tonight I'd hear the best truck driving story ever told. I'm waiting ....."

Everyone looked around at each other in a quizzical way, and then they all sort of shifted their gaze to Toby. He knew there was no use in sidestepping. It was his turn. Every time the JETS got together, they all took turns telling stories.

"Well Chris, I'd be glad to tell a truck story. I don't know if it is the best ever told, but it goes something like this. Way back when God decided to put men on Earth, He knew that at some point in time Satan would unleash an all-out assault on everything that is good. And God knew that truckers were just the kind of men to stand up against the evil being thrown at humanity. Why did He know truckers were the men for the job? Well, number one is this. Truckers are men of tremendous faith. Who else in their right mind would leave their homes for months at a time and go to far-off places that a little computer on their dashboard told them to go?" Everybody around the fire laughed and chuckled.

"And who else besides truckers could live in a nine foot by nine foot by eight foot box with no women and more importantly, no running water?" More laughter.

"So, anyway, God had a special place in his heart for truckers. And when the end of the world was getting close, you know, Armageddon, well, God had a very special job for one very lucky trucker."

"What was it?" Chris asked, now getting into the story,

"God had chosen a trucker named Ernest to drive Jesus around to inspect the entire Earth before He would actually come back to save us all. That's right; Ernest was going to be the lucky driver to have the ultimate honor of being the chauffer for Jesus. But you know what happened?"

"No, what?" Chris said.

"Ernest had lost the keys to his truck, so he missed out on the greatest assignment he would ever be given. And so, do you know what the real moral of the story is?"

"No, what?" Chris said.

"Always carry a spare key to your truck. The best thing to do is to wear it on a leather strap or a chain around your neck." And he showed off the spare truck key hanging from a thin leather strap around his own neck.

"Now that was the craziest truck story I've ever heard," piped Windjammer. The rest of The JETS voiced their affirmations to Windjammer's words.

But Chris thought the story was pretty good, and before turning in for the night, he told Toby that the next day he would be wearing a spare house key hanging from a thin strip of rawhide around his neck. No, not a truck key, but to Chris, something just as important to him – the key to his house.

The campfire was lower now. Chris had gone to the camper to get much needed rest before he would start early in the morning on his thirty miles. Windjammer, Old Soft Shoe, Big Montana, and Whiplash had gone to their trucks. Only Jabez, Toby, and T.P. were left poking at the embers and dying flames with long sticks.

T.P. still had the smile and was still in a euphoria about all that Chris had accomplished so far. He couldn't keep it to himself any longer, "Just a month and a couple of days since he received the instructions from God! Look at all that's happened. He's run thirty plus miles every day. The research study linked the seed to the attacks. The new laws are working. The attacks have almost ceased. How many since the laws were passed, four? The last one was three days ago. He's a national hero, maybe the greatest since George Washington or Abraham Lincoln. Somebody smack me hard. Wake me up. Am I dreaming it all?"

Toby added a few thoughts of his own, "And you know what I think is really wild ….? All of those young folks out there running. We've been seeing more of them every day. Not just the ones that run with him, but all over the country. They're even trying to look like him. Wearing the same outfits, cutting their hair like Chris, you name it!"

Wise old Jabez was considering it all. He didn't particularly like the feel of all the adulation the country was pouring out on Chris.

The question of whether or not the cross country anti-seed marathon was even necessary any more was a question that Jabez had privately raised with Chris earlier in the evening. But Chris seemed as determined as ever to continue. "I have to run until the attacks have completely stopped. I told God I'd run all the way across the country, and that's what I'm going to do."

*That may be,* Jabez thought, but he also knew there were evil forces still out there that would love nothing better than to end the life of Chris Remington.

The next morning Chris was up an hour before dawn. He intended to get at least eight miles completed before any of the JETS were up and moving about. His thinking was it would shorten the day for them. He'd felt bad about all the time they'd been taking away from their normal driving jobs to provide security for his run. *Anyway, I don't need the security any more,* he thought. *Those guys have done way too much already.* When he'd tried to persuade Jabez last night to end the security blanket so the JETS could get back to their normal lives, Jabez had stood fast, "As long as you continue running, we're going to be out here with you."

So, Chris drank a quart of Gatorade and ate two bananas and began his runner's stretches. He knelt and prayed for a short while, much of it focusing on Cindy and Charly. Next, he threaded a thin strip of leather through the small hole in his San Diego house key, tied off the ends of the strap, and hung it around his neck. In five minutes he jogged off, slowly at first, then after a mile or so he increased his pace to seven and a half minute miles. It was a great morning, cool and quiet, very little traffic at this hour. Running alone! He wasn't all that thrilled with the groups of runners that had been running with him lately. Oh, he appreciated the support they wanted to show for him, he really did, but running in a group just wasn't the same as running solo. Oh well, he'd created the anti-seed marathon, and who could argue with its results? It almost seemed as if all of the young people in the country were on the roads running, and by so doing, they were making a statement and a commitment not to use seeds. Unlike the *Just Say No* movement of another era, this time the country's commitment held strong.

*Oh well,* Chris thought, *I'll run with whoever shows up later today. For now I'll enjoy the peace out here alone. Look at those mountains to the east, the pink oozing around them. The sky will explode with color in a few more minutes, maybe like a novel I read recently about strawberries being attacked by a blow torch. This is beautiful!*

He didn't notice the cargo van pulled over on the deserted shoulder three hundred yards in front of him.

# CHAPTER 15

The JETS were up drinking coffee and making plans for the security umbrella they would keep around Chris. Today's route north would provide scenic vistas of the Sierra De Salinas to the west and the Diablo Range to the east. Also, the Mission Nuestra Senora de la Soledad Ruins would see Chris running by them late in the afternoon. San Jose was still three days away and San Francisco five days away.

At 7:30 a.m. Diane Warner's news van pulled into the small camp where six big trucks and Chris's camper had spent the night. She spotted T.P. and Jabez outside drinking coffee. "Good morning Mr. Jabez, Mr. T.P. Where's our American hero this morning?"

"I reckon the big old campfire and storytelling last night went a little too long. We ain't seen him stirring about yet." T.P. finished his coffee and continued, "And how about you Miss Warner? You got a big day planned?"

"Absolutely! I wanted to see if Chris would be interested in doing a live 'question and answer' broadcast later today at the Soledad ruins."

"Well I reckon we'll just find out. Let me go see if he's crawled outa' the sack."

T.P. walked back to the camper, disappeared inside, and a minute later was returning to Diane Warner and Jabez. "He's done vamoosed. Left a note saying he went out for an early eight mile run."

T.P. and Jabez exchanged worried looks and then immediately assembled the JETS.

Jabez made sure the others took this as seriously as he did. They were each assigned roads, trails, pastures, wherever Chris might be running, and told to stay in phone contact with Jabez every five minutes until Chris was found. They all dropped their trailers and bobtailed out to find Chris.

An hour later Windjammer was driving along a back road five miles from camp and spotted a solo runner a quarter mile ahead. *That's got to be him. Looks just like him.* He called Jabez. "I've got him, about five miles from camp. He looks fine."

Then as he got real close to the runner, he said, "No, sorry Jabez. It's not him. You know how all these runners out here dress like him. Sorry Jabez, I screwed up."

"That's okay, keep looking."

Twenty minutes later it happened again. Whiplash spotted a solitary runner and thought it was Chris, but it turned out to be another young runner who was probably so taken by the effort Chris Remington had been demonstrating to the whole world that he was training to do the same thing. He intended to run all the way to the east coast, carrying the same anti-seed message Chris was carrying. He told Whiplash that in California alone there were over a thousand other runners who intended to do the same thing. Many of them, he said, were planning to run in groups of fifty or so.

Three hours had now gone by since Chris was discovered missing. The JETS had called in more local truckers to expand the search. After that had produced no Chris, and no evidence of his disappearance, Jabez reluctantly notified the state police and the local police.

Diane Warner was in tears and wasn't sure she could tell the nation in her next broadcast that the national hero, Chris Remington, was missing. Jabez and T.P. were with her and assured her that Chris would be found, but for now, she would have to do her duty and report the bad news. She knew they were right.

At 1 p.m. in the afternoon, at the sight of the Soledad Ruins, Warner's broadcast crew gave her the thumbs up and said, "four, three, two, one, rolling."

"This is Diane Warner, and this afternoon I'm at the Soledad Ruins near Soledad, California. Chris Remington has been missing for approximately eight hours. Other than a note he left in his camper saying he was going out for a pre-dawn eight mile run, there is no evidence of his disappearance. A massive search is under way being led by state and local police. The trucker group, the JETS, has also been involved in the search since 7:30 this morning. Toby Etheridge, a spokesman for the group, has issued a request and a statement that he said is directed to the entire nation. I now read it to you: 'We ask that every American pray for the speedy and safe return of Chris. We all know what's he's done for our country, and now, it's our duty to pray for Chris. We know our Father in heaven will hear our prayers and return Chris to us.'"

That night Acting President Rawlings spoke to the nation from the Oval Office. "Good evening my fellow Americans. As you probably know by now, there is a massive search underway for Chris Remington. It is with a heavy heart that I report to you the search has to this point been unsuccessful. I have personally been in almost constant communications with the authorities in California and have made available to them the full scope of federal assistance to find Chris Remington as soon as possible. This includes the FBI, the Federal Marshalls, the ICC, the Department of Homeland Security, and any other federal assistance that might be necessary. I want to point out that the rumors of Chris Remington's disappearance being the result of a cowardly kidnapping for ransom plot is totally unsubstantiated at this time. We have as yet, no evidence that such a plot is the cause for Chris's disappearance."

"As we all know by now, Chris Remington was the catalyst for the successful investigation that led to the hiatus of the unprecedented evil attacks caused by the seed. In our nation's history it would be hard to find any one single individual who had more to do with saving the country from ruin and destruction  than Chris Remington. And now, our national hero is missing. Tonight I ask all Americans to be active in the search for Chris. Even the slightest bit of information concerning his disappearance or whereabouts will be followed up and pursued. We will find him! Also, tonight I announce that a private consortium of concerned citizens and businesses has posted a ten million dollar reward for information leading to the location and safe return of Chris Remington."

"Finally, my fellow citizens, I want Chris's wife Cindy and son Charly to know that we will not stop until we find Chris. As a trucker in California stated this morning, 'Now it's our duty to pray for Chris. We know our Father in heaven will hear our prayers and return Chris to us.' I think we would all agree that because of Chris and his unwavering faith in the Almighty Creator who made the inception of our nation possible over two hundred and thirty-five years ago, we have witnessed in the last two months what can happen when God is trusted. We've been saying for a long time, "In God we trust", but it's only been lip service. Chris Remington has taught us what it means to put our trust in God. The trucker was correct; now it's our turn. As a nation we need to pray a fervent and immediate national prayer for the safe return of Chris. Good night my fellow Americans. God bless America."

And so, for maybe the first time in a long time, an unapologetic speech linking God and nation was broadcast from the Oval Office. Christians loved it, non-Christians were stirred by it. They couldn't deny the plain unvarnished truths to which it alluded. The ACLU and left wing activists were thoroughly disgusted, and the next day they were calling for the removal of Edgar Rawlings from his seat of acting President. Be all that as it may, and the country's sudden leaning toward a stronger faith in God, nothing could change the terrible truth – Chris Remington was missing, unaccounted for, had disappeared, and vanished without a trace.

# CHAPTER 16

The next month saw only two attacks that were caused by use of the seed. A total of fourteen had died including the two attackers. The follow up investigations, once again, proved without a doubt that the two attackers fit a now familiar psychological profile. They'd both cared deeply about morality – what makes right right, and what makes wrong wrong. And as had been proven over and over again, post mortem lab results of their brains detected slight amounts of the God enzyme, some natural and some synthetic from the seed.

These were to be the last two attacks in, other than the Civil War, the darkest period of history the country had ever seen. To be sure, the sentences of death or banishment were deterrent enough to keep people from using, possessing, manufacturing, or trafficking in seeds. But there was another factor that was the more subtle factor. It was their new found spirituality the country was reaching out for. The acting President was correct. Chris had taught the country how to trust God. People who were pro-seed just two months ago were now strongly anti-seed. Other street drug users began to reduce or stop using completely, and heroin, PCP, marijuana, crack cocaine, barbiturates and other drugs all saw drastic reductions in demand and use.

Maybe the most dramatic change in the American landscape in the month since Chris Remington disappeared was the number of runners who were on the roads all over the country. Many attempted to take on the actual physical appearance of Chris Remington. They wore a tee shirt with the anti-seed slogan just like Chris had done. They even wore the same brand of running shoes Chris had worn. And thousands of them were running toward Washington D.C. They left jobs and family to finish what many now believed Chris would never be able to finish. They were doing it not only to continue the anti-seed marathon that Chris had started, but also as a tribute to Chris himself. In roughly three months Chris would have taken the anti-seed marathon as far as Washington D.C. Now there were plans for a huge celebration to commemorate Chris's run. A great Chris Remington tribute was to be held in three months on the mall at the nation's capital on the same day that Chris would have been scheduled to arrive there.

As to the whereabouts of Chris, the police, the government, and the JETS were completely baffled. The FBI had been able to pick up a spotty trail of Chris's running shoe imprints on a dusty shoulder about four miles from where the JETS had made their truck camp the night before the dark morning Chris came up missing. But the prints suddenly disappeared. Where they disappeared was found a set of tire treads that would have matched untold numbers of vehicle makes and models. So the investigation was stumbling about blindly. Thousands of "Chris Remington sightings" were investigated. All turned out to be Chris look-alikes who had taken to the roads to honor his memory, many of them running east toward Washington D.C.

The JETS, though discouraged, weren't about to give up the search. Jabez, Toby, Whiplash, T.P., and Windjammer were in a truck stop diner outside Sacramento. Big Montana, Old Soft Shoe, and a couple of other JETS had returned to northeast Tennessee a few days earlier. Everyone agreed it was about time someone checked on the Christian Mountain School for Children. The professional staff and faculty who operated the school were used to members of the JETS visiting on a regular basis. Jabez, in fact, lived on the property when he wasn't trucking. It was his land the school was built on, and in fact, it was his idea to build the school in the first place.

Windjammer looked across the table at Jabez, "You're right. The Heavenly Father must be using him for something. He'll get him back to us. There's not much more we can do."

Sadly, they all agreed. They were praying almost constantly, and they had crisscrossed every road in the Bay area and central California daily since the disappearance. Still they would not quit. They couldn't quit. It wasn't their style.

Jabez spoke up, "We need to get back down to San Diego and keep a prayer vigil over Cindy and Charly. It hasn't been easy for them. Everybody else will continue searching here for a few more days and then start drifting back east."

They all caught the hint in Jabez's voice, of something good that could come from the eastward expansion of the search. And they all knew that when Jabez had sniffed out a direction that God had alerted him to, well …. always something good had come out of those situations.

Whiplash and two other JETS said they'd go back to San Diego to pray with and for Cindy and Charly. They all agreed that would help her a lot; just letting her know that none of the JETS were giving up praying and searching.

Jabez, T.P., Toby, Windjammer, and hundreds of other JETS would start turning the search back toward the east.

# CHAPTER 17

A lone runner struggled toward the summit of the mountain, still a mile up the way. He opened the top of his jacket to release a little of his body heat. *There that's better. Cool my neck and chest a little. I wonder if that big group of runners will be on top? Somebody this morning said they probably would. Tried to catch them yesterday. They were only twenty miles ahead of me. This morning …. Where was I? Coming out of Salt Lake City, I think. Must have been, there was a ski resort right off the interstate, had that huge ski jump ramp; I've seen it on TV, looks strange in the summer season, no snow, no jumpers. Everybody says don't worry about running on the shoulders of the interstate; the cops don't hassle anyone; they encourage it; safer for the thousands of runners than the secondaries. Plenty of runners on them too.*

The runner opened his running jacket a little more. He removed his ball cap and slapped it against his thigh to knock off some of the dripping sweat. He put it back on and lifted his arms over his head even as he continued running up the increasing slope toward the summit. Now he was Ferris-wheeling his arms around and around in three sixty arcs. It broke the tension in his shoulders and neck. He would do it every twenty minutes or so. Likewise, about once every hour he'd stop running and go through a quick series of leg stretches. He'd always done it. He couldn't remember when he began doing it. For as long as he'd been running he assumed. When *had* he began running? He didn't know. But it must have been a long time ago. That's all he ever remembered – running.

*A half mile to go. Sure is plenty steep up here. Wispy smoke some-where up on top. I bet they are up there. A couple of weeks ago I came up on a big bunch of runners. They had a fire too. Plenty of hot dogs. Hot dogs for everyone. They saw I was a runner and just brought me right on in. I must have eaten eight hot dogs. Boy were they good! We all started running the next morning, I think; not really sure. Their pace must have been too slow. I don't remember what happened to them. I probably did over forty miles that day. Maybe these folks up on top have plenty of food. Oh well, I've got granola and water for tonight, and I'll stop somewhere tomorrow and gobble down a hot meal. I hear a lot of restaurants are feeding runners for free. If they know the runners are headed for Washington D.C., they say they're feeding them for free. Whew, take it easy. Don't overdo it. Slow down. Don't tear a hamstring getting to the top. Drop the pace down to a crawl. About a nine minute pace. Almost on top. It's a good thing, only twenty minutes of twilight left. It'll be a little more than just chilly up here tonight. I've got my body wrap if there's no room in a van or camper. What would I have done without it out in the desert at night? Likely would have frozen to death. I suppose I could have kept running, and slept in the daytime. Yeah, that would have worked. Oh well, deal with one problem at a time. Wow, look at that sunset behind me. Awesome! The mountains, the sparkling, crystalline, blue silver-gray sky with early stars already winking on and off. I know who controls the switch! Awesome! I know HIM .... And then the runner thought about it .... But I don't know myself.*

The mountain sunset triggered another fleeting thought in the runner's mind, or was it a flashback? It came and went so swiftly that it left no trace when it was gone. It was as if a strong wind swept through his mind. He felt it, and then it was gone. He *saw* it, and then it was gone. Something about running on the beach. He saw it clearly, and then it was gone.

*There they are. Looks like maybe eight or ten support vans and campers. A big bon fire, maybe thirty-five or forty runners around it. Here come five of them, walking toward me.*

"Hey, man! That was some hill to climb wasn't it?"

The runner dropped his nine minute mile pace to a walk, "You can say that again," and he went into his lightweight runner's back-pack for his water bottle. He quickly noticed that the five who had come out to greet him were just like most of the others he'd seen at all the nighttime running camps. They wore identical anti-seed t-shirts, and they had their hair cut the same way and tinted the same color. Except for the scraggly beard the runner had, they looked a lot like himself.

Another runner in the group of the five put his hand out, "I'm Ron Weston. I bet you're the guy our van driver told us about. He said there was a solo runner on our tail who was running below seven minute miles. We all said , 'You're crazy; only Chris Remington himself could run a pace like that for thirty miles a day. You're not Chris are you?"

Everyone, except one runner, got a big kick out of that. When the chuckling died down, that runner said, "It's not funny. God only knows what's happened to Chris. Let's take this whole thing a little more seriously." Then he extended his hand to the lone runner who just topped the hill, "I'm Bill Tarpley."

The lone runner smiled at the other five, "I'm Jeremy Barnsdale. Would you mind if I sleep in your camp tonight?"

"Are you kidding? Come on in. We've got plenty of room in my brother's camper. He's got a bum knee; hasn't been able to run for five years. But he wanted to be a part of the big deal coming up in Washington, so he's our supply clerk, nurse, scoutmaster. You name it, he does it."

They all walked about a hundred yards off to the southeast of the shoulder of the interstate. It was flat and the eight or ten vans and campers had no trouble setting up a sort of semi-circular perimeter around a big fire. Runners and supporters were milling about, talking and eating. Bill Tarpley led Jeremy to a table that had been set out to hold the group's nourishment for the evening. Green salad, barbecue beans, and a huge kettle of pasta were getting plenty of attention from the carbohydrate starved runners. Breads, soups, and fruit were also on the table. It would all be gone in another fifteen minutes.

Jeremy got plenty to eat. He was sitting near the fire with Bill Tarpley, his brother Raymond, and four or five others. Raymond was explaining to Jeremy how this ragtag group of runners had gotten together and adopted the nickname of Remington's Raiders. "When Bill said he was running to Washington D.C. to honor Chris Remington's memory, I thought he was crazy. Then I got to thinking where the country would have been without Chris Remington. We had sixteen attacks in Oakland. Two hundred dead and another two hundred injured. Ever since I tore up my knee five years ago I've missed running terribly. So I started thinking, maybe I can't run in memory of Chris Remington, but I can be with them, and I can be at the Mall in Washington on the big day. I knew I couldn't sit back there in Oakland and watch it on TV, so, when Bill and I started, it was only a week after Chris disappeared. By the time we got to the Nevada line, we had nine others running with us. In Reno we met two ex-Oakland Raider football players who joined us. See those two big guys over there? They're not as big now as they were six weeks ago. They've both lost over fifty pounds. So anyway, from then on, we've been Remington's Raiders, and we've grown to forty-two runners and a support team of ten vehicles and eighteen humans."

Jeremy was not the talker that Raymond was. All he said was. "You've got a good group here. You won't have any trouble making D.C." Mostly he was thinking about something Raymond just said – "to honor Chris Remington's memory." They all said that. Every running camp he'd been in lately. It confused him in a way he could not understand. And tonight, sitting here with the Remington's Raiders, it set off another vicious windstorm through his mind, another flashback. He saw a little boy. The little boy was running, his arms out, reaching toward a man running in front of him; reaching out, trying to catch him. Then it was gone. It left no trace of its existence in Jeremy's mind.

Raymond noticed the faraway look in Jeremy's eyes. "How about you Jeremy? What set you off to run to D.C.?"

"Oh, I don't know …." *Here it comes again. Why do they always ask me this stuff? I don't know why I'm running. I'm just running. I've always run. I feel like I have to keep running east. That's all I really know. I don't even know who I am. My ID says I'm Jeremy Barnsdale. Ha! I have no idea who Jeremy Barnsdale is. Maybe it's me, maybe it's not. I guess I'll answer Raymond the same way I answer all the others, even though I don't know or understand anything at all about Chris Remington, the seeds, the attacks, or any of it. I'll answer the same way I always do. It's the easiest way. It's the easiest way out of their questioning. One day I'll figure it out. I'll figure it all out. I'll have to. One day it will all come clear. But for now, I'll tell them what I always do. It's the easiest way.*

"I guess the same reason everyone else is running. I want to be in D.C. when they have the big tribute for Chris Remington." Nobody in the small group questioned him anymore. That answer said it all. He was one of them.

Jeremy sat with the group by the fire for a while longer. He listened as they talked about tomorrow's thirty miles, the increasing excitement and sense of accomplishment, and honor and respect each of them felt he was offering toward Chris Remington's memory. As Jeremy sat and listened, he touched the key dangling from the rawhide strip hanging around his neck, and he wondered why he was wearing it.

# CHAPTER 18

The next morning Jeremy Barnsdale was up early. The eastern horizon was a red bubble, stretching, stretching, about ready to pop. The big red ball pushing it outward was steadily rising, and Jeremy put on his running sunglasses. He'd already breakfasted on bananas and granola trail mix, and he'd already performed ten minutes of his perfunctory runner's stretches. As he was leaving camp, Bill and Raymond Tarpley were just beginning to stir. They saw Jeremy heading out toward the interstate and start running eastbound.

"I didn't think he would stay with us," Bill said.

"No, I didn't either. What was it Bear Bryant said about Forrest Gump? 'That's one crazy young man, but he sure can run.'" Raymond laughed at his re-creation of the line from the movie.

"I'm not sure that's the words he used to describe Gump, but the running part sure would describe Jeremy."

Two days later Jeremy was running on a secondary road in southern Wyoming. He'd decided to stay away from the interstates for a while. It was really annoying and frustrating him, when people wanted to know who he was, what his background was. It got to him, not because people asked the questions, but because he couldn't answer them. Be that as it may, his sense of confidence was growing that one day he'd be able to answer the questions. He felt this would happen sooner by his staying away from the running crowds. He was developing a sense that this is the way it's supposed to be. To find out who he was, he needed to stay away from the running crowds. Being around the crowds just made it harder.

The road Jeremy was on might have been listed as a secondary, but in rural Wyoming a secondary road takes on a whole new meaning. It had been two hours since Jeremy had seen any sign of life – human life, that is. There were plenty of antelope, prairie dogs, rattle snakes, horses, cattle, and even a couple of eagles overhead. Sage, prairie grass, and wild flowers fairly well permeated the ground whenever rock outcroppings, mesas, arroyos, coulees and random boulders didn't control everything. The northern Colorado Rockies could be seen on most days. Puncturing the low clouds, their white peaks looked like melting vanilla ice cream.

Jeremy had fifteen running miles behind him already today, and he was thinking about stopping soon to have a bite of lunch. He knew there wasn't much to eat in his pack, so he started looking up ahead for any signs of civilization. Hopefully a crossroads country store would show up soon. If not, maybe a nearby ranch would sell him some food. He had plenty of money. He hadn't even counted it. His wallet was loaded with twenties and hundred dollar bills. He didn't know where the money came from, just like he had no idea of why his photo ID driver's license had the name Jeremy Barnsdale on it and actually did look just like himself.

Another couple of miles behind him now, the hunger was getting to be a real issue, and the wind seemed to be intensifying. He quit running and took his last Gator Aide out of his pack, along with some cheese and the last of his bread. He ate and drank as he walked, the afternoon shadows growing longer. Finally he saw a speck on the horizon. Maybe a ranch house was up ahead, probably another four miles away. He'd stop and see if anybody was home.

Another mile behind him … was the ranch house any closer? Jeremy didn't think so. Distances out here were deceiving. He began to notice that the sky was darkening rapidly all around him, and the wind seemed to be gusting with an alarming fury. *It's a little early for sunset isn't it?* He looked behind him to try to locate the sun. It was gone, swallowed up by an angry black cloud that was in control of everything back to the west. Everything! Left to right, top to bottom, whatever was between terra firma and the top of the ozone layer was devoured by this blackest of all black clouds. Some would describe it as a "wall cloud."

The sight of the black monster kick started his running pace. He thought it very wise to get to that ranch house up ahead before the black monster did. The rain and hail storm caught him before he could get close to the ranch house. Golf ball size hail began pelting him and hitting him hard on his head. He removed his skimpy back pack and tried to shield his head from the assault. He was taking a serious beating by the ice, then it let up. If he'd known what was coming next, he would have chosen to keep the ice. It was at this point that he realized his race to the ranch house was lost. A wall of water hammered him and he couldn't see a thing. But his ears still worked and when he heard the thunderous whirling roar of the train about to engulf him, he dove for the ditch. He never did find it. Then he was swirling wildly, ripped from a hundred different directions at the same time. Torn and tossed, swirling, swirling, still swirling, unable to breathe, unable to see, the life being sucked out of him. His shoulder hit solid on something and he was tumbling and then dragged a short distance, and then he was out.

When he awoke the sky was a gray-blue satin in one direction and a blotchy dark gray maelstrom in another direction. Overhead it was a little of both. Jeremy felt the stabbing pain of his busted shoulder first, then he began noticing the less severe damage. His face was cut and bruised, elbows, knees, and hips all banged up badly. *My clothes, where are my clothes? Running shoes and socks gone. T-shirt and jacket gone. Back pack gone. Running shorts …. Running shorts? Gone. I'm naked …. No, no I'm not. I've got that leather cord around my neck with the key on it.*

Before he tried to get to his feet he looked around to see if maybe he could locate some of his things. Nothing. *Where is the road?* He couldn't see it. *What's that?* He saw a pile of rubble two hundred yards away. He slowly got to his feet. Everything was wobbling. He was dizzy and nearly fell back down. *Hold steady …. That's better ….*

*Just stand here a minute.* The pain in his shoulder almost took him down, but no, he persevered, standing there shaking. He was very cold.

He looked toward the rubble pile. *Can I make it there? I don't know, but I can try.* The closer he got he could see that the rubble pile had, just a few minutes ago, been a house. Two walls were left standing and some of the cinder block foundation was intact. Roofing, furniture, and all sorts of debris were scattered all about. He could see where a corral and barn had been. A good deal of hay looked untouched. A big gray horse appeared to be a survivor.

Jeremy stumbled on toward the wreckage. A couple of chickens were pecking around, and a light cloud of smoke was coming from somewhere under the rubble.

As he walked around one of the still standing walls, he saw a woman on her knees, her chin dropped to her chest, her hands clasped together. She was praying. Jeremy stopped and was looking at her, but she seemed lost to the knowledge of his presence. He went back around the other side of the wall and looked for something to cover up with. He found a bed sheet still semi-attached to a mattress and used it for a cover. He walked back toward the woman. She was still on her knees, bent over in prayer.

"Are you okay?" Jeremy was twenty feet away.

She looked up, surprised, "Yes, I think so. Would you pray with me?"

"Sure." He came a little closer to her.

She said, "Come over here beside me."

He knelt next to her, and she began to pray again. "Glorious Father of Creation, keep her protected. She's with You now. Hold her in Your hands. Oh Father hold her so close. Oh please hold her close. I know she's with You. Now Your angel is here. I know she's with You. Your angel has come for her. Thank You for sending him. Thank You Father. Thank You, thank You for sending him. In Jesus name I pray. Amen."

She turned slightly and lifted a small broken body wrapped up tightly in a blanket. It was her daughter. The woman gave her to Jeremy and got to her feet. She looked at Jeremy and smiled one last smile for her daughter. She walked to the horse, mounted it bareback, and rode off toward the north.

# CHAPTER 19

Jeremy sat there in the rubble a long time, still holding the blanket-wrapped little girl. While he held her he kept seeing images of the little boy who had been running after a man. These images were persistent. They would not go away as they had in the original flashback. Eventually he laid the little broken body down.

Before the light of day vanished, he poked around the rubble and found a pair of sweatpants to wear, some kind of a winter coat, and some socks that he put on. He found some food that had not been blown completely away. He ate just a bit, then sat back down and put the little girl's wrapped-up body back in his arms.

The sheriff arrived an hour after sundown.

"Here son, we'll take her. You say her mother rode off on a horse?"

"Yes, sir."

"Don't worry. We'll find her. But first we better get you to the hospital."

"Sheriff, have you seen any of those running groups pass through?"

"Yeah, sure have. None for a couple of days, but we hear there's one scheduled to come through the interstate tomorrow afternoon. We've got a reception party set up for them at the rest area."

The next night Jeremy was waiting for the runners. The vans, campers, and support crew showed up first, then a slow moving column of forty-two runners. He couldn't help but notice the two ex-football players were leading the pack. Some distance back he spotted Bill Tarpley and several other familiar faces.

Bill spotted Jeremy with his shoulder and left arm in the sling and his face all bruised, cut up, and swollen. "Jeremy, is that you? You look like you ran right through that tornado yesterday."

"No, actually it ran right through me."

"No way! I want to hear all about it. Let me get cleaned up and get some food in me."

That night Jeremy told Bill, his brother Raymond, and about ten others the entire story. They were in awed fascination.

Raymond said, "I guess you'll stay with us for a few days. That dislocated shoulder ought to keep you out of action for a while."

"Well, I hope not. I'm going to see how it feels tomorrow morning. But all my running stuff is gone. When I woke up yesterday I was naked."

"Aw, no problems there. We've got plenty of running gear. The shoe companies were fabulous. We've got extra shoes, shorts, sweats, socks, whatever you need. But seriously, you're not going to try running with that shoulder, are you?"

"We'll see."

That night Jeremy went into a serious prayer mode. The woman at the destroyed ranch house had made a huge impression on him. The fact that her prayers created an angel escort for her little girl's journey to heaven ...., well that really dug into him. Also, the entire event, especially the woman's praying, reminded him of something and begged the question – when was the last time he himself had prayed? He couldn't remember. It was strange. He knew he was a man who often prayed, daily. He was sure of it. But for the life of him, he couldn't remember doing it. So now, in the nice bed that Bill and Raymond had provided him in Raymond's large camper, Jeremy began to pray: "Well God ...."; he couldn't even seem to remember how to pray. He started again: "God I'm awfully confused. I don't even know who I am, and who I might have been – Jeremy Barnsdale. He blew away in the tornado yesterday. My ID, money, clothes, it's all gone. It looks like I'm going to have to start all over again. I'll do it. Of all the things I don't know, there is still one thing I do know – You are real. You have always been real. You have always been there for me, and I know You are now. I guess I'm asking You

God …. to ….” He had to stop and regroup again. “I guess I want to ask You to help me remember things. It seems like all I can remember is being out here on the roads, running. Don’t I have another life? A life before the running? I’ve been seeing things God. I’ve been seeing a little boy. He’s running after a man. Is that me God? Running toward You? Or, is it someone else?”

What Jeremy didn’t know was that it was a little of both.

The next morning Jeremy was up and moving around camp with all the others. The two ex-Oakland Raiders led an impromptu prayer meeting. Not all of the runners and support crew participated, but most of them did. They asked God to intervene in the seemingly failed investigation to find Chris Remington, and they prayed for protection and safety as they struggled to maintain their running miles every day. There was growing worry that Chris never would be found. This wasn’t voiced openly, but many were thinking it.

Bill Tarpley and his closely knit crew of eight or ten runners had adopted Jeremy. Before the day’s run started, Jeremy was outfitted with all new running gear; but they all told Jeremy they thought he ought to give the shoulder at least a week before he tried running again.

When the forty-three runners pulled out of camp in a slow jog, Jeremy, Bill, and the two ex-Oakland Raiders were up front leading the pack. Even with a consistent, throbbing pain running from his neck all the way to his fingers in his left hand, Jeremy began coaxing them all into a faster pace.

“Come on Raiders! We can do better than this! Let’s go! Let’s go!”

At the five mile water break Bill walked over to Jeremy, “How does the shoulder feel?”

“Not bad. Just a little pain. I’m thinking I’ll be able to get my old pace back soon.”

“I thought you were getting it back in the first five miles.”

"No, I've got a ways to go, but I'll tone down the verbal macho nonsense when we go back out. I get a little juiced up sometimes. I don't mean anything by it."

"I understand." Bill knew Jeremy was far and away the best long distance runner he'd ever seen. And, he was beginning to wonder about this newcomer to Remington's Raiders. He got to thinking, *we all try to look like Chris. It's just natural I guess, but Jeremy, he even runs like Chris.* Bill had seen TV follow Chris for three weeks, so he knew exactly what style runner he was, exactly what his stride looked like. *He sure does. He runs just like him. It's funny too. I've been wondering what Jeremy would look like without his beard? I think he'd look exactly like Chris.*

At the fifteen mile lunch break, many of the runners were attending to blisters, cramps, indigestion, hydration, and other normal bodily functions. But not Jeremy. No, he'd gone back to the interstate and was running back through the slow stragglers. When he got back two miles to the last runner, he stayed with him all the way to the lunch camp.

Bill saw Jeremy do it and then he remembered a bio some female TV reporter had recently done on Chris. One of the things she emphasized was Chris Remington's inclination to always do that very same thing. When he'd win or finish up in the lead pack of a race, Chris Remington ran back down the race course to the last few stragglers and escorted them to the finish line.

As the group started out for the remaining fifteen miles, Bill Tarpley was muttering to himself, "No, can't be. Impossible, no way."

The running became drudgery for some of the Remington Raiders. For some, the daily abuse their bodies took became just too much. Some would call it quits and go back home. They were still vehement supporters of the anti-seed campaign which by now ruled the country, and they encouraged the remaining runners with their emotional and financial support. But for every runner who succumbed to the limits of endurance his body was capable of, there was a new runner or maybe two new runners to take his place. By the time the Remington Raiders had crossed the flatlands of eastern Colorado and the entire state of Kansas, their numbers had swollen to one hundred ten.

Jeremy and Bill had become really good friends. Bill never questioned Jeremy about his background. He was just so very pleased that Jeremy had stuck with the Raiders because Jeremy's spirit lifted the entire group. When he wasn't helping less experienced, less gifted runners, he was doing something else around camp to pitch in. He did more than his share. Bill was sure of that.

The entire group was now feeling the increasing excitement of making it well over halfway to Washington D.C. There was only a thousand and seventy-four miles to go; just thirty-five more days. And at the pace they were running they would be on time for the Chris Remington tribute celebration on the Mall. The excitement was high, and the expectations were building.

Jeremy himself was beginning to get very excited. In the thirty days Jeremy had been with Remington's Raiders, he'd learned a lot more about the entire Chris Remington phenomenon by just simply listening to the other runners, and of course watching some of the TV news on the satellite TV in Raymond's camper at nights. He saw the way the country had nearly been destroyed, and how a single distance runner from San Diego had claimed that he knew what was happening because God had told him. It was not nearly as confusing to Jeremy now as it had been a short time ago. Not only that, but Jeremy was now receiving a steady stream of images from what he assumed was his previous life. He attributed it to the daily prayer sessions he was holding for himself with God. Also, his shoulder was almost back to normal. It still hurt, but it didn't slow him down very much.

# CHAPTER 20

*Washington D.C. - The Oval Office*

"**G**ood morning, Mr. President." Thomas Kinnison, the Acting President's Chief of Staff, had a calm and collected demeanor early in the mornings.

"Good morning Thomas. Let's start with the President's situation."

"Yes sir. The mini stroke, as you know, occurred at 10:20 p.m. last night. It was not unexpected. Just like the last three, the doctors had no problem stabilizing the President. This morning they say there has been no change since yesterday. He recognizes his family and salutes the doctors. Other than that, I'm afraid it's still hopeless. There is still the occasional incoherent babbling, but that's about all."

"I see. Thomas, would you bow your head and join me in prayer?"

"Yes sir."

"Almighty God, we pray this morning that You would be with President Whitley, his family, and our nation. Heal us all from the scars and pain caused by the recent turmoil, anguish, and horror we've witnessed and endured. And if we might ask again .... yes again, and again, please help us find the young man You used to stop the madness. Please return Chris Remington to us. This is our solemn prayer. Amen"

"Now Thomas, what's next?"

"Sir, I respectfully submit that we are not finished with President Whitley's situation."

"Ah yes; the Blair House and my impending departure from it."

"Yes sir. The Congress will undoubtedly make the official announcement today. Your family will be moved into the White House this weekend. All arrangements have been made for President

Whitley and his family to move back to their family home in Indiana."

"Yes. As much as I hate it, for the President's family, I realize it must be done."

"Yes, sir."

"Thomas, what are the polls showing on the job I'm doing? You know I'll need to make a decision soon. The party seems to be indicating it's automatic, there is no question that they will run me as a shoe-in incumbent. But I'm not so sure."

"The polls right now would support the party's thinking. You have a favorable rating with seventy-nine percent of voters. That's unheard of. Of course we know that a good deal of that is simply the backwash of getting the country out of the seed war."

The President corrected him, "I had very little to do with it. All of the credit should be going to Chris Remington."

"I understand, Mr. President, but I think your modesty is slightly overdone. After all, you listened when the FBI sniffed out the Remington lead, and you got Congress to act swiftly on the banishment and death sentences."

"What about the chatter from the hard left? I understand they are not exactly enamored with my weekly prayer broadcast for Chris Remington?"

"That is putting it mildly. They are threatening to have you impeached. The ACLU is leading the charge. It's the same old argument they are making – separation of church and state. The thing is, and I know you see this as clearly as we all do. If it got to the Supreme Court, we would probably lose."

"Yes, I suppose we would." He looked away for a moment and then seemed to acquire a happy and expectant look on his face. "Now I believe we have an unusual visitor this morning. I wonder how many working truck drivers have had an appointment with the President?"

"I looked that up, sir. I believe Jabez is the first."

"Was he surprised when you called him?"

"No sir, I don't think he was. Strange, but I sensed that he antici-pated the call and your wanting to see him."

"Before you bring him in, run his bio by me again."

"Born and raised in the east Tennessee mountains. No records exist for his mother or father. Raised by an aunt and uncle. No crimi-nal record. He's been a truck driver over forty years. A few years ago he and other JETS took down an international sex slave ring in Montana, and recently the JETS opened a school and home for abandoned children on his property. The rest, I'm sure, you are up to date on – the JETS ran security for Chris Remington up until his disappearance."

"Thank you, Thomas. Let's welcome Mr. Jabez to the Oval Office, and please have them fetch fresh coffee and two mugs, not those dainty china cups."

"Yes sir."

Thomas Kinnison returned quickly with the leader of the JETS and left them in private. Coffee and mugs arrived via a white-jack-eted waiter and were placed on the beautiful antique coffee table.

"Come in, come in Jabez. I'm so happy to meet you. I've heard a lot about you."

"Thank you, Mr. President. It's an honor to meet you."

After a hearty handshake the President and the truck driver stood in the middle of the Oval Office making a quick appraisal of each other.

"Please sit down. We have fresh coffee. It's my understanding that a truck driver never turns down good coffee."

"Yes sir. I suppose that is correct."

An awkward silence snuck in between the two men. Jabez might have seemed a bit nervous and out of place, all spruced up in his truck driver finery – clean, almost new jeans, shined cowboy boots, his top drawer white cowboy shirt trimmed in purple and orange Indian designs. He held his ball cap stitched with the message "Hammer

Down – Heaven Bound" in his hand. Yep, he'd put on the best he had when he came to the White House, but he wasn't nervous at all. He sat waiting for the reason the President had called for him. He let his eyes take in the room, admiring the portrait of Lincoln and all the other accoutrements.

"Jabez, I've asked you to visit with me in order to invite you and the JETS to the Capital next month when the Chris Remington tribute is to be held. I'd like you all to be my guests and join me beside the podium on the steps to the Capital overlooking the wading pool and the mall. I can't think of anything more appropriate than the JETS being there – the men who knew Chris, the men who loved him the most. Not only do I want you there, but we know that the country wants you to be there. What do you say? Can we count on you?"

"Well, Mr. President, of course we would be honored to attend, but there's one possibility that could damage all of your planning for the big tribute to Chris."

The President looked somewhat surprised, but when he looked into Jabez's deep, steadfast, eternal, hazel eyes, he knew that whatever Jabez was about to say would be the unassailable, the untouchable, pure, clean truth. The President shook in the realization that this old, gray fuzzed, road hardened truck driver was an emissary from God – FROM GOD! The President had an eerie feeling that whatever Jabez was about to say was the will of God.

The President stretched to return his coffee mug to the table, as he was trembling a mite and about to spill the coffee. "Uh, .... I hadn't thought about such a possibility ....and what might it be Mr. Jabez?"

"It's what you're praying for, Mr. President. It sounds to me like the planning for the big day is for a wake, not the celebration we all want to be a part of when God returns Chris to us. Don't you believe your prayers will be answered? Not just yours, the nation's. Do you believe in what you are praying for? Do you not believe The Father's Word?"

Again a palpable silence ensued. The President looked startled and confused. He wasn't able to respond.

"Jesus tells us that, 'Whatever you ask in My name, that I will do, that the Father may be glorified in the Son.' Do you believe Chris will be returned to us, Mr. President? Isn't that what you've been praying for? Jesus also said, 'If you abide in Me, and My words abide in you, you will ask what you desire, and it shall be done for you.' Not just you Mr. President, the nation is praying. Do you believe the Bible? 'Ask, and it will be given to you; seek and you will find; knock, and it will be opened to you.' Do you believe it?"

"I'm a believer. I grew up in a churched family. I have always believed, but I think you are on to something. A key element may have been missing. The fever is not in me."

"Mr. President, I like the terminology you just used – "the fever". And I agree with you, it is not in you. I sense it is all around you and that it's been trying for years to get in you. But you've put a wall up, not to all goodness but a wall to the most important goodness, to Jesus Christ, The Holy Living Lamb of God. Am I right?"

Edgar Rawlings was stunned. He sat there in shock, not aware of place or situation, and barely aware of the truck driver across the coffee table from him. Bared naked, he sat and contemplated the awful predicament he was in; stripped now by Jabez's hunch that he didn't know Jesus. Oh sure, he could make saintly prayers echo across the land, and he could claim a great record of church attendance, and he could produce receipts for hundreds of thousands of dollars for charity. But he could not say he'd asked Jesus into his heart.

"But I do believe in God, and I've studied the Bible, the Old Testament and the New Testament. I think Jesus was a great prophet, a great teacher. Look at the influence he's had on civilization. You can't say I don't know a lot about Jesus."

"I never said that." Jabez only had a passive look on his face.

"Well, what are you saying?" The President's volume and frustration were both on the rise.

"I simply made a hunch, and asked you if I was correct. I was asking this : Do you know Jesus in your heart? Not the historical Jesus, but the Living Messiah, The Alpha and The Omega, The Son of God, The Resurrected Tree of Life, The Living Water we need to drink from, our Redeemer, our Savior, do you know *that* Jesus? Do you want Him? That's what I was asking."

"Oh boy, I knew this day was coming. Do you know how many preachers have given me virtually the same speech you just gave? But none of them could ever get me over the fence. It is very strange, Mr. Jabez. For some reason that I can't explain, I think maybe you are about to get me over."

"No sir, I don't think so. You see, that is the reason you've never gotten over. You, and I suspect the preachers too, figured it was up to them to get you over. The only way you will ever get over is for you to do it yourself."

"How would I go about it?" The President didn't just ask it, he really did want to know.

"Mr. President, I've seen folks do it in many different ways. I've seen churches require a whole list of procedures and doctrines, and certain scripture, and so on, but the way I see it, all you really have to do is ask Jesus to take you. You have to mean it when you ask; really mean it, really want it. I've never seen it fail."

"Just ask Jesus to take me, and mean it, really want it, and I'll no longer be a hypocrite, I'll be the real thing?"

"Yes sir; four simple words, 'Jesus please take me'."

The President was silent. A lot of things were streaming through his mind.

# CHAPTER 21

It was Toby Etheridge this time. It was Toby who felt it first. Many times in the past it had been Jabez. Many times Jabez's antenna had plucked the message from God out of the ether sphere first – a message that something big was taking shape.

Toby had pushed his truck hard to reach the Mountain School for Children before the sun escaped to the west where it would sink below the Clinch Mountains and then sixty miles north the Cumberland Mountains in Kentucky. He gunned it out of Big Bubba Bucks Belly Bustin' Barbecue Bliss at Munfordville and whizzed past Horse Cave, and Cave City, and jumped on 68/80 at Glasgow. At Corbin, Kentucky he went southeast on 25, then through the Cumberland Gap.

Approaching the wide spot in the road at Dogwood Heights, Tennessee he had a flat tire and limped into a little run down tire shop on the side of the road. He backed his trailer under the eighteen foot high shed where the tire man could repair his right rear outside trailer tire just before some ominous black clouds caught up with him and opened the faucet. The rain started with a whimper, then strengthened to a consistent pelting, then grew into a serious downpour accompanied by booming thunder and blue-white explosions of lightning.

Toby was talking with the young black tire man as he worked the tire off the rim after he'd removed it from the hub. "You ever hear of the Mountain School for Children?"

"No suh. Never did hear no such thing. Why you askin'?"

"Oh, just wondering, that's all. It's a school for homeless children that me and some other truckers helped set up a couple of years ago. It's not far from here, about forty or fifty miles down the road."

"Oh, I see. Well that was good of yal' to do that."

The tire man's strong body didn't interrupt the rhythm it always took up when working on a tire. He used his considerable strength to manhandle the big black doughnut. The art in his labor showed with every move he made. Toby had seen many a tire man work, but this fellow was as good as he'd seen.

Toby noticed an old gray haired black man shuffle slowly into the shed from the attached office. The man slowly and carefully felt his way along with a walking stick out in front of him poking here and there to check for a clear pathway. When he got to an old ragged thread bare chair a few feet from Toby, he sat down and started to speak, gazing straight ahead, his eyes seeing nothing through the dark sunglasses.

"You might's well sit on down. That storm gonna' be a spell."

Toby spotted a rusty, grease stained metal folding chair a few feet from the old man. He walked over and sat down. "Yal' get a lot of storms up here?"

"Aw .... fair 'mount. But these mountain storms, they ain't nuthin' like them teeth rattler's we used to get back in Alabama."

"I heard that. I'm from Lake Thomas. Where you from?"

"Down around Mobile. They called it Freedom Woods. The slaves would run off the plantations ya' know. None of the whites would go in there after 'em. The gators was heavy back in there. My granddaddy used to tell me about it."

The thunder and lightning was getting closer, and the tire shed trembled and rattled each time the black sky erupted with ear splitting electricity.

KABOOOOM! This time a teeth rattler from Alabama found its way to Dogwood Heights, Tennessee. The seventy foot Elm behind the tire shed felt itself falling – half of it in one direction, and half of it in the other direction. It was split down the middle.

The old man removed his sun glasses and was rubbing his eyes with the palm of his hand. "I seen it! I seen the lightning! Oh God A'Mighty,I seen it! It was like the feelin' of a cold river runnin' over your naked skin. Maybe like a snake on fire and the fire comin' out everywhere. I seen it! The first thing I ever seen in my life!"

"Shakkel, go take a look. See if it hit anything."

The young tire man and Toby both headed toward the back of the shed, and a minute later came back in.

"No suh. The tree didn't hit nuthin'. We's lucky. It come close to the propane tank."

Toby sat back down.

"Mister, I seen more than just lightning! It's you ain't it? You the cause of the lightning! No, no I ain't a blamin' you, but you's the reason the lightning come."

Toby was still a few wave lengths behind the old man, but he had the ears to hear, or at least to listen.

"My people, we always believe that when a blind man sees lightning, it's 'cause of the person nearest to him. It's you. And the folks believes when the blind sees the lightning he also see something about the person nearest to him. That's you. I seen something more than just lightning. I seen something that's about to happen to you."

"What did you see?"

"I seen you been lookin' for someone. You and a lot of people been lookin' for somebody. And I seen, yes suh, I seen …. You gonna' find that somebody, and when you find him, there's gonna' be a million people around."

"Mister, what's your name?'

"Well my momma named me Aristotle Deepstep, so that's what I been goin' by for a long time, but I feel like changin' my name. I think I'll be Bright Eyes from here on."

An hour later as Toby was nearing the Mountain School for Children, he was still thinking about what the old man said. More so, he was thinking about the way he was feeling when he had the flat tire. He *knew* something was about to happen. The feeling arrested him. He was captive to it. All he could have done was hold on and ride with it – just wait to see what God was going to do.

This time as he wound his way through Wilson Holler past the Matlock Crossroads Country Store, just a couple of miles from the Mountain School for Children, he had no such anticipation – no sense that God had another surprise in store for him. But He did.

It was nearing twilight, a light mist came off the pastures and hay fields and a few low areas had some shallow puddles from the rain. The smell was late summer Appalachia – fresh cut hay, lingering honeysuckle that wasn't quite ready to give up, pine scent from the forest, and sharp oak and hickory tones from nearby logging. The mountain ridges cast shadows that draped the low valleys in such deep, dark, green that you could feel it. You became a part of this mountain and valley world when you came into late summer Appalachia.

Toby's eyes looked for the sign for the school he knew was just around the next curve to the left. He and Jabez had taken two weeks to build the sign. It was six feet high and twelve feet long and only had two words – Mountain School bordered by a ten inch hickory frame. The letters in the two words were hickory strips, each uniformly handcrafted to a four inch thickness and nothing was between them and the frame but air, except where their tops and bottoms were secured.

Toby slowed down and turned into the entrance drive and drove a quarter mile. There were Jabez's log cabin and barn off to the left, two hundred yards away, tucked back in tight against the lower braces of a lofty mountain

*What's that up ahead?* A big tree was lying across the road that led into the school's dorms, class rooms, barns, stables, and other buildings. Toby pulled over on the grassy wide spot the JETS often used to park their rigs temporarily. He got out and walked to the fallen tree where Jabez, T.P., and several other JETS were hacking away at it with chain saws.

"What happened?"

"A storm passed by and I reckon all the water in this old Sycamore was just too tempting. It came right down when a fearsome tongue of fire hit it right here at the base." Jabez led Toby down a few feet to where the tree snapped right off.

"And look there," he was pointing to where the burned out splinters and trunk of the Sycamore protruded in a ragged heap only a foot off the ground. "It followed the tap root right on down, about half way to Hades it looks like."

"When did it hit?"

"Exactly an hour ago; me and T.P was sittin' over yonder on my porch."

"An hour ago …. Jabez you ain't going to believe this. I got news about Chris, and I got it exactly one hour ago when lightning split an Elm tree clear down the middle." And then Toby thought to himself, *Of course he's going to believe it. He was made for moments like this.*

He was right; that is exactly what Jabez was made for.

Later that night Jabez, Toby, T.P., and four other JETS were talking over all the latest events, including Jabez's recent visit to the White House.

"So, he changed his name to Bright Eyes, did he?" Jabez couldn't hide the big grin on his face.

"That's what he said."

T.P. was chuckling to himself. "And he said you're going to find Chris? Well, we all knew that was going to happen or at least *somebody* is going to find him."

Toby looked toward Jabez and T.P. "He didn't say Chris, but I got the feeling that's who he was talking about. And don't forget, he said there's going to be a million people around. That probably means the big day coming up in Washington. And now we get the invite from Edgar Rawlings to be up on the podium." He stopped and let his eyes drift away a moment, and then he looked back at Jabez, "It looks like it's all coming to a head on the big day in Washington. Is that it?"

Jabez scratched his head and started to say something, but didn't. He got up and walked to the door of his cabin and walked outside.

He scanned the heavens for a while searching each galaxie, each constellation, and each bright star.

When he came back inside he sat down and with a calm look that revealed no emotion, he said, "Maybe it will be the big day in Washington that we get him back. It all depends on one individual who has a big decision to make."

All seven of them knew who that individual was.

Toby took the conversation off in another direction. "I think it's storytelling time. Seven of us here tonight, right? Seven, a pretty good number, and I bet all seven of us know whose turn it is."

Everyone shifted their gaze toward Old Soft Shoe. The eighty year old trucker squirmed a little and tugged on his suspender straps.

The youngest JET of the seven, a fifty something trucker named Garnie Ray Beardon said, "Soft Shoe, I'd like to hear that yarn you spun about your ship leaving you ashore in China."

"That wasn't a yarn. That's a true story."

"Well, whatever. Tell it again." Garnie Ray Beardon knew it wasn't a yarn. He just liked to yank Old Soft Shoe's chain every now and then.

Old Soft Shoe looked around the group of JETS and said, "Well Garnie, I'll tell you what. I'll save that one just for you a little later tonight. Okay? Windjammer was telling me about something that happened to him and I think it would make a great story. How about it Jammer?"

Windjammer looked excited. You could tell he really wanted to tell what happened to him. "Well fellers, it's a bit of an unusual story, but I guarantee it's true. It just happened two weeks ago."

Everybody settled back and opened up their ears. They didn't want to miss a thing.

"I was coming out of a truck stop in Salt Lake City when I noticed a hitchhiker up ahead on the shoulder. You know how you always feel when you pass a hitchhiker up – rotten. Yes sir, I certainly felt guilty. This guy had a ton of junk sitting there next to him. Why, you'd think he was dragging a small household along with him. I thought he should have used a Mayflower moving van. But that's not why I was feeling guilty. You know what else he had?"

Everybody had a blank expression. Finally Garnie Ray Beardon said, "He had kids with him."

Windjammer smiled and said, "No, he didn't have any kids, but he did have a sign. It said "God Saves". I felt terrible passing him up, but I was anxious to get on down to L.A., and really, I didn't have any room in my cab for all his stuff. Well …. I guess I could have made room …." His voice trailed off somewhere, and he just stared straight ahead.

"I got to thinking it over. Why *did* I pass that man up? I thought about it all the way to Las Vegas. I never did come up with a good reason. Instead I set my mind to try to make up for it. I planned to keep my eyes open for the next hiker I saw with his thumb out or a sign with a destination down around L.A. It took a while but I finally spotted a likely candidate. I had stopped at another truck stop just east of Las Vegas. All I planned on doing was fuel up and grab a sandwich. As I was coming in I saw a feller on the outbound side of the truck stop with a sign. I couldn't see what it said. I went on in and fueled up and grabbed a sandwich and put it in the truck. Before I pulled out, I walked around the front where that man was standing. I went up to him and asked him where he was hitching to. He said he wasn't hitching anywhere. I looked at his sign. It said "Will Work – Need Help – Thank You – God Bless." Well, he certainly looked able to work. I mean he was clean and very healthy looking. I asked him how long he'd been out of work and he said about four months. He said the old lady he'd worked for in Oregon died. He was her chauffer. Well, we talked a little more and the impression I got was, he really had been trying to find work but so far he'd come up empty. I wished him good luck and went back to the truck.

I honked at him on my way out and he waved back. Then I spotted another man on the shoulder and his sign said "L. A." He looked very neat and tidy, only had one good sized piece of luggage, a small overnight bag, and a small pet cage. I said to myself, 'Windjammer, there's the hitchhiker you've been looking for'.

I pulled over and used the switch to lower the passenger –side window. He climbed up on the safety steps and I asked him, 'Do you have any drugs or weapons?' 'No,' he said, 'I don't smoke, drink, or do drugs.'

'I'm going to L. A. Get your stuff in here if you want a ride.'

It didn't take him long, and in a minute we were back on 15 heading for L.A. He had what sounded like a British accent. I asked him, 'Where are you from?'

'South Africa.'

'How long you been in America?'

'Five years, maybe a little longer.'

'What are you going to L.A. for ?'

'I've got a new job. Actually it's in San Diego. I put L.A. on my sign just to get that far, but really I'm on my way to San Diego. I thought I might try to earn passage to Hawaii on an ocean liner and get back to San Diego in time for my new job.'

'What kind of work do you do?'

'International finance, actually. My last job I was a global hedge fund manager.'

'What happened to it?'

'You know how uncertain the markets have been, and all the problems with the Euro, and the general economic uncertainty. The company I was with bailed out. They let us all go. There's no other way to put it – we were laid off.'

Naturally I felt that this guy was not your typical hitchhiker. How many times do you see a global hedge fund manager hitch hiking? We talked and talked and sure enough, it didn't take long for me to see that he had a whole bag full of other unique characteristics. He was extremely articulate, knowledgeable in history, politics, anthropology, religion, and about anything else you might want to talk about. Then somehow our conversation drifted to physics and mathematics, that is, *his* conversation drifted that way. I was mostly listening, just asking a question now and then. He went on and on. I followed everything he said, although I sure didn't understand much of it. Eventually he was making a point that God was mathematics. And he had plenty of evidence, but of course I didn't understand it."

Windjammer paused. No one spoke up. Finally, he started again, "Well, you know me. I had to question his theory. I said something like, 'That doesn't sound like your theory leaves much room for Jesus.' He came back with some really neat stuff. It didn't rule Jesus in or out in any way. I can't recall any of the specifics. We talked all the way to L.A. By the time we got there, I honestly couldn't tell you whether he knew Jesus the way we know Him or not. You see, his depth of knowledge and ability to keep me mesmerized had disarmed me. I never asked him if he was saved, but I did tell him about the way many of us got saved. You know, the four words, Jesus please take me."

Everyone around the room in Jabez's cabin shifted in their chairs and they all had uncertain looks on their faces. But they weren't about to leave until they heard the rest of Windjammer's story.

T.P. was the first to speak up, "What happened when you got to L. A.?"

"It was after dark, so I offered to let Anderson, that was his name – Anderson Wheeling – I offered to let him sleep in the truck. He said that would be great, that he had to conserve what little money he had left. I didn't deliver the load 'til the next morning, so this way we'd get a good night's sleep, and he'd start hitching on to San Diego the next morning. Well, I fixed us up a couple of sandwiches, and then we got ready to hit the sack. He walked his little dog Gennie first. She was the cutest little cocker spaniel. She never made a noise in her little cage. He put her back in her cage then he climbed up in the top bunk. I was about ready to turn-in myself, but I decided to get back up in the driver's seat and listen to a little radio. You know,

I always try to check and see if there's any news about Chris before I turn in. So anyway, I turned it on and scanned the dial for a news station. The first one I came to had a lady interviewing some man. You'd never guess the first thing she said. 'Dr. Wharton, your book makes the case that God and mathematics are one.'

Well, we both chuckled a little and didn't say much about it. We both went to sleep. The next morning I delivered the load before the sun came up, and I was telling Anderson about my plans to look up an old friend of mine. He's a bartender in Santa Monica. Anderson sounded like he might be interested in tagging along. Since he said he wasn't in a hurry to hitch on down to San Diego, I invited him to join me on the two hour trip to Santa Monica. We didn't leave 'til around four o'clock that afternoon. After I dropped my empty trailer at the company yard, we set off for Santa Monica.

It took a while to find the bar and another twenty minutes to find a parking place within a couple of blocks. As we walked I told Anderson a little about my old buddy, Jerry the bartender. I told about the days nearly forty years ago when we had worked at the Ramparts night club in Waikiki, and that it had been six or seven years since I'd last seen Jerry. We walked into the bar and there he was, behind the bar talking to a couple of customers. We came in and sat down on the far end of the bar. Jerry walked toward us, but he didn't recognize me. I said. 'Barkeep you got any Kentucky Bourbon back there?'"

"Windjammer, you old son of a gun!"

Well, we had a big night. You know I'm not the big drinker I once was, but I definitely was throwing a few down that night. And Anderson was too. I told him when we walked in to order anything he wanted – everything was on my tab. We ordered food from outside, and Jerry was spinning a lot of old stories. Then the strangest thing started happening. Anderson and I were talking whenever Jerry was busy with other customers. Anderson's story started coming undone. I don't remember what triggered it, but he admitted that he'd lied to me about his "new job" in San Diego. He said that the truth was he did have a couple of potential jobs but nothing would be certain for four or five weeks, and that he was down to his last twenty bucks. He told me that he was headed toward San Diego because the weather should be warmer there when his money finally dried up.

I was pretty flabbergasted, not just that he lied, but I guess I sort of felt like he was taking advantage of me. But then I started thinking, who is taking advantage of whom? I picked him up didn't I? Who wanted company and conversation? Which lonely truck driver wanted those things? I knew which one. And what about my making sure he knew what the four words were? Is that all there is? You tell somebody what the four words are, then you let him slip-slide into starvation and let him die. Is that what you do? And then I thought about the guilt trip I had dealt with, you know, when I passed that first hitchhiker outside Salt Lake City with the sign that read 'God Saves'. There it is right there. I was thinking about that …. and then it hit me. I knew what the whole Anderson experience was about. It was about God's giving me the second chance, the second chance to actually help somebody who needed help. But then I knew it was more than that. It *was* about telling him the four words. It was actually about both. God, in His wisdom, gave me a chance to atone for my first mistake, and He showed me that this man, Anderson, *did* need to learn about the four words.

We were still drinking and talking and by now Anderson's strength and confidence had deteriorated down to mush. He was a lost soul. I said, 'Anderson, you remember the four words I told you about?'

'Yes.'

I said, 'All you have to do is say them, and mean it, and your whole life will change. You will be free. You will be saved.'

He said, 'I've already said them.'

'Then you are a saved man, Anderson. Did you notice anything change when you said the words?'

'No.'

'You will. You just gotta' give it some time. If you really want Jesus, He will take you. Jesus will never let you down. You are a saved man Anderson!'"

Windjammer stopped, and everything was quiet. Finally somebody asked, "Is that the end of the story?"

Windjammer said, "Pretty much. I tried to get him to stay in the truck with me when we left Santa Monica. I told him I thought I could get him some labor work. But he decided to go his own way. I was really hoping that you guys would pray for him."

Everyone said they would. Then somebody asked Jabez, "What do you think will come of him?"

"I know exactly what will come of him, if he meant it."

# CHAPTER 22

The mayor of Kansas City welcomed The Remington Raiders to Missouri by giving them a police escort through the middle of downtown. Approaching from the west on 12th Street, the skyscrapers up ahead on the hilltop city looked like castle spires disappearing into medieval cloud banks. It was 10:45 in the morning, and despite the heavy cloud cover, the temperature was already eighty-two degrees. The runners were exhilarated. Several thousand citizens and office workers lined the street, cheering and shouting encouragement as the runners sped by. Coming out of downtown the caravan of foot slappers dropped south to route 50 which they planned to follow into Jefferson City, the state capitol.

Five days later Lone Jack, Warrensburg, Knob Noster, Sedalia, Tipton, California, and St. Martins were all behind The Remington Raiders when they set up camp at a state park on the banks of the Missouri River, just outside Jefferson City.

"The locals say that on certain nights you can see Tom Sawyer, Huck Finn, and Jim the runaway slave, just north of St. Louis, floating down the Mississippi on their raft." It was Bill Tarpley spinning the tale, and he was so caught up in it he let it rip for all he was worth. "They say you can even catch a ride with them if you are willing to swim out to the middle of the river."

Bill's brother Raymond responded, "Yeah, right, and they say that Big Foot will welcome you into his cave up around Mt. Rainier and give you a foot rub."

Another runner quipped, "Everybody knows that Smoky Bear gives private tours through Yellowstone. All you need to do is show up with a Ranger hat."

Jeremy listened to the banter, but as was his custom, he didn't participate. He only listened. He really didn't understand much of the conversation, joking, and storytelling that went on around the nightly campfires. Also, the frequency of what he assumed were flashbacks from his former life were increasing dramatically. The little boy he had seen running after a man now had a name – Charly. A Navy ship would sail across his visual screen two or three times a day. Certain names and places that he felt he had some connection to would come to mind. He knew he was getting closer to his real identity, and he was sure it was because of his prayers.

It was later now, and runners were slipping into the many support vans and campers to get some much needed rest and sleep. Jeremy started for Raymond's camper, but then he turned back for the river. The ghostly image of a raft on a shimmering moonlit river just would not give him any peace. He had to go down by the bank and get as close to the river as he could so he could see …. whatever there was to see.

He had on the same running shorts, tee shirt, and shoes he'd run in earlier that day, and in addition to that, he wore a nice new running sweat suit. There were some scattered trees along the steep slope to the muddy Missouri River bank. Jeremy held to a tree and let go to chop step to the next one. Same to the next one and the next. When he let go again his feet slid out from under him, and he was tumbling down toward the river. The last thing he saw was the little boy named Charly, calling …. Daddy, Daddy.

He quit rolling and tumbling when his head bounced off a solid Sycamore stump about fifteen feet from the water. It didn't knock him out. Worse, it set his memory recovery back about forty days, to just about the time he'd first run into The Remington Raiders camp, east of Salt Lake City. All the recent images, names, locations, and the little boy Charly were all gone, as was his name of Jeremy Barnsdale.

When he got to his feet he cleaned the dirt and mud off his running sweats as best he could, and then he did the only thing he knew to do. First he climbed back up the bank, and then he started running. He saw a lot of vans and campers at the top of the hill, and there were a few people milling about, but he had no interest in anything he saw there. When he got to the first major highway, he saw the sign for St. Louis and started running east.

He ran for two hours and came to a little town. An all-night convenience store was the only place open. He went in and asked the clerk for water. The clerk said help yourself and pointed over toward the soda machine. He went over and filled a big plastic cup with water and drank it down and repeated that maneuver two more times. He filled it again and was about to walk out but stopped at the checkout and said, "How much do I owe you?"

"Aw, we're supposed to charge thirty-five cents for the cup, but if you're one of them runners on the way to Washington, then we don't charge anything."

And so the solitary runner had his new education jump started yet again. It would take several more days, but he would learn again that if he just told people he was running to Washington, free food, beverage, and even lodging would be happily extended to him.

He crossed the Mississippi River into Illinois in only two more days. Now that he was a solitary runner again, there was nothing to slow him down. He was doing over forty miles a day. During the day he used his running jacket to carry water and food. He tied off the arms around the front of his waist. It was a very efficient fanny pack.

His beard was now a full flowing wild looking bush of a thing. One day someone said, "Look! It's Forrest Gump running along with all the Chris Remington look a-likes." So he adopted the name Forrest Gump. It sounded to him as good as any other name, and after a week or so of solo running, it dawned on him that he needed a name. But he couldn't understand why people would look at him in such a strange way, and why many would laugh when he told them his name was Forrest Gump.

None of that kept him from what he always had known he must do – run. He must run! And run he did. In three more days he came to Indianapolis. A middle-aged couple insisted he stay with them for at least two days. They explained that at the pace he was running , he'd get to Washington a full week and a half before the tribute to Chris Remington would take place. He stayed, and by the time he hit the road again he'd been reeducated once again on who Chris Remington was and why the country held him in such lofty regard.

By the time he entered Ohio he was beginning to re-align some of the memory chips he'd knocked loose that night on the banks of the Missouri River. A little boy started showing up again, and his lost driver's license ID with the name Jeremy Barnsdale popped up prominently in his mind. He thought, *that might be me, maybe if I go by Jeremy Barnsdale instead of Forrest Gump people won't laugh any more.* So the solitary runner was still a solitary runner, but at least he once again had a legitimate name.

A few days later he found himself running a secondary road in eastern Ohio. The up and down, up and down of the hills taxed his running only slightly, *But oh what a treat for the eyes*! thought Jeremy. It was sheep country and between each village were lush green valleys with perfectly kept pastures between the stands of hardwoods. Early in the morning the fog and mist raised just enough to frame twenty or thirty fat, contented sheep grazing on a sloping hillside. Jeremy thought it was a perfect scene, beautiful! Later that day he ran through the tiny hamlet of Londonderry, Ohio and the name Londonderry triggered something in Jeremy's slowly recovering memory. Somehow he fused the fascinating sheep country and the name Londonderry into an image he was sure he remembered from somewhere back in his past. He could actually see English sheep farms out in the countryside north of London, and he knew he'd toured there while on leave from the Navy.

In the next three days he began seeing ships, ship yards, and faces he couldn't connect with a name except the little boy who was without a doubt, Charly. Also there was a pretty blond woman who began to vibrate not only in his mind's eye but in his finger tips and in his veins. Who was she? He didn't know. But he knew he didn't want her to go away. *So, I'm Navy, or ex-Navy,* he thought.

Western Pennsylvania hit Jeremy hard. The long mountain grades were relentless, so he had no choice but to drop his mileage back to thirty a day. He knew he was about eight days from Washington D.C., and he knew the Chris Remington tribute was ten days away. The highways were swarming with runners converging on the capitol. Running camps of varying sizes were spotted here and there along all highways leading into Washington. The excitement and anticipation of the big day looming a little over a week away was something America hadn't experienced in a long time. Unity wasn't always the thing America could call attention to. But it was now.

# CHAPTER 23

As the solitary runner got closer to Washington D.C. and six days before the nation would stage the national tribute to Chris Remington, Acting President Edgar Rawlings went live on every media outlet in the country at 9:00 p.m. EST. The speech was described by Rawling's press secretary Jimmy Brinkman as personal, far reaching, and a speech that might change history. The press secretary said that's all he could elaborate on as that is all the President had divulged to him. In effect, no one knew what was coming.

"Good evening my fellow Americans. Tonight I bring to you a message that many would say is unlike any other message an American President has ever before made, but they would be wrong. I could talk to you for hours about the deep belief many past Presidents may have had in the principal object I lay before you tonight. Instead, I will denote two specific speeches, one by President George Washington and one by President Abraham Lincoln. Also, I will read for you, several things President Ronald Reagan had to say on the subject at hand.

Here is an excerpt from George Washington's first inaugural speech:

'No people can be bound to acknowledge and adore the Invisible Hand which conducts the affairs of men more than those of the United States'.

Many have said that President Washington's use of the two words "Invisible Hand" means he was not talking about God. I say they are wrong. Why would he have capitalized the words?

And here is an excerpt from President Abraham Lincoln's second inaugural address:

'Fondly do we hope, fervently do we pray, that this mighty scourge of war may speedily pass away. Yet, if God wills that it continue until all the wealth piled by the bondsman's two hundred and fifty years of unrequited toil shall be sunk, and until every drop of blood drawn with the lash shall be paid by another drawn with the sword, as was said three thousand years ago, so still it must be said, 'the judgments of the Lord are true and righteous altogether.' With malice toward none, with charity for all, with firmness in the right as God gives us to see the right, let us strive on to finish the work we are in, to bind up the nation's wounds, to care for him who shall have borne the battle and for his widow and his orphan, to do all which may achieve and cherish a just and lasting peace among ourselves and with all nations.'

And finally, President Ronald Reagan had this to say:

'If we ever forget that we are 'One Nation Under God,' then we will be a nation gone under.'

'The Constitution was never meant to prevent people from praying; its declared purpose was to protect the freedom to pray.'

'Within the covers of the Bible are the answers for all problems men face, if we'd only look there.'

As you can see, these Presidents were not afraid to tie the destiny of our great country to the will of God. Recently we have seen a vigorous and exciting rebirth in our trust that a sovereign God really does care about us, really does listen to us, and really can and does lead and direct us. The example Chris Remington set for us all not only saved us from ruin but reminded us that we are a nation which must follow God if we wish to survive.

Yes, I know, there are groups within our midst, powerful factions, which have for years and years tried to disavow our allegiance to God. Under the guise of separation of church and state, they have tried to remove God from our schools, the government itself, the military, our families, and even our very souls.

My fellow citizens, I tell you tonight, the time has come for us all, for this cradle of freedom and liberty that we call America, to finally and forevermore return to the throne of God. If recent events and the legacy that Chris Remington has left us don't affirm the fact that now is the time, then I'm afraid nothing ever will. We must act now!"

Edgar Rawlings paused and looked as if he might be saying a silent prayer, his head tilted forward a bit and his eyes were closed, but the silent prayer started leaking out for the entire world to hear. "Father, give me the strength to lead this nation, to tell them the truth about myself, and give us all the strength to finally prove to You that we want to come back, we want to be Your children, we want this nation to conform to your will. In Jesus name I pray. Amen."

He looked up, back into the cameras. "I have a sad confession to make. You know the weekly prayer broadcast I have been making for the purpose of God to bring Chris Remington back to us …. This is hard for me to say, but here's the truth …. I didn't believe it. Like everyone, I have wanted Chris to be returned to us, but I really didn't believe that he would be. How shallow and thin was my faith in God? Yet I led you to believe that I trusted God, when actually I had given up on Him."

He paused and again lowered his head and closed his eyes. "Oh Father, let this country see that their acting President has not been true to You, and that by making this confession, I do hereby proclaim that from this moment forward, I will be true to You."

Whatever notes and prepared lines he had intended to use were forgotten. Edgar Rawlings was speaking now as a child of God. He looked back up at the cameras and the assembled audience and said, "Soon our nation will hold another Presidential election. I know that the consensus is that I will be my party's nominee and that we will ride the success we had in the seed war to a certain victory to retain the executive branch. But I submit to you that it may not happen. It will not happen unless God Almighty returns Chris Remington to us. As I just pointed out, I had given up on God actually bringing Chris back. Now, of course, I see the cowardly, two faced stance I was taking – outwardly saying God would bring him back when deep down inside of Edgar Rawlings there was no such confidence. But now the time has come for the leaders of the United States to proclaim our allegiance to God, to publicly declare that we are a nation of God, by God, and for God. And for me to be your leader there is only one way I can do that, and that is to actually believe in the prayers we submit to God for Chris's return.

"My fellow Americans, what I'm saying is this: I now believe God will do it. He will bring Chris back to us. I believe it, and I believe you believe it. I don't know how He will do it or exactly when, but I do know it will happen before or on the day of the tribute for Chris. How do I know it will happen? I know it because we are God's children, and yes, we are God's nation! And what we ask for in His name will be done! Jesus said so. Goodnight my fellow Americans. You can sleep peacefully in the comfort of the knowledge that America is finally back to being a nation under God."

The left wingers, humanists, the ACLU, the mainstream news outlets, and the Sunday morning political talking heads all went ballistic. "How could Rawlings do that? Can't we just yank him out of office for suggesting what he just suggested?"

Two of Washington's most savvy news producers were having a drink at a quiet lounge in Arlington. Trent Woodridge started his career at Harvard by editing the student newspaper. After stints at the Washington Post as domestic legal affairs editor, then international correspondence editor, he moved over to NPR where he quickly ramped up the radio stations pro Muslim, pro-choice, pro-gay, anti-military platforms even more than the previous program director.

Roger Benton was a Mississippi farm boy, who like Abe Lincoln, was self-educated. By the time he'd entered his local community college he'd read all the classic Greek philosophers. He also read Tolstoy, Dostoyevsky, Ayn Rand, Dickens, Freud, Lenin, Marx, Shakespeare, Thomas Payne, Jefferson, Thoreau, and many others. And of course he read Lincoln. He never ceased to be amazed at the seemingly endless depth of Lincoln's thinking and ability to bring his sharply honed lawyer's research skills to bear on any argument. Benton was viewed by many as being one of the few unbiased journalists in Washington. He was just as likely to be seen hobnobbing with power brokers from the progressive side as well as the primary players in the hard right conservative camp. His writing and editing confirmed the view.

"He's certainly gone out in the deep end. He seems to think he knows what he's doing." Benton took a sip of his bourbon and chased it with salty beer nuts.

"Deep end? You think? He's just committed political suicide. He had the party nomination in his pocket. What is the man thinking? He didn't have to stoop down to this cheap trick. He's doubling down, quadrupling down; he's putting it all down on the fantasy that somehow Chris Remington is going to magically appear out of thin air."

"Maybe he knows something we don't."

"I doubt it. He's just trying to ride the current God wave, and he's just set himself up for a wipeout."

# CHAPTER 24

Abdul Aleem Isam was born in Jerusalem in 1978. His father moved the family back to Gaza four years later, thinking that finally Palestine was on the brink of reclaiming the same land that had been in dispute for thousands of years. By the age of twenty Abdul knew that the only way his people's rightful claim on the homeland would succeed was for young people like himself to carry the fight to Israel's only true ally - The United States of America, the great Satan.

Abdul had been trained in revolutionary tactics, weapons, and espionage by whatever radical anti-Jew terrorist group happened to be in vogue at the time – the PLO, Mujahedeen, Hezbollah, and Hamas to name a few. But eventually he came to see them all as ineffective. They each had their particular weakness, many times being a power hungry figurehead at or near the top. Abdul was very bright and very cunning. When he finally decided it was time to act on his own, he devised a plan to enter the USA as a student and then, through the use of false ID's and computer record hacking, Abdul became a native born U.S. citizen – Jeremy Barnsdale. The assortment of lethal attacks against U.S. infrastructure that Abdul had considered was impressive. Suitcase nukes against the capital and key military bases were at first high on Abdul's list. But as the scope of such attacks became clearer in his mind and the expertise required to make them happen became daunting, Abdul shifted his thinking to less exalted targets. Taking out a couple of key bridges should be doable, maybe the Golden Gate and the George Washington in New *York*. Another possibility always lurked around the pernicious corridors of his mind – a Presidential assassination. *Ah, to look into the evil President's eyes the moment I plunge the dagger up under his rib cage; to see that he knows Allah has sent me to destroy him, and thereby, all he represents, and to do it on a stage for the entire world to witness. Yes! It would be a virtuous conclusion to my mission which would also provide instant martyr status. Allah would be pleased!*

The day Abdul saw the silly Christian, Chris Remington, on TV declare that his God had told him what caused the attacks, Abdul sensed that an opportunity to assassinate a President had presented itself. What if the gullible, imbecile Americans actually got behind Remington, actually supported his cause? What if Remington actually was able to run across the continent? Forget the idiocy of his claim about a "God message?" What if he was successful in actually running nearly three thousand miles – regardless of whatever anti-seed, save America nonsense he tossed out along the way? If he actually ran to Washington D.C, it would be the kind of thing the American Jew-lovers would desire to see. They would embrace Remington, they would celebrate wildly! Remington would be the newest capitalist pig hero, Super Bowl winning quarterback, home run hitting World Series champion – the new Babe Ruth, Knute Rockne, Ronald Reagan. He naturally would be invited to a meeting with the President; all American heroes are.

*But what if I get to Remington first? What if I hypnotize him? What if Remington is programmed to remove the dagger hidden in one of his running shoes and kill the President for me? Surely Allah would have no hesitation to approve such a tactic. The main objective, the assassination of a U.S. President, would still have been achieved. No, I will not become an instant martyr, but the assassination would probably be more likely to have success than if it were my very own hand on the dagger.*

That was Abdul's thinking about how to assassinate the President – grab Chris Remington, hypnotize him and sit back and watch the murder on TV.

Things didn't go exactly to plan, though. Plucking Chris off the road he'd been running on south of San Jose and near the Soledad Ruins had been easy. Chris had been agreeable to helping Abdul change the flat tire on Abdul's cargo van. That's when Abdul covered

Chris's face with a pillow soaked in chloroform. The struggle lasted almost twenty seconds, but Abdul prevailed and drove an unconscious, limp Chris Remington to a secure first story condominium two hours away.

Later as Chris began emerging from the fog, he faked his continuing unconsciousness. He would open his eyes slightly and survey the room he was in. When he heard Abdul approach, he was back to the flaccid, listless pile of bones he'd been. Eventually he was able to understand his predicament – feet duct taped together, hands duct taped, and mouth duct taped. He was in a well lit room with only one outlet door that seemed to be locked except when his lone captor would enter or depart. There was another door, half open, that seemed to lead into a small bathroom. Chris noticed that the lower of two hinges on that door had not been set perfectly square or it had a very small edge on it that extended out from the wall maybe an eighth of an inch. He thought he might be able to use it to tear the duct tape from his hands. He wriggled himself over there and managed to get the duct tape torn and loosened considerably just as Abdul re-entered the room. *It's now or never,* thought Chris. One more vicious swipe at the protruding hinge freed his hands. Abdul in three long strides was across the room and aimed his foot at Chris's head. Chris grabbed his leg and twisted him down. On his way down Chris put a shoulder into Abdul's chest knocking him hard against the open door frame. Then Chris threw an elbow at Abdul's head and caught him solid, knocking the back of his head against the same door frame.

Abdul lay there stunned for a moment. Chris used the time to free his feet and legs. As Abdul was getting back to his feet, he grabbed a wooden chair from a nearby table. Chris saw the chair coming and knew it would find his left arm and shoulder. Still, Chris's charge hit Abdul chest high and Abdul's head once again bounced off something very hard, this time the table. The wallop Chris took from the chair sent him careening back toward the open door. He lost his footing and fell into the small bathroom, his head slapping heavily against the edge of a low vanity cabinet. Slivers of jagged light exploded in Chris's head. Connectors to memory banks bounced inside his head. Years of experiences and history were compressed and rendered useless. The physical Chris Remington was left intact. The running animal, Chris Remington was unaltered, but the cognitive Chris Remington disappeared, was a void, a blank slate.

It was this Chris Remington who got to his feet and like a lethargic rain drop that you're not sure will slide all the way down your windshield, he slowly walked out the bathroom and the other room, barely even noticing the slumped body of Abdul half under the table. In the next room Chris was headed for the door to the outside but noticed a leather wallet on the dinette counter. He picked it up and took it with him. When he left the parking lot he started running. That was the only thing he knew he must do – start running.

Abdul staggered to his feet and felt the blood trickle down the side of his face from the gash on his forehead. He looked everywhere in the condo apartment but found no trace of Chris Remington, not even a blood trail. He went outside quickly. No Remington. When he came back inside he tended his wound, grabbed the keys to the cargo van, and went to the dinette to get his wallet. It wasn't there. No time to fret over the missing wallet. He must find Remington. He couldn't have gone very far. He hustled out to the cargo van and started searching all the nearby streets.

After almost an hour, he halted the search. He went back to the condo to ponder his next move. As soon as he walked in, he realized he couldn't stay. *Remington probably has my wallet, ID and all. The cops are probably on the way here right now.* He grabbed his clothes, laptop, papers, and all the documentation and IDs he possessed which would allow him to become someone else immediately. He drove a hundred miles away and checked into a motel as Winston Balthrop.

Within the next month Abdul was able to devise a new Presidential assassination plot. He couldn't believe his good fortune – the fact that Remington had disappeared. *He must have gotten run over somewhere and perhaps his body had rolled into a ditch or a deep canyon when he escaped my condo. Maybe he got mugged and the perpetrator hid the body. Look what's happened; the stupid Americans have already made him a hero, just as I predicted. What if the body turns up with the driver's license photo ID with Remington's picture and Jeremy Barnsdale's name? That would not be a problem. I'm no longer Jeremy Barnsdale. In fact, it would only enhance my original plan. I placed Remington's picture on the driver's license simply to throw the police off track. If something had gone wrong and I were investigated or even arrested, Remington's picture on Jeremy Barnsdale's ID would be my perfect escape. A Remington impersonator "gone off the deep end." Sure, that's what they would have thought. It would have bought me valuable time, but that's all history. Now I must concentrate; I must put all of my energy and love for Allah into the revamped plan. Now that Remington is gone, I once again will have the honor of sinking the dagger into the President's chest.*

Nearly three months later Abdul was shocked once again by the stupidity of the Americans. *Edgar Rawlings must have camel dung for brains. Telling the fools he expects his phony God to deliver Chris Remington back to the nation before or on the day of the big tribute. That is …. that is the height of stupidity, and it is the key to Rawling's death, by the dagger which I will joyfully plant in his chest. Idiots, all of them!*

# CHAPTER 25

Jeremy had spent the night in a friendly, jovial, up-beat running camp some sixty miles east of Pittsburgh. The evening chatter amongst the runners was buoyant and cheerful. Everyone was expectant and excited to be close to the end of this grueling marathon. Jeremy listened as four or five runners were talking:

"I'm really feeling good about the whole thing. What about you guys?"

"Absolutely. Just look …. We've been a big part of history. I'd do it all over again. The country has never been as united as it is now."

"And to think one runner started the whole thing."

"Not to mention having a one on one with the Big Man Upstairs. I still catch myself wondering about the way that conversation went down. I took the seed two or three times myself. Thank God I didn't have the genes or chromosomes or whatever it is that can set off the nasty stuff."

"Poor Chris. Whoever killed him will without a doubt burn in eternity."

"So you think he's dead?"

"What do you think?'

"I don't know for sure, not a hundred percent. I'm in the camp that thinks he just might show up."

"He better hurry if he plans on making it to his own party."

Jeremy shared a mattress with another runner in the back of a pickup truck after eating all the food he could hold. At sun-up he was among the first to be up and stretching and drinking coffee. He packed some fruit and sandwiches and a water bottle in his makeshift fanny pack and started off solo, running into the rising sun.

In twelve miles he came to another running camp that was ready to get moving. The camp was in a big grassy area between the interstate and an off-ramp. He asked the first runner he encountered about a detour sign that caught his attention.

"Oh, I think that's for state vehicles only, something about a registration office for some of their trucks or something, but a local runner told us it's a beautiful road to run on, and it comes back out on the interstate about eighteen miles down the road."

Jeremy said thanks and started chugging off down the secondary detour route.

In three miles he passed a state highway building with a lot of state trucks in the big parking area. He kept running and had to agree, it was a beautiful area to run through. In a couple more miles there was nothing but forest and mountains on his left and a deep lush valley dropping off to his right. He could see a few farms scattered in the valley and a few pockets of livestock grazing the fields.

As he continued running he realized the road would soon be down in the valley, and he was thinking about maybe taking a dip in a river or creek he hoped he would find. He was running easily downhill, into shade provided by the forest, then back into the warm sun. Next was a big easy curve, more shadow, then broken sun and shadow, followed by a gentle breeze off the valley floor. When the road curved back the other way, the mountain was still playing out to the waiting valley, not far now. Jeremy the solo runner, saw the breeze swaying the trees gently which made the leaves shuffle and created a song of leaves, more shadow, more sun, and more running. The downhill grade finally flattened out, and with his head high, shoulders high,  Jeremy the solo runner was relaxed, breathing as smooth as silk, and running easily,.

Jeremy found the stream and walked back into the forest to follow it as it flowed through flat, blue-gray outcroppings of Pennsylvania limestone on one bank and broken pegmatite in the stream itself. He walked the bank for a while until he came to a wide spot of peaceful water. The tree silhouettes waltzed on the surface of the water as if orchestrated by an unseen long-haired maestro. A few leaves spotted the surface of the water, and a frog launched from a rock and dove for the bottom.

Jeremy removed his shirt and fanny pack as well as the key on the leather strap from around his neck. He waded out slowly until he was waist deep. He went under quickly the first time, then stayed under and kicked off to a glide the second time.

When he came out he perched on a big sun drenched flat rock to dry off. He removed his running shoes and socks, wrung the socks out, and snapped the shoes against the rock to get most of the water out. He looked at the leather strap with the key for a long time, and not knowing why, he put it around his neck. He closed his eyes and his fingers went back to the key. He turned it over several times and tried to see the key through his closed eyelids. Instead, he saw a man, a tall man who wore a leather strap around his neck with a truck key on it. The man was near a campfire, and his tractor trailer was illuminated by the fire. Jeremy could see the four small letters painted on the tractor just below the driver's window – JETS. His eyes still closed, Jeremy said, "Toby". The next thing he saw was a cargo van in the early morning light and a man bent, over working to change a flat tire, and Jeremy saw himself stopping to help.

# CHAPTER 26

As the Earth sped along its annual trek around the sun, it twirled its last three hundred sixty degree dance on its axis. It was the day before the greatly anticipated national tribute to Chris Remington. Creation held its breath. There was a palpable excitement, an electric anticipation, a hopeful pleading that something big, something prodigious was about to take place

That night Edgar Rawlings huddled with his chief of staff, several key advisors, the lead secret service agent in charge of all security planning for tomorrow, the FBI director, and Jimmy Brinkman, the Acting President's press secretary . Brinkman was to be the master of ceremonies for the big event.

Thousands of citizens were already camped on the mall, and more were arriving every hour. Thomas Waynick, the lead secret service agent, had told the group that a gathering of more than two million citizens was expected for tomorrow. You could see the worry in his face when he said it.

The program would consist of opening statements by the press secretary, an invocation from a prominent Christian preacher, a tribute to Chris Remington by Edgar Rawlings, a word from Chris's wife Cindy, followed by one of the JETS. Next the independent news reporter Diane Warner would speak. After special music performed by more than three hundred musicians from the military bands, the New York Philharmonic, choral groups, and leading popular vocalists, Acting President Edgar Rawlings would speak again and make closing remarks. Somehow security would attempt to deal with the aftermath of two million Americans, either extremely jubilant, or extremely dejected, depending on whether or not Chris Remington was in attendance for the tribute being paid him.

Stewart Menkoff, the FBI Director, wished he had a better response to Edgar Rawlings' question about any new leads, but he wasn't in the business of wishing or spinning fantasies. All he could do was report the facts. "Mr. President, I'm afraid not. The last credible lead we had was two weeks ago. We had sixteen agents on the case. We are no closer to finding him now, than when he disappeared back in California."

Neither Menkoff nor any of the others wanted to suggest to the acting President that any thoughts of a miraculous reappearance by Chris Remington between now and tomorrow afternoon would be pure balderdash. Certainly none of them would tell him that the dismal gloom that was certain to engulf the nation after tomorrow would be the beginning of the end of his political career, but most of them were sure of it.

That same night twenty JETS were parked near the Vietnam Memorial. They'd spent a good part of the day cleaning and shining their tractors and trailers. The chrome twinkled in the sun as if a furnace had ignited millions of diamonds to an eye burning metallic silver cascade shifting constantly as one gazed on the big trucks.

Time was running out. Chris was still missing. The JETS were sitting in chairs, hands firmly chained to others to form the prayer circle. They'd been at it since dark. It was mostly silent. Occasionally someone would vocalize his deepest desires – The Father would return Chris to an adoring nation.

Indeed, all across the National Mall groups of prayer warriors prayed through the night. Other groups expressed themselves in a much different manner. Partying, dancing, and music was their way of celebrating tomorrow's national tribute to Chris. Even in the camps of the partying rabble rousers there was the hope and expectation that maybe it was possible, just maybe it wasn't too late. Maybe Chris would still show up.

# CHAPTER 27

The morning broke with a cosmic anticipation. The sun itself seemed to vibrate to a strange and dreamlike frequency as it pulled itself out of the low predawn gray-blue broken clouds behind and to the east of the U.S. Capitol Building. The mall was a sea of humanity. Overnight another half million Americans had worked their way into Washington and staked out a small piece of ground on which they hoped to be a part of history.

The Secret Service, The Capitol Security, The Washington D.C. Metro Police, and six battalions of National Guard troops were all very worried. The estimate now was that three and a half to four million citizens would be massed in and around the mall by the time the event was scheduled to begin – 2:00 P.M.

Some of the security officials were imploring Acting President Rawlings to call the whole thing off. They said they never anticipated a crowd this size. "Mr. President, we simply are not prepared to manage this size population, particularly not under these unusual circumstances. There is no way we could contain such a mass of humanity if, for instance, they were to rush the podium. Patton's army would not have been capable of stopping them."

Edgar Rawlings listened intently, then stood up and walked around the Oval Office. "And what, pray tell, do you think would induce them to rush the podium?"

"Well, sir ….." The security official knew he was treading on a touchy subject, "let's say, and I know how you feel about this sir, let's say the day is …. uh, uneventful."

Rawlings cut him off, "Are you trying to say that what if Chris Remington isn't found today, or doesn't , in fact, show up on the mall?'

"Yes, sir."

"Well, let me tell you, let me tell all of you, Chris Remington will be found today! I expect you all to accept that fact and prepare this town for the biggest party it's ever seen!"

They all looked at him as if he had lost his mind.

By 10:00 A.M. the two and a half mile stretch from the Potomac River to the Capitol Building was full of red, white, and blue Americans. All parking areas near the mall were filled, and no additional parking extending into interior Metro Washington and across the river into Northern Virginia was available. The bridges across the river had never seen the onslaught of foot traffic they were seeing today. Runners, solo and groups, were continuing to swell into the mall. Families, school groups, entire church congregations, all were filtering into the National Mall. One jailhouse in West Virginia had allowed thirty jailbirds to run to the mall, under tight security, of course, by twenty volunteer police runners.

By twelve noon the excitement, the drama, the raw spiritual passion of over three million brought even the non-believers to a fervent emotional glow. They didn't know *what* was going to happen, but they knew *something* was going to happen.

Jabez was on his cell phone, talking with Toby. "I saw you pull out about sun-up. Where are you looking?"

"Glen Echo right now, about a mile and a half from 495. I've been all over Arlington, McLean, Tyson's Corner, Potomac, and Rockville. I just figure that's where I'll find him, somewhere on the west side."

"Ten-four . I guess it's about time for the rest of us to go with the security detail the President sent down here this morning. They got a bus waiting for us."

"Who's going to do the talking on the podium?'

"I've asked Old Soft Shoe to do it. He said he'd be glad to."

"Roger that. And Jabez ...."

"Yes."

"Don't worry. I'll get him in."

"I know you will Toby. I know you will."

By 1:45 P.M. everything was in place on the podium that was situated on the west side of the Capitol Building looking out toward the millions on the mall. Security had been in place for hours. Now all the speakers and other guests, including the JETS, were seated behind the bullet proof plexi-glass protected rostrum. The bands, orchestra, choral groups, and vocalists were all in place. Everyone was waiting for the President. He and his wife and an entourage of VIPs and political cronies would be escorted by his secret service detail from the Capitol Building.

And now everyone could sense his arrival to the podium. The increasing roar from nearly four million continued for five minutes until finally Press Secretary Jimmy Brinkman was able to hear his words getting through on the massive public address system.

"Thank you, America! Thank you, Thank you ….."

Another three minutes of continuous human thunder.

"Please, please ….. Thank you …."

He let the thunder roll another thirty seconds until it began sub-siding. "Today is for Chris Remington!"

The deafening rumble exploded again, this time for a full two minutes.

"And make no mistake, Chris is here! Either the Spiritual Chris Remington whom we all love, or the physical Chris Remington we all want to see, or both! Chris Remington is here! And this day is for him!"

Glassware in the bars on 15th Street and E Street and M Street rattled. Windows in the Smithsonian vibrated. The dome on the Capitol Building thought about launching, then on second thought, decided to stay put. Eye witnesses, years later, would swear that the Washington Monument swayed fifteen degrees, and that Abraham Lincoln smiled from the memorial where he'd been perched for years and years. Pandemonium! And Edgar Rawlings hadn't spoken a word.

"Ladies and gentlemen …. Please …. Thank you ….. Please …. Ladies and Gentlemen please welcome Pastor Antonio De Costas from Grace United Methodist Church, Chris Remington's home church in San Diego, California. Pastor De Costas will deliver the invocation."

As Jimmy Brinkman stepped away from the rostrum and invited Pastor De Costas up to the microphones, the lead secret service agent, Thomas Waynick, was whispering something in Edgar Rawlings ear. "Mr. President, we have a solo runner about a mile and a half out on Independence Avenue who says he is Chris Remington."

Rawlings was sitting between Cindy Remington and Old Soft Shoe. Thomas Waynick had leaned over a bit from behind Rawlings to make his report. Edgar Rawlings turned his head and shoulders slightly to respond to Waynick. "Excellent. Has his identity been verified?"

"No sir, the two D.C. uniforms out there say he looks exactly like Chris Remington, and that a group of about two hundred runners have a perimeter around him and are escorting him up here to the podium."

Rawlings just caught a few words of Pastor De Costas's invocation echoing out to the clustered masses, "And Heavenly Father if our petition today is answered, and surely it will be, then we, God's people, God's America, we …. "

Rawlings turned back toward the mall and was looking out toward the left, toward Independence Avenue. *My God, my God, it's happening! Here he comes!* As all the others on the podium still had their heads bowed and their eyes closed, Edgar Rawlings could see a human wedge opening a hole through the four million. A tiny dot was in a vacuum in the middle. It was Chris Remington. The two hundred running his wedge were bringing him right toward the podium.

"Agent Waynick, get a corridor opened up for them. Get them to bring Chris right on up to the podium."

"But Mr. President, you know we can't do that. We have no conclusive ID on this guy."

The invocation was over and Jimmy Brinkman was back at the podium, preparing to bring the President up front. And by now, those sitting next to or near the President knew something was going on.

Edgar Rawlings sensed this was the defining moment of not just his political career, but of his entire existence. It all came to this moment. He'd prepared the country for it, he himself believed it would happen, he really did, and now the only thing left undone was his acting decisively, his resolve to lead the country back to God as he had said he intended to do. He must act now!

"Agent Waynick, you will remember these words for eternity. We will make a path for that runner to get to this podium, and we will make it now. This country will follow the will of God this moment, and I believe forevermore. Do you want to be the one who tries to stop it?"

"No, sir."

"Then see that the path is cleared for Chris."

The President approached the rostrum not to deliver a tribute (actually a eulogy) to Chris Remington, but to welcome him back.

# CHAPTER 28

**A**bdul Allem Isam felt the lower neck portion of the custom prosthetic full face disguise slip just a bit a little below his collarbone. At that particular spot he had attempted to leave a tiny aperture to allow sweat to drain from his face. The designer and builder of the mask had assured him there was no need to worry about normal perspiration. The disguise was breathable. Naturally Abdul didn't tell the designer he would be running for three or four miles, and of course that would amount to more than normal perspiration. The mask was a lightweight composite of silicone and polyurethane and after it had been molded to an exact sculptured replica of Chris Remington's face, the designer had painted on the final touches, and made the wig to be the identical copy of Remington's hair style. Also, it didn't hurt anything that Abdul fit Remington's body build - five-ten, a hundred and sixty pounds. How very fortunate. Surely Allah was deeply involved in the removal of the American President!

Abdul had been living across the Potomac in a studio apartment in Arlington for two weeks before the big tribute to Chris Remington, which was plenty of time to learn the lay of the land on and around the mall. For the last three days he'd crossed the river and walked around in the midst of the early arriving campers. He talked with lots of them, many of whom belonged to running groups. He was trying to get the feel of the growing crowd. Why were they really here? To party? To show their love and sense of loss for Remington? Were they here for the spiritual miracle all of the Christians anticipated and expected?

Then on the third day of his reconnaissance of the enemy held mall, he found a running group that had run all the way from Wisconsin for all of those reasons. Abdul quickly discovered, however, that partying and drinking was becoming their primary passion. They were camped in the vicinity of the Lincoln Memorial.

That afternoon and evening Abdul spent a lot of time with them, and just when he thought they were at their peak susceptibility he explained to them that he had a strong feeling. No, he was positive that Chris Remington would actually show up. Moreover, he was sure this running group from Wisconsin was destined to run with Remington and lead him up to the podium. Even the moderately sober members of the group were thinking to themselves – *wouldn't that be something?*

The day of the tribute Abdul inserted the dagger in the false sole of his right running shoe. The compartment was spring loaded and would eject the dagger only when Abdul pushed his finger in a certain spot at the side of the sole. The mechanism worked flawlessly and didn't impede his running stride much at all, at least not more than he was able to conceal for only three or four miles.

He dressed in the same running outfit all the other Chris Remington look-a-likes wore, the main article of course being the anti-seed T-shirt Chris had worn. He saved that until he had carefully pulled the mask over his head and down across his face. He flattened out the lower portions on his upper chest, shoulders and lower neck. Then he put on the T-shirt and got in front of the mirror to affix the wig and make any other final adjustments. *Perfect,* he thought. *Even my eyes by virtue of the contact lenses are now tinted that hideous ice blue that many of the Jew lovers have.*

He laid his prayer rug out and went to Allah one last time on his knees. Now he was ready. He walked to the Arlington Memorial Bridge with a hooded sweatshirt covering most of his disguise. The bridge was closed to all but foot traffic. When he crossed the bridge he tossed the hoody aside and began running at a decent eight minute mile pace.

In just a couple of minutes he was coming around the Lincoln Memorial and ran across the grassy area toward the camp of the

Wisconsin runners. He hit a preset code on the cell phone he was carrying and then tossed the phone aside. Instantly the simple three word message he had recorded earlier began belting out from the four speakers he had secretly placed in front of the Lincoln Memorial in the middle of the night. The message in an excited Anglo voice, not his natural Arabic accent, repeated loudly, over and over, "It's Chris Remington, It's Chris Remington!" All eyes were quickly scanning the area. There he was! It was Chris Remington! THE Chris Remington!

Abdul ran right into the camp of Wisconsin runners shouting he must get to the podium on the other end of the mall! He must get there! Not a single one of the Wisconsin runners doubted that! Within fifteen seconds two hundred of them were off, running as a human wedge ice breaker, cutting a passage through the steamed up, hysterical human mass. They angled off a little to the south and continued toward the podium on Independence Avenue.

Abdul felt confident he would get his opportunity. He continued the visualization rehearsal of every move he would make once he climbed the side steps to the podium and got within five feet of the head of the Great Satan, Edgar Rawlings. He would bend as if to pull his sock up or tighten a shoe string, then release the dagger, then the lethal uprising plunge, the target just an inch below Rawlings's sternum, the blade a relentless, cutting, tearing, agent of death.

Closer now. Maybe a mile and a half to go. Two uniformed police tried to penetrate Abdul's security curtain. All they heard from the throng was, "It's the real Chris Remington!"

Indeed, now the entire mall was aware that the real Chris Remington was here. The miracle they came to witness was taking place! By the time the Wisconsin herd had Abdul up close to the podium, the four million had begun a tumultuous, ear shattering chant – WE WANT CHRIS! WE WANT CHRIS!

The President was at the rostrum and had tried without success to get control of the crowd. It was impossible to quell the mob. Even if he'd screamed into the microphones it would not have overcome the blasting uproar of the mob. Now Chris was about to climb the steps to the podium. Waynick had ordered three of his men to meet him at the bottom and at least frisk him thoroughly. When they had performed their assignment and looked back up to Waynick to indicate he was clean, Waynick waved Abdul to come up. The word was spreading amongst the four million, and they could see it happening on the huge jumbo-trons, Chris Remington was on the podium. The maelstrom of noise and chaos rose to another level. Communicating verbally up on the podium or anywhere else was impossible. Everything was in eyes, arms gesturing, and body language; there was no other way. Edgar Rawlings threw his arms up and out wide as he nearly bounced across the podium to embrace Chris Remington. He got very close, but Chris for some reason bent over to grab his shoe. Waynick was closing fast from the six feet away he had been. As the flashing blade bolted upward toward Rawlings's chest, Waynick kicked Abdul's wrist with the force of a jackhammer. The dagger sailed toward the rostrum, and within three more seconds five secret service agents had a perimeter around Rawlings, their guns drawn, looking around intensely for a target.

Waynick and three others had Abdul down fast, crushing his face into the podium floor. After feeling the rubbery texture of the back of Abdul's neck, Waynick began to understand what he was dealing with. He got his fingers under both sides of the bottom of the mask and quickly peeled it over the failed assassin's head.

# CHAPTER 29

The running in western Maryland was wonderful for Jeremy. Much of it was a long downhill gradual grade. He ran so smoothly and effortlessly you never would have guessed he'd come three thousand miles. And Jeremy's hopes and prayers that he would figure out who he was , where he was from, were paying off. Every day some new information, some new clue would come sprinting into his consciousness. He'd even shaved the shaggy beard and trimmed his hair to something he felt comfortable with.

By now he knew someone had hurt him in California, but he didn't know who or why. Also he knew he had a wife and a little boy named Charly. And, he knew he had some connection to a group of truckers called the JETS. He also knew he must continue running to the Capitol to be there for the tribute to Chris Remington, whom by now he understood was the national hero who followed God's instructions to run across America to warn the country about the dangers of the seeds.

The morning of the big tribute Jeremy was just east of Rockville, Maryland, twenty miles from the Capitol. He started running solo an hour after sunup but with all of the traffic still trying to get close to the Capitol, it was slow going.

By 1:30 P.M. he was in Brookmont, only six miles from the Capitol. All inbound traffic was clogged up. Police were barely able to keep a safety lane open for emergency vehicles only. Thousands and thousands of motorists were parking wherever they could and walking or running the remaining six miles. Despite the difficulty of all the compressed humanity, everyone was in a festive mood. The energy and anticipation ran unhindered among the crowd.

Jeremy felt it too. Everyone was all smiles and shouting things like "We love Chris, God bless America, Mine eyes have seen the glory". Everywhere he looked people were happy. As he scanned his surroundings his eyes stopped on a bobtail Peterbilt tractor that was on a side street waiting for the police to let traffic cross. He stopped running, now only a slow jog because of all the congestion. He stared at the tractor and noticed that driver was looking toward him, right *at* him. He saw the letters JETS just below the driver's window. He started walking through all of the people toward the tractor. The driver was opening the door and getting down.

The solo runner walked up to the driver, "Toby?"

"Chris?"

The solo runner looked very confused. "I'm not sure who I am."

Toby reached out and placed the house key around the runner's neck in his fingers and said, "You are Chris."

Toby wanted to give him a big bear hug but instead asked, "Are you all right? Where have you been?"

"Yes, I'm fine. I'm just not sure of very much; just that I was supposed to run here for today's celebration." He looked pleadingly at Toby as if to ask, *Can you help me?*

Toby understood perfectly, and he knew what to say, "You sure you're alright?"

"I feel great."

"Okay, try to hold on just a little longer. Everything will come back to you soon. Your wife and son are waiting for you right up the road."

"Charly? He's here?"

"He sure is and a lot of other folks!"

"You said my wife?"

"I sure did."

"What's her name?"

"Cindy."

A lot of things started clearing up in Chris'ss mind.

Just a moment after Waynick had pancaked Abdul Aseem Isam, Jabez answered his beeping cell phone. "Yeah."

"I got him. We're about five miles out. He's in good physical shape, but seems to be in a mental fog. I believe he's had amnesia."

"Ten-four. Let me inform the President and see what he wants to do. We've just had a Chris impostor get all the way up on the podium and nearly take Rawlings out with a dagger."

"You're kidding!"

"Do I sound like I'm kidding? I'll get right back with you."

Jabez knew better than to try to approach the President. He probably would have been gunned down. Not only that, the secret service were hustling Rawlings off the back of the podium presumably to be whisked back to the safer confines of the Capitol building.

Still, something clicked in Jabez, and he knew he must act. He stood up and took two or three steps toward the surrounded President. "Stop! Stop! Please! Just a second, I have a message for the President from the real Chris Remington."

Waynick knew that all of the guests on the podium had been screened and had no weapons. He went to Jabez. "This better be good."

"One of our drivers has Chris five miles from here. As God is my witness, I swear it's Chris Remington. Do finger prints, DNA, search him thoroughly, whatever. It's him. If we can get the route opened up a little, Chris can be on this stage in twenty minutes."

Waynick searched Jabez's eyes looking for a hint of anything threatening or untruthful. He couldn't find anything like that. He *did* find just the opposite – goodness, conviction, eternal love. He stopped the removal of the President and stepped inside the ring they had around him and told Edgar Rawlings all Jabez had told him.

A couple of minutes later two fire trucks from the Brookmont Fire Department, six police cruisers, and one red Peterbilt tractor were leading Chris Remington down the MacArthur Boulevard, then the Rock Creek and Potomac Parkway toward Constitution Avenue.

In the meantime Edgar Rawlings had been released by the secret service, and on his way to the microphones on the rostrum he stopped to tell Cindy Remington that her husband had been found and in just a few minutes would be here with her.

The crowd, having witnessed Rawling's near assassination, had relinquished most of the revelry and frenzy to a low hubbub filled with questioning and concern.

Rawlings began speaking, "My fellow Americans, trust me when I say this: I truly regret the ugly scene we've all just witnessed. I am fine, our brave and splendid secret service have the suspect in custody. Such a shame that thoughtless plots such as this still plague free and God- fearing men. But let us move on to the business that brought us here today. We will never back down from the cowardly attempts by some to injure and destroy our spirit. Not today, not ever!"

A reasonably enthusiastic response drifted up from the four million, but nothing like it had been just a few minutes earlier.

"As I said, we have important business to get on with. Recently our country passed through an incredibly difficult period which threatened our very existence. We all know about the heartwarming encounter Chris Remington had with our Creator and that Chris had the faith required to respond to God and follow His directives. Sadly, forces beyond our control took Chris away from us. As you know I outwardly voiced my belief God would return Chris, but as you know now, it wasn't in my heart. Then something happened to me. A trucker shared with me the power of four simple words – Jesus Please Take Me. Yes, that's all I said, and then I believed. I really believed God was in control and that God would bring Chris back.

As you know, today was to have been a tribute to Chris. From individual to individual, feelings differed. Was it to be a tribute to the memory of Chris? Or was it to be a thank you and a tribute to a living Chris that would one day return? Citizens of the United States of America, I tell you this: We no longer have to wonder what kind of a tribute this day was meant to be. It is a tribute from a nation of God's children, a nation who loves God and His Son, The Light of The World, Jesus Christ. It's a tribute from *you* to Chris Remington, who is at this moment running down Constitution Avenue toward this podium!"

Jumbo-trons all around the mall flashed the live footage simultaneously. Two red fire trucks, a red Peterbilt tractor, and now twenty police cruisers were coming east toward the Capitol. Chris Remington was in the middle, running strongly, waving to the crowd, running toward the podium, running toward Cindy and Charly, and thanking his Heavenly Father every step he took, thanking Him for being such an awesome God.

This time, when the festive pandemonium cut loose, the uproar literally shook the Capitol to it foundations. The event was later known as the Christian Woodstock. It continued for four days.

That  day Chris had run down Constitution Avenue and was about ready to climb the steps to the podium, he couldn't make it. Cindy and Charly were running down the steps and Cindy wouldn't relinquish the bear hug she'd put on him for a long time. Eventually the three of them made it back up and that's when the party really began. After everyone put a hug on Chris, and cannons were going off somewhere on the south side of the podium, the strangest sights were beginning to reserve for themselves a unique place in American history. Edgar Rawlings and Jabez were locked at the elbow, prancing to some kind of other worldly jig. FBI agent Bart Duncan and FBI profiler Dr. Kate Wenderson were doing the same thing, as were T. P. and Diane Warner.

And while the VIPs on the podium were engaged in gaiety and merriment, the masses were no less immersed in their own riotous celebration. A quarter mile west of the podium, lost in the bedlam and the sea of humanity, two men were making an attempt at communicating. "Bright Eyes, I wished you could see it all. Them big TV screens is showing the President up there dancin' like a corn crib rooster."

"Oh, I feels it Shakkel! I feels it! Hallelujah! What a day!"

Neither the two men, nor anyone else, paid much attention to the darkening clouds overhead. If a storm was coming, well then, it might as well come on. These four million weren't going anywhere soon. Then it hit. KABANNNNNNGGGGGGG! A cord of lightening so intense and powerful, your very thoughts were erased as they bounced off an unseen wall of disbelief. A tree off to the south of the podium burst into flame. Fortunately no one was hurt.

Bright Eyes grabbed a man next to him. It was a man he didn't know. It wasn't Shakkel.

"Mister, what's your name?"

"Anderson Wheeling."

"Mr. Anderson Wheeling would you believe me if I told you that you is the reason that lightning hit so close to all these people?"

"And what is your name sir?"

"Well now, my momma give me the name of Aristotle Deepsteps, but I changed it to Bright Eyes."

Anderson Wheeling looked at the old blind man next to him and said, "You know Mr. Bright Eyes, actually I think I could believe anything."

"Well good, 'cause you is the reason for the lightning, and not only that, but I know something else about you."

"You do? That doesn't surprise me either. What is it you know?"

"You said four words recently that changed your life."

"That I did, my good man."

"And you know what else?"

"No, but it's not going to surprise me."

"You and me and Shakkel here, we is going to shout out those four words and see what happens. But we going to change the last word to "us". You ready?"

"Yes sir, I believe I am."

"Shakkel, you ready?"

"Yes suh, I is."

"Jesus Please Take Us, Jesus Please Take Us."

They kept the chant going, and in a minute or two, everyone around them joined in, "Jesus Please Take Us, Jesus Please Take Us." It kept growing and growing and in a couple more minutes four million Americans on the national mall were crying in unison, "Jesus Please Take Us." Many watching on TV around the country joined in, as did many from around the world.

Those on the podium were caught up in the pleas also. Many were openly weeping, many were unsure of what was happening, but they found themselves chanting the four words despite their confusion.

Charly was with his dad and asked him, "Why is everyone crying?"

"Because they are happy."

"Oh. Dad, can you and me go running together? I feel happy too."

"Sure."

Chris asked the President if a narrow trail could be forged through all the people to create the semblance of a path about a quarter of a mile around the podium, and in a few minutes Charly was running with his Dad.

# The 1986
# Just Say No
# Marathon:

# Running
# and Walking
# with God

# Chapter One

It all began in 1976. I popped open my fifth can of beer. The ball game I was listening to on the radio was in the late innings, but I had long forgotten the score or who was at bat. I was thinking about a lot of other things. One was the night my mom, my sister, and I had returned to Honolulu from Maui. We had crossed the Molokai Channel on the Windward, an inter-island ocean going airfoil which ferried tourists and islanders throughout the Hawaiian chain. I had never used it before; although, I had flown to the outer islands four or five times and always marveled at the brief, fifteen minute flight.

My mother and sister had been in town visiting with me for several days. It was a good time for all of us. I think they were pleased to see how my college work was going in my junior year at the University of Hawaii. The trip was also the classic reward trip to paradise for my mother, who along with my dad had raised four children. Mom was fifty-nine and was in the early stages of an insidious killing brain tumor which finally took her in 1992. Her golden years of retirement were never to be. They were replaced with operations, pain, paralysis, fear, and depression. But Mom was a real trooper, a true inspiration. Never once did I see her lose her dignity, her will to live, or her love for all of her family. Mom's days in Hawaii with me were probably the best days she and I ever had as mother and son.

She never did know that I almost died that night after the Windward had tied up to the pier at Honolulu harbor. It had been a long day. We had made many of the tourist stops on Maui, and by the time we had arrived back in Honolulu we were all tired. I advised my sister, Donna, that it would be best for her and Mom to catch a cab back to their hotel in Waikiki. They agreed, and after seeing them off in the cab, I walked to my VW bus parked nearby. I was already anticipating the buzz I was longing for even before I lit the joint that I had tucked under the dash just for this very occasion. My return to Honolulu after having spent an entire day on Maui showing the sights to Mom and Donna would have to be rewarded with a dynamite joint. After all, an entire day without so much as a single toke and nothing to drink was an unthinkable proposition. But now everything was going to be fine. My reward for staying straight all day was now burning down my throat. The cannabis was in my lungs now and beginning to enter my bloodstream. In a few seconds it would be in my brain and then, well, and then, yes, it would, it would, oh yes. Oh yeah, sure enough, I was stoned again.

Pulling out into traffic was a slide onto a wavy trail. Everything felt fine. The day was behind me. I'd done my family duties. Now, it's drive back to my dorm room, make a few calls, find another late-night friend, everything was going to be fine. But the buzz was a good one, a really good one. Stop and phone a good friend first. Share it with him. Tell him how loaded you are. Tell him you've got more stash that ought to be shared tonight. He says have a good trip, but he can't make it tonight. The wife has friends over, and it's just not a good night. Did I detect a hint of apprehension or worry in his voice? Forget him. Who needs him anyway? This is really good stuff.

Back in traffic, the headlights around me all have a very large and a very warm glow about them. They seem to be floating, not really attached to automobiles, but completely independent, in full fight. A warm and secure envelope began hazing in around me.

Wait a minute. Something is wrong. The lights are coming at me. They are no longer in full flight. Their beams of light are lasers going right through me. The automobiles they are attached to are skidding off the road left and right. Why are the lights approaching me? Why aren't they taillights? No, they are headlights. I'm driving about fifty miles per hour going the wrong direction on the four-lane, median divided Kamehameha Highway, one of Oahu's busiest thoroughfares between the airport,

Pearl Harbor, downtown, and Waikiki. My mind is going about 150 miles per hour. What happened? What's going on? Surely this is a bad dream. Luckily as I'm trying to piece this scene together and make sense of it, my rote driving reflexes, those that somehow escaped the stupor induced by the cannabis, took over. My foot came off the accelerator; I'm coming to a stop. There, now I'm stopped dead center eastbound facing two lanes of westbound potential head on collisions going by me at fifty.

Now my mind is catching up with my physical reflexes. It says, *"Get off this highway NOW!"* I see a break in traffic. Cars are still swerving and skidding to avoid hitting me. There, now. No traffic for a block or so. *"Turn this hippy van around, you crazy fool."*

The ball game was over now. I popped another can of beer. I looked around at my surroundings and tried to count how many nights I had been as lonely as I was tonight. Listening to a Hawaii Islander baseball game, sitting in my parked van, drinking beer, and wondering how life got to be so lonely. I bet I had done this very same thing ten of the last thirty nights. If not this same thing, then something very similar, like spending as much of an evening as my money would allow drinking in one of Honolulu's "pu pu bars," as I called them. As long as you ordered a new drink on a regular basis, the hostess would keep bringing you excellent dishes of Oriental and Hawaiian hors devours, known in Hawaii as pu pu's.

Whether it be local bars or drinking alone, usually in my van, I was beginning to see a frightening pattern emerging. I was alone, and it began gnawing on me. I knew I was supposed to be happier than this. Why not? I was young, only twenty-seven, healthy, a bachelor living in paradise. I'm sure that to many people I was living the good life, but for some reason, I was miserable. I didn't see all the drinking and the marijuana as the real problem. After all, that's what everybody in my circle did for relaxation .

Well, not everybody.

There was Wendell Davis, a classmate in many of the physical education classes I was taking at the university. He was a thoughtful, serious young local guy, younger than myself by seven years. He entered the University of Hawaii straight out of high school where he had played football and basketball and seemed to be a natural athlete in about everything he did. Like me, he was a physical education major, and like me, he was serious about getting his degree and going on to a teaching and coaching career. Unlike me, he stayed away from the orgiastic drug and alcohol scene in and around the Waikiki nightclubs.

No, I didn't see the marijuana and alcohol as the problem, even after the near-fatal event on Kamehameha Highway and other similar near tragedies. I wrote such experiences off as the risk you take when you're living life to the fullest. Once in a while, you might cross over the line a wee bit. You might over-indulge with a drink too many or get some bad weed that you didn't know had been cut with opium or elephant tranquilizers. So what? It didn't happen often. It was just a risk you'd be willing to take. I was in the early stages of denial, but of course I didn't know it.

Now that I look back, it would be interesting to hear the Madison Avenue crowd respond to this scene. It might have been the perfect, all-American picture. The young happy-go-lucky athletic crowd. Half the time on the beach with a cold one in their hand, half the time in a pool hall or a bar with a cold one in their hand. Hot babes promising everything just so long as you've got a cold one in your hand. What would the Madison Avenue image makers say about me? I fit into their picture perfectly.

But what happens when the game is over, the lights go out, and bars close? I was what happens. An empty shell trying to fill it up with alcohol and drugs. The alcohol and drugs were probably just symptoms. Something else was wrong.

The real problem. What was it? A character flaw perhaps? I didn't think so. People liked me. Locals seemed to like me, I think because I didn't quite fit the free and easy California beach bum profile. I was a born and bred Southerner. I had a light Kentucky drawl or I suppose, to some, a twang. When I tended bar in Waikiki to many I was known as "Kentuck." Others dubbed me with "Joe Buck," the role played by John Voight in *The Midnight Cowboy.* I accepted the nicknames with no ill feelings. In fact, I think I liked them.

So what was the problem? As I sat there thinking about it, I was becoming aware that this evening sitting here in my van alone, half-soused, melancholy, retrospective, and worried about the direction my young life was going in, was somehow going to be a pivotal point in my life. Something was about to change, either for the better or for the worse. I didn't know what was about to change, but I started to sense a quiet rumbling from somewhere within. Maybe as a reflex similar to a drowning person reaching and clawing for something solid to hold onto, I began a methodical process of eliminating the options I had before me.

I began a somewhat rational self-evaluation of how serious the problems I faced were. Can I even define the problems? I began to realize that was the hard part. Knowing you have a problem and knowing what the problem actually consists of are two different things. This thought process was going nowhere fast. Realizing this dropped my spirits lower. I kept asking myself, "What can I do?" There must be a reasonable and understandable solution to this nowhere existence I found myself in. I was going down fast. Every attempt I made to seek a direction to take ended in bitter frustration. I just did not have the ability to define, analyze, or construct a solution to my problems. I was utterly lost. I was at the lowest I had ever been. I was at the bottom.

"Jesus, please take me," were the next words I uttered.

# Chapter Two

It was cold on the evening of January 3, 1986, belying middle Tennessee's reputation for very mild winters as compared to more northern parts of the United States. This evening was not only cold, but also had a couple of inches of snow left from several days ago. Even the roads had enough ice on them to require your attention if you were driving. I wasn't driving. I was running. I started from my house and jogged slowly the first half mile down the narrow country two-lane that ran into state Highway 46 which is a remote, never busy, north-south route. I took the south turn on 46 which if I had a couple of hours to run, would have taken me into the small town of Dickson about thirteen miles away. However, this evening's run wasn't intended to be training for a marathon, only a four or five mile maintenance run which I had to have every two or three days in order not to feel lousy.

When I got to Highway 46, I picked up the pace and was starting to warm up considerably. I had become pretty decent at layering the parts of my running outfits in cold, windy weather. I probably found more uses for a pair of white tube socks than any runner you ever knew. Their primary usefulness as mittens was only a small part of their repertoire. As a reflector at night, they were effective. If your hands were warm, but you needed a scarf-like head wrap to block a stinging wintry wind, they fit perfectly by knotting them and then tying off at the back of your neck or under your chin. I also used them as belts, headbands, and so on.

I was glad I got out of the house on this cold, clear night. I loved the solitude and the silence of a winter night's run. Having lived here in the country where I had lived now for more than a year, I still was amazed by the lack of noise. In fact, there is a preponderance of silence where I live.

I remember when, as a kid, my family drove down to this remote little Tennessee village called Edgewood on at least an annual schedule. My house was then owned and occupied by my paternal grand-parents, Marvin and Laura Baker, and my great-uncle Henry and my great-aunt Lizzie Bellar.

When we arrived after the seven-hour drive from Louisville, I remember it took hours for the ringing noise in my ears from the highway to subside. How strange it was to sink slowly into perfect silence, broken only occasionally by a farm tractor rumbling now and then, or maybe a dog barking in the far distance. I have since theorized that the silence itself has a subtle ring to it or maybe a remote frequency that you feel probably more than you hear. At any rate, if you wanted a place where city hubbub and noise were not desired, then you could hardly go to any better place than Edgewood, Tennessee.

I continued running. I was approaching Ruskin Cave. Having run nearly two miles now, the rhythm of my breathing and pulse were not at that perfect, harmonious place that they get after you've run five or six miles; still, I was feeling good and decided to stop and stretch a few minutes. It was around 6:45 p.m. There were no cars or humans anywhere about. I was absolutely alone on this cold country road with only the black night and the twinkling stars above.

I had no idea what was about to happen, that in the next forty-five seconds the rest of my life was going to change. God was about to communicate with me in such a way that was both miraculous and prophetic in the sense that I had been asking for this night all my life.

Then I saw the airplane. I should say, then I saw the commercial airliner. It was low, very low. It was on a westerly bearing and appeared to be directly over Ruskin Cave. The altitude I judged to have been between five and eight thousand feet. I could hear no noise from the engines. I knew its configuration was that of a commercial airliner not only because of its size, but also because I could easily make out the line of windows running fore to aft down the starboard fuselage. Years later I would still be in contemplation over the windows. If I had judged the altitude correctly, would I have been able to see the windows at all? Not only could I see them distinctly, but I could also see the illumination from the interior lights. It was kind of like seeing the aircraft from a much close vantage point. I felt like I could see into the aircraft, but I couldn't. I felt like I could make out human silhouettes, shadow-like head and shoulder silhouettes. As I gazed above me and focused on the airplane, I had at this point not begun to formulate any theories or explanations as to the status of this mysterious object in the sky. For a brief moment I felt like it might be in trouble and possibly looking for an emergency landing area. I soon discounted that idea and was about to dismiss the episode as nothing really abnormal. In a moment the aircraft was gone. It vanished over the low Tennessee hills out into the night.

There was one more very noticeable thing I saw on the aircraft before it disappeared. Its nose light and its red and green marker lights on the tips of the wings seemed to be brighter than you would have expected.

This is going to be hard to explain.

It was as if these three lights were more than just lights. It was as if their importance was elevated way above being mere marker lights. They made me feel like they were in some way a protector of the aircraft or its guide. It was just a feeling I had that they were providing some spiritual significance to the craft or to those onboard, or as I would come to believe – me.

The aircraft had been gone for a couple of minutes. I was just standing there in the middle of the road, gazing off into the west where it had disappeared. I might have been a small child following the flight of a wonderful butterfly.

You might expect me to say that now I should have considered these events as abnormal. I really didn't feel that way. A strange occurrence? Yes. A feeling that something way over my head might be going on? Yes. That was already entering my psyche.

I stood and looked off towards the west. The everlasting silence of middle Tennessee encompassing everything. *Starting to cool down now. Don't want to stand out here much longer. My wet, sweaty running glow cooling down now, cooling me down. Got to get moving. But still I stood. Maybe it will come back. Why was it so low? Why did I not hear engine noise? I should have; it was low enough. It could not have been on a landing glide path to Nashville International Airport. It was on a westerly heading. Nashville International is sixty miles east of here.*

Nothing seemed to be making any sense. There still were no cars going by. No homes anywhere close by. Only me, the now gone phantom airplane, the cold winter night, the low hills, the silence, me running, Ruskin Cave.

Did you ever see the movie *Close Encounters of the Third Kind?* I was beginning to feel like Richard Dreyfus as he played the role of the ordinary guy who after having witnessed an alien presence, started building a mountain in his living room from dirt he wheel-barrowed in, from garbage, fencing, anything he could get his hands on. He was being driven by forces so utterly overwhelming and disproportional compared to his tiny existence; he had absolutely no control over what he was doing. Little did he know, he had already been selected to be a part of a cosmic event the like of which the earth had never known.

This vague sense of my involvement in something huge that was at this very moment beginning to evolve was overtaking me. What could it be?

I was standing there getting colder physically but starting to heat up mentally. Looking across the creek and through the narrow swath of bare winter trees; even in the darkness I could make out the outline of the enormous opening of Ruskin Cave, some three hundred yards away. Why was I still out in the cold looking at Ruskin Cave? Why had the airliner been directly above Ruskin Cave? Why had I been running when all of this happened? Why was I here? What was happening? Why was I still looking at Ruskin Cave? I was trying to put the pieces of the puzzle together.

Ruskin Cave! Phantom airliner! Running! Memories of my crying out to Jesus when I knew all other roads were useless. My involvement with Paul Ritchey and his band of misfit recovering alcoholics. My own personal history of alcohol and drug use. My very recent encounter with one of Nashville's finest – the night I should have been locked up for DUI but was somehow granted an escape.

I said earlier that I had been asking for this night all my life. Thoreau was quoted as saying, "Most men lead lives of quiet desperation." I think that this is probably one of the most accurate statements ever made. I certainly fit the mold. Even though my life had changed drastically after the night I asked Jesus to take me, I was still searching for that soul–fulfilling calling, that great life's work that fulfilled your deepest yearnings. For me it was the search for a great adventure. I've had several people suggest that these unfulfilled dreams of mine and what they led to were the quintessential midlife crisis. Whether or not this dream included a vocation wasn't important to me. What was important was that it be a tremendous challenge, that it be something that I threw myself into, something that would require all of me to be good at. The running I had been doing for the last ten years was soaking up some of this unfulfilled energy (the searching for the ultimate escape valve), but the running wasn't soaking up nearly all of it.

Standing there in the cold, I did a quick review of the last ten years. Maybe there was a connection with my 'Jesus night' and the phantom aircraft I just saw. The only thing that registered was the fact that my life had changed big time! I had completed not only my B. Ed. in Health and Physical Education at the University of Hawaii, but had gone on to earn a Masters degree in Education from Indiana University. I had met and married a wonderful girl who gave me the best children in all America! Things were different from the nights of drinking alone, and they were certainly different from the one night I was truly at the crossroads, the one night I truly chose the right path. I had toned my drinking down and had given up drugs completely. Ten years ago I didn't think that would have been possible. I attributed the turn around and the good fortune to God the Father, Jesus the Christ, and to the Holy Spirit. The night ten years ago I asked Jesus to take me changed my life. As I had often explained to people, the change occurred instantly in one all-important way, and over time in other ways.

The night I said those four words, "Jesus, please take me", I knew immediately that all the weight of the world was removed from my shoulders. No, I didn't hear a chorus of angels singing. Nor did I hear a voice from heaven calling me. I *felt* God's presence so deeply it was startling and was unmistakable. I knew God had heard my call for help! I knew Jesus was my savior! I knew from that moment my life was changing. Years later I would come to believe that night was my born-again experience you hear so many Christians talk about. I still believe it to this day. More than that – I know it! That was the instant change. The other changes would evolve over time and I believe are still evolving.

So, yes, I had been waiting for this night at Ruskin Cave all my life. Up until ten years ago, my "Jesus night", I obviously had been spinning my wheels. From then until the night at Ruskin Cave my wheels were on the ground but weren't sure of the direction to take. In terms of the big adventure of a lifetime, I was still very much in the dark. That is until now. Until this night at Ruskin. Like my "Jesus night" the presence of God in the deepest fibers of my soul was instantaneous and overpowering. He told me what I was to do. Standing there on that deserted highway, the puzzle of the phantom aircraft, the running, the anticipation of something happening at this moment, looking at Ruskin Cave, and the you-can-only-grab-it-once adventure of a lifetime ordained and now even created by God; it all came together. God told me what I was to do.

I was to run across the United States to raise money for Paul Ritchey's band of misfit recovering alcoholics who were at this very moment across the creek, beyond the narrow swath of bare wintry trees, probably huddled up near the wood stove in one of the several houses on the eighty-acre grounds of Ruskin Cave, a mere three hundred yards from the very spot I was standing on. It didn't take long to understand that this God-given instruction was indeed the very will of God.

I turned toward home and started jogging in that direction, already accepting of my fate. I could have been a drone, that when activated by a code, proceeded methodically almost mechanically to perform my preprogrammed instructions – in this case to run across the United States of America. I felt like this was the big answer to all my questions and certainly was the answer to what form the big adventure might take. I knew where my marching orders had come from. I also learned from the last ten years that when God is in control, good things happen. There was no mistaking who was in control on this night. My mind was already racing with the "what-if's" and "how can I's". I can honestly say that from that moment on, the rest of my life up until now, that I have relied totally on God to take even one step in any enterprise I've been involved in. That's not to say that I've done everything I was supposed to do or that I've been a good Christian. I've tried and come up short every day. Through it all, I've known God was with me.

I made two phone calls as soon as I got home. The first was to Paul Ritchey. Paul was a recovering alcoholic who had been dry for a good period of time. I don't remember how long that period was. He may never have told me. My guess would have been less than five years. Paul was the founder and driving force of the Touchstone Foundation, a treatment center for recovering alcoholics. The facility was located at Ruskin Cave. It was being held together purely by Paul's will. He was determined to make it a successful treatment center; although it faced an uphill battle. The financing was the big problem from the outset which was only a few months earlier.

The Touchstone Foundation had a rental contract with options to purchase the Ruskin Cave property, and Paul already had five or six patients living on the grounds at Ruskin. The big old house served as office, dining room, sleeping quarters, church, and treatment center. Another old house served as residence for the staff which consisted of Paul, his wife Sylvia, and a few of their friends who had cast their lots to help Paul and his dream of eventually making this place a state of the art treatment facility. It was far from being state of the art at the present time. At times it was a real struggle to keep the patients warm and fed. The best thing this facility had going for it was Paul Ritchey. I had met him only a couple of months previously in early November. Performing my duties as a salesman for Standard Coffee Company, I had called on Ruskin Cave to sell my company's program to them. Paul was interested in our service and after two more visits with him, the Touchstone Foundation at Ruskin Cave was Standard Coffee's newest customer in the state of Tennessee.

Paul and I became friends. He was a charmer. A tall good-looking man, Paul carried with him off the stage the same southern man of hard living yet gentle and peace-loving persona he presented on stage as a country singer. At one time his star had risen near to the top around the cut-throat Nashville music industry, but the alcohol did him in. These days his band was in demand mostly at AA gatherings. Never the less, Paul's devotion to his dream of making the Touchstone facility at Ruskin a success, and his energy to do so elicited admiration from myself as well as others. He had a real spiritual side and a deep, throaty yet soothing and gentle voice. He could have been one heck of a salesman and, in fact, was. As I eventually came to understand, it was only his persuasive skills and his true spirit that wanted to help his fellow alcoholics that enabled Touchstone at Ruskin to have any hope of success. Ruskin was off to a slow and stumbling start, but it was open, and they actually were ministering to five or six lost souls that otherwise would have been on the streets or in jail.

The phone on the other end rang. "Hello?" I reached Paul at his home in Nashville fifty miles away. His nights were mostly spent there. Only in emergencies or on special occasions would he stay overnight at Ruskin.

"Hi, Paul. This is Gary."

"Hey, Gary. How are you tonight?"

"Real good. You're not going to believe what just happened." I was peeling off my wet running clothes and had only been in the house a few minutes.

"Give me a try brother. Anything is possible."

I hesitated, cleared my throat. "Well, I uh, I was out running tonight, and I uh…" How do you tell someone God had just spoken to you through a miraculous vision, if that's what it was. Or even more difficult to explain, He had spoken to you through a ghost airplane that logically could not have been where you had seen it with your own two eyes.

"Gary, go ahead, tell me what's going on." He by now was probably starting to worry that something was wrong at Ruskin.

"Yeah, sure, I'm sorry. Look, here's what happened. I was out running tonight, and stopped in front of Ruskin to stretch for a minute, and there was an airliner above Ruskin at a low altitude, and well, Paul, I'm sure God was sending me a message. Paul, I want to run across America for Touchstone. I think I can raise some money for you." To a guy who was working everyday with people who were going through DT's, seeing strange things, hallucinating about this or that, my report on what I had seen and felt didn't rattle him at all.

"Well, Gary, I'm not sure what to say." He paused, "Hallelujah, brother! Any man that gets a direct message from God, I think ought to be listened to." I told you Paul had a real spiritual part to him. "Look, let's just take it slow and see what happens. You say this happened tonight?"

"Yeah, I was on highway 46 in front of Ruskin, and I noticed this plane directly above the cave opening. It was low enough that I could see the interior lights coming from the windows. There was something about it... I just knew somehow something was going on. It was gone in less than thirty seconds. It was flying west, Paul. What would a big airliner be doing that low over Ruskin?"

"It could have been off course, or lost, or something. Why don't you call the airport and check that out?"

"You're right. That's exactly what I plan on doing. I wonder if I can talk to anybody tonight?"

"Well, I don't know, but keep me informed on what's going on. There could be some real possibilities in your idea of running. Again, let's just take it slow and see what happens, okay?"

I must have already been looking for a way out of this encounter I had had with God, because I am usually headstrong enough not to take well-intended advice from anyone. Paul's insistence on slowing down and not getting over-excited on what I thought I saw, I normally would have disregarded. I said, "Yeah, okay. I think that's the thing to do. I'm going to call the airport, get a good night's sleep, go to work tomorrow; and oh yeah, maybe a prayer tonight will give me some answers."

"All right, Gary, that sounds good. Give me a call tomorrow, and we'll see what happens."

Now the call to the airport in Nashville. I didn't think anyone at the tiny small-town airport in Dickson would be able to give me any answers. I doubted if anyone was even there at this time of the evening.

"Is this the FAA at Nashville International?"

"Yes, it is. Can I help you?"

"Yes sir. I'm wondering if you could tell me whether or not the air traffic controllers in Nashville have noticed any airplanes off course or in trouble tonight?"

"I'm not sure we can provide that information to you. Can you tell me why you want this information?"

"Yes sir. It's simply that I saw a very low altitude airliner out in the Dickson area about thirty minutes ago. It appeared to be flying west." I think I had his attention this time.

"Can you wait just a minute? I'll check on it." He didn't wait for my response, and in a moment he was back. "Sir, we have no information of any aircraft off course, lost, or any that might be at a low altitude in the Dickson area this evening."

I could only counter with, "Really, the air traffic controllers don't see anything out this way at a low altitude?"

"No sir. We've checked on that, and we don't see a thing."

"Okay. Thanks a lot. I appreciate your help."

Over the years I've taken some raised eyebrows and in a few cases flat rejection of what I saw that night, and what it meant, but not as much as you might think. For one thing very few people other than my wife and Paul Ritchey ever heard what actually happened until now. Another thing – I've learned that when God gets your attention the way he got mine, the road ahead will have more surprises, more supernatural events (I prefer "God's attention getters"). It seems to me that he also paves the road ahead with lots of other spiritual people that you will be dealing with along the way. What this does to you (to me) in the long term is the strange events that occur along the way become perfectly natural. When you give God total control, you don't get overly blown away by miraculous events. They just come and go. You know why, and you go on. In fact, over time you start forgetting the unbelievable nature of these events, and you can even forget the events totally if you allow yourself to. That's one reason I'm writing: so they will be preserved, at least on paper, before I may be guilty of letting them slip away.

As the ensuing weeks and months slipped away, I would also gain an insight about this night that would make perfect sense – at least to me. The message (instructions) that God gave me that night were really the answer to a dream I'd been having ever since I started running. Ten years earlier back in Hawaii, I had read a book that told the story of a solo backpacking trek over the Sierra Nevada mountain range. The adventure lasted several months and traversed some of the most rugged wilderness area in the United States. I wanted to do something similar. I don't know if the book made much money, but like the author, I wanted to write a book that I hoped would make some money.

For all those ten years since Hawaii, that desire to accomplish a very demanding trek on foot haunted me continuously. I had planned it out in my mind a thousand times. More often than not, the fantasy journey had me running across the United States from one coast to the other, completely self-contained and self-reliant. I would carry with me everything I needed right down to the shelter for bad weather, sleeping bag, food, water, the whole works. In other words, this trip would have been the ultimate cross-country backpack trip with one all-important difference – I would be running. I had actually researched similar adventures but could not find one that met the exact guidelines that I had been conjuring up in my mind.

My thinking was that this had to be a can't miss, money-making enterprise in the context of "what big time publishing company could afford not to beat a path to my door for the rights to the best-selling book I would write?" Well, you know what? I still believe a well written nonfiction book chronicling the adventures of the ultimate cross-country runner would be hugely successful. But for me it was never to happen. I believe it could have, but something was missing. Some crucial component was missing. If the obvious hasn't already jumped on you, let me tell you what was missing. God was missing. While the concept of the ultimate cross-country running adventure may have been totally doable as a money-making scheme for myself, it lacked the one thing it needed, an element that redirected it away from my selfish ambition. It needed to be about something bigger, something aimed at helping others.

What one aspect of my life could give me any insight into the needs of others? I had been pretty selfish my entire life. Most of my decisions, I would have to say, revolved around my personal comfort level. I don't believe I had really done much for others most of my life. So, how could I help others? It all came clear that night at Ruskin. God said, "Look over at that house next to the cave. Forget the phantom aircraft. I just used that to get your attention. Look at the six lost souls in there. You know, Gary, except for the grace of God, excuse the pun – hah, hah- you might have been number seven. That's right, Gary. You were a bartender for, let's see now, how many years was it? Seven, I believe, wasn't it? How many heart-ache stories could you tell? How many times did you see the devil at his worst? When were you the loneliest you've ever been? Come on, Gary. You know. You know, Gary! And how about two months ago? You yourself know you should have been locked up that night. The Nashville police officer that pulled you over doing sixty in the forty mph construction zone looked you square in the eye, and he knew you were wasted. You knew it too. You knew it when you left the bar, didn't you Gary? You even said to yourself, 'I better be careful on the drive home. I can barely see ten feet in front of me, much less the road.' You did say that to yourself didn't you, Gary? And then when you got in the forty mph construction zone on the interstate you said to yourself, 'Dammit, I've really got to watch it through here. They'll bust my ass for sure.' Yes, Gary, I noted your foul language that night, and all the other nights, for that matter. But the real crux of the situation that night was it was your destiny to be pulled over by one of Nashville's finest, wasn't it? But why did he let you go and only give you a warning? Because I told him to. You know that's true, don't you? It took you a couple of months to really figure it out, right? But now after tonight it should all be pretty clear to you."

It was clear. Of course. Now I see. I do have an insight into the lost opportunities of alcoholics and drug addicts. I have seen the havoc chemicals produce. I have seen the destruction, the lost families, the loss of all hope, and of course, eventually death. Yes, oh God, yes! I do see your plan for me. I do understand why you've instructed me to run across America to benefit anti-drug and alcohol programs. I do see that only through your wisdom could I possibly convert a once selfish scheme into the adventure of a lifetime and help others at the same time.

Now I know why you brought me here to Edgewood, Tennessee a year and a half ago. It wasn't only to be with my dying grand-mother, to allow her the dignity and dream she had of dying in her home with family around – not in a nursing home or the small elderly care home she had been in which was operated by a local couple out of their home. That was important not only for Granny, but for me. Granny had been one of the few links I had with believ-ers, Christianity, and the whole God thing. Now I see the move here was also for this night at Ruskin. I have often wondered how many people are fortunate enough to receive the unmistakable, direct will of God. That night I was convinced I had.

I told my wife, Debbie, what had happened not long after I had talked with Paul. She wasn't overly surprised by the events of the evening. I think that she probably did not pay it much credence. She dutifully nodded and in so many words gave me her acknowl-edgement that she'd support this, yet another plan I was developing for running across the country. She had heard it all before. I actu-ally told her when we first got married that one day I would be off on the run across America. No, this didn't surprise her. The angle of a vision of a phantom airliner being associated somehow with a direct communication from God – she probably thought I was way out in the deep end, even for me. But like she always had before and like she always did in the difficult days ahead, she loved me and sup-ported me. I sure didn't deserve her then, nor do I now. God had blessed our marriage from the outset.

I have always told Debbie and others as well, that when the preacher said the words that our marriage could only be successful if God was at its core, I bought into that concept so deeply that I know it is the truth. Yes, we both bought into that concept, and we both know it to be true. Thank God it is, for without it, we never would have made it through the rocky days ahead.

# Chapter Three

I talked with Paul Ritchey almost daily after the phantom airliner night at Ruskin. By the time two weeks had elapsed, I'm certain he was convinced that whatever happened that night had a solid grip on me and had made substantial inroads into his own thinking – even as far out as it sounded. His thoughts went something like this.

"Gary just might be able to pull this off. After all, he's a pretty good salesman himself. First, he sold us his company's coffee service, and undoubtedly he is convinced he can run across this country, and as a fund raising bring in millions for Touchstone. If he was successful at raising $100,000 for us, that could be the difference in our success or not. God, how I want this place to be successful, but God, how I underestimated the financial burden. Sylvia and I have put all we have into Touchstone. My brother, George and his wife, Tammy Wynette, have done more than I could reasonably ask for. As for the other members of Touchstone's board of directors, the same is true. Johnny Cash, Mo Bandy, Johnny Rodrigues are all inundated every single day by charities, non-profit organizations, hospitals, etc. to lend support financially, public appearances, or just their implied support of a project."

This implied support, I would learn a whole lot more about. A star's name, or a big politician, or dignitary's name, on the list of the board of directors, or better yet having written a letter for your cause, I would come to learn is a powerful tool and can open some big doors.

A month after God's wake-up call in front of Ruskin, Paul had done more than just think I might really be onto something. He told me Touchstone was committed to support my run for them any way they (he) could. Unfortunately, this would not include any financial support, because they simply did not have the ability to do that. But there were several things they could do that would be as important as finances.

Being in and around the country music industry in Nashville, Paul and his brother George had many connections that Paul said he would put to use to help get the "American Marathon of Help" up and running. First, he wanted to hook me up with a Nashville PR firm that handled some of Tammy Wynette's publicity. Paul thought they could help do most of the planning of the trip and all of the publicity an enterprise of this nature deserved and required. He said the highlights of the publicity and PR campaign would be an appearance of myself on the national morning TV shows. Next, he said he'd be able to provide me with a support van to accompany me along the way across the country. The organization and administration of the national fundraising portions of the run, he said could be handled by Touchstone's accountants. Lastly, he said there was office space available on Nashville's famous Music Row. George Ritchey had run his publishing business and his wife Tammy Wynette's publicity office there for years.

I was stunned. From the Ruskin night until Paul told me of his plans for how he could support my run, I certainly had the commitment and the motivation to make the American Marathon of Help a success, but I had no idea how I was going to pull the run off. It appeared things were starting to fall into place. As grateful as I was for Paul's implied help in all these things, my big problem was, of course, money. I didn't make a lot of it selling coffee. Debbie's teaching salary was ... well it was a teaching salary. We had two growing boys to feed and were still recovering financially from Debbie's having missed a year of work while she so gallantly helped me take care of Granny.

Having very little savings, I had no idea of how I could manage to take time away from my work to run across the United States. So yes, Paul's offer to help with a van, publicity, and accounting firm to handle the money, and office space shocked me. Believe me, it was a welcome and joyous shock. More than that, it told me there was someone out there other than myself who believed in the run. It meant a lot to me that a real player in the music industry believed in me enough to let me run "for" a worthy organization, that is, to raise money for the facility at Ruskin. Financially strapped as that organization was, they would still do all they could for me in other ways. That meant a lot to me.

In that first month, I had been busy myself. I started physical training a day or two after the Ruskin phantom airliner night. I had increased my running schedule from three days a week up to six. By the end of January I was logging over forty miles per week. I was still working nine to five for the coffee company, but my heart and mind were no longer focused on my work. Practically every minute of the day, my mind was working on the American Marathon of Help. How would this adventure pan out? How long would it take? How would I live on the road? How could I pull it off financially? Would my employer grant me a leave of absence? These were constant worries.

# Chapter Four

Still I continued training. The training was the easy part. After all, I loved running. I had loved running ever since John, Yvette, and Jeanette Cotté had introduced it to me back in Hawaii. John had three daughters. Yvette and Jeanette were twelve and fourteen respectively. Yvonne was twenty-six. I remember the night I met Yvonne. It was October 30, 1973.

George and I were bored, but the evening still had possibilities. We could drive to Kaneohe in less than an hour if we decided to try and make the Halloween party. It was on the windward side of Oahu, thirty miles from my house near Waikiki. It would do us both some good. Getting away from Waikiki every now and then was always good. I normally had three to four nights of work off, but it was unusual for George and I to be off on the same nights. There were three main night shift bartenders in the nightclub we worked at: George, Frank, and myself. There were two separate bars, so it was just fate that a backup bartender had wanted to trade a day shift with me to free me up this particular Halloween Eve.

It was close to 8:00 p.m. "Come on George, we better aim the van over the mountains (pointing to the Koolau mountains to the north) if we plan on making an appearance at this Halloween festivity."

"Now Mr. Baker," with a measured self-assuredness, "I reckon the fine ladies and whatever feeble excuse for menfolk that venture out to the get-together this splendid evening … well, Mr. Baker, they'll just have to wait. There's absolutely no point in scurrying about, driving like hell just to say we made it on time."

"Why, George my fine fellow, I quite agree. I believe another Jim Beam would be in order whilst we plan our evening in more detail."

It was funny sometimes how George and I seemed to possess the same general mindset on most everything. Of course, we didn't really discuss many items that were "important" as the world would define important. Many of our conversations involved the character and depth of interpersonal relationships – ours and others around our immediate environs. Many drinkers dwell on similar topics. I believe it's a way you can discuss the nature of your drinking habits. That is, by discussing which friends you can count on to go drinking with you. Also, a talk with George would invariably lead to a deeper sense of communication and definitely a deeper sense of language.

One similarity George and I had was that we certainly seemed to be attracted to the same kind of women. Take Ann McKinley for instance. Ann and I had a pretty good go at it for a couple of months two years prior to this Halloween Eve. She was older than I and did a good job of financing her wander-lust by cocktailing stints at some of the noted tourist cities around the U.S. and Canada. She had worked at our club in Waikiki for a while, and we dated a few times and then laid our plans to make an extended mainland trip together. She probably thought that my talk of wanting to tour from Canada to Mexico on a Harley was rooted in actually having the money to do so. When the trip actually got started, we settled for a '65 VW square-back wagon.

Ann didn't seem to mind the loss of glamour and excitement from the Harley to the VW. But within thirty days she had definitely lost her interest in me. It might have had something to do with the night we were in Las Vegas. We had saved the last of some marijuana that friends had given to us in San Francisco for a special evening. The night in Las Vegas we chose to smoke it was special only in that we were running out of money and that my friends in Las Vegas were either in the hospital dying of cancer or too busy with their growing family life to see us. The first was a bartender and the second an old Navy buddy of mine. Ann and I soaked up some of those negative vibes and felt like this would be a good night to fire off the last of the dope – sort of lift our spirits, you know.

The first joint got us going. We were driving down one of the broad main business corridors a mile or two from the strip. We were feeling pretty good and decided to pull over at the nearest vacant lot to explore the small cargo compartment in the back of the VW station wagon. As the exploring got underway, we somehow lost most of our clothes. It was about that time that we noticed a police squad car was turning into our vacant lot. It was also about that time that we noticed that our vacant lot really was an empty bank parking lot and for some reason I had decided to park within twenty feet of the front entrance.

"Where's the dope?" we both screamed. By the time the police had pulled up close, Ann had managed to get the few remaining bits of marijuana down her throat. I'm sure the police saw us trying to get our clothes back on and were too busy laughing to seriously consider that they might have come up on a bank robbery in progress. They eased on out of the bank parking lot and didn't even look back at us. Ann and I were in no mood to feel good about dodging the bullet. Ann was spitting dope back up, and I was now fully dressed and scrambling back into the driver's seat. We never mentioned the incident to anyone.

Unfortunately, other near-disastrous events occurred on our mainland tour, and after a month, she boarded a jet back to Hawaii. We were in Denver, and I guess the thought of going on with me all the way to my parents' home in Kentucky was just too much for her. When I made it back to Hawaii a month later, she was doing quite well with a new boyfriend.

It wasn't long after that when Ann and George got together. They pooled their money and boarded a jet for Tokyo, Japan. Their plans were to ferry up to Vladivostok and then take the Trans-Siberian Railroad all the way to Moscow. The only problem was, as George later explained it to me, that he drank and gambled all of their money away, forcing an early end to their Russian adventure. Poor Ann.  In her quest for first-class travel and adventure with the two of us, she received instead second-class accommodations and sordid memories in the ilk of that classic Bohemian traveling story by Jack Kerouvac, *On the Road.*

Yes, George and I might have been clones when it came to life-style department, including the women, who for some reason, came along with us.

What a night for a Halloween party.  George and I were feeling great.  We weren't drunk at all, and what's more, we had not lit up any joints – a rarity for sure.  We were just feeling good, and why not?  We had every right to expect this party to be like a lot of parties we had experienced in and around Waikiki.

Although this party was on the other side of the island, it was being thrown by some friends we knew from the Waikiki bar crowd.  Normally these events were thick with Waikiki profession-als on their night off:  cocktail waitresses, bartenders, musicians, a few locals, a few surfers, and a couple of dope peddlers.  This night's crowd was not much different.  A lot of times spontaneous music would break out, or the drunkest in the crowd would fail miserably by trying to climb a palm tree.  I never saw any violence at these parties, but always saw plenty of alcohol and marijuana. Tonight's party had a contingent of California transplants and the overall mix of cultures, ideas, book and movie talk, and music was somehow special.  It was a good party.  Certainly there were some comely ladies, and they all seemed to be friendly.  George and I knew a lot of the people here tonight.  We also knew that several of the ladies were spoken for and their boyfriends were here.  We didn't care.  We flirted with them anyway, and we joked around with their boyfriends.

The wine flowed.  The joints were passed around.  Everyone was having a good time.  Then we noticed Yvonne.

You know you always remember those first exhilarating moments when you meet someone special. Her voice, her words were magical. She had been invited to the party by Eslie, a gorgeous 25 year-old Californian whom we had known for some time. But we had never seen Yvonne Cotte' before. The daughter of a French-Canadian father and Puerto-Rican mother, Yvonne was a beautiful dark-haired girl. The three of us talked and talked and it was all Eslie could do to get in a few words. We were like children playing. I didn't want this to end, and I know George felt the same way. Not much later, Eslie needed to drive back to Waikiki, and since Yvonne was staying at Eslie's, she was leaving now too.

"You can't go. We don't know anything about you yet!" George and I blurted out simultaneously. "Oh yes we can, watch this," Eslie and Yvonne responded, then proceeded to say good-bye to everyone, complete with all the hugging and laughing that ends really good parties. As they went outside to leave, George and I were in hot pursuit.

"Hey, you can't drive all the way back to Waikiki without an escort, you know. We'll just make sure you get back okay." George and I were hoping that more than just thank-yous would be our reward after we had seen them safely home, but they weren't buying. All of this had a very light and innocent feel to it. Yvonne was capable of making everything light and innocent.

Still we persisted. "Listen girls. We'd feel terrible if something happened! It would be our fault. We're going to be right behind you on the way over the mountain." Our big grins probably didn't support our stated intent all that much.

"Well, you'll have to catch us first." They laughed and roared away. George and I leaped into my VW van with the peace sign on the front. We were in not-so-hot pursuit. Have you ever seen a VW outrace anything? Before it became evident that we had no hope of staying with them, I told George that if we caught them and followed them home, and if anything else developed, that I was going to propose to Yvonne. He said I probably wouldn't have to; she would probably propose to me first. He had seen it. He had to. He was right there with us the entire evening. I knew something had happened, but I wasn't sure what. Thirty years later, I asked George about it, about his side of it with Yvonne that night. "Yes," he said. "I felt it too, but I don't think with the intensity that you did."

But that particular night Yvonne and Eslie were long gone. I didn't know if I'd ever see Yvonne again.

A couple of days later she called me. "Hi, sailor. Remember me?"

Did I ever! "Hmm, let's see. Were you the girl that tried to chase me back over the mountains a couple of nights ago?"

"Maybe I was."

"Well, well. To what do I owe the pleasure of this call?"

"I'm at Eslie's, not far from you. I thought I might pay you a little visit. That is, if you'd like." She came over, we talked awhile, and within four days Yvonne had moved in with me.

For the next ten weeks we were pretty much inseparable. The only thing that kept us apart was my work, my classes at the university, and her work. Yvonne was a stewardess with Pan American Airlines. Because Eslie was here, Yvonne had requested that Pan Am transfer her to Honolulu as home base. They did so. She had only been in town a few days before we met at that fateful Halloween party. Yvonne's flight schedule had her roaming all over the Pacific Ocean and the Far East. A typical trip might last four or five days and take her to Tokyo, Hong Kong, Bangkok, Manila, Tahiti, Samoa, and then back home.

Christmas came. I remember Yvonne cooked a big turkey with all the trimmings. After Christmas we both had several days off and had planned to do nothing but go to the beach. Then towards the end of January, Pan Am called and asked if she would be willing to trade trips with another stewardess. Something personal had come up with a girl on another flight crew, and they were really in a jam.

Would she help? She loved her work and was always ready to pitch in any way she could. She said yes and was off to the Far East. They left on January 24, 1974.

The phone rang at 4:30 in the morning on the 30th of January. "This is Pan American Airlines, crew center in Honolulu. Is this Gary Baker?"

"Yes, it is."

"Mr. Baker, our records indicate Yvonne Cotté's address of record is 832-A 16th Avenue in Honolulu. Is that correct?"

"Yes, it is. What's going on?"

"Mr. Baker, we have information regarding flight 80631. It appears that there has been some trouble with the flight as it was on landing approach in Pago Pago, Samoa this morning. We can't confirm any details at this time. It's our procedure to notify family and friends if there appears to be any kind of a situation developing. We will be back in touch with you as soon as we have solid information about the situation in Pago Pago."

"I don't understand."

"Mr. Baker, we are very sorry to disturb you this morning with only partial information. We will call you immediately when we confirm more about the situation."

"Okay, okay," I muttered. They said good-bye and hung up.

The next hour and a half I stumbled around the house not knowing what to do. Then they called back and reported that ninety-six of the one-hundred and one people on the plane died in the crash. Yvonne was gone. Of the five survivors two were crew members: the co-pilot and another stewardess.

I fell in a corner and cried until noon. I cried so hard it was difficult to breathe. Then I got up and called Mike Thompson, my best friend. He came over and spent the remainder of the day with me. I was completely empty and nearly through with my crying. I had to get out of the house. It was already becoming that oh so terrible place that those left behind hate so much. A place that every square inch, every fiber, every shadow had a memory. A jail cell so fraught with emptiness and pain that escape became the omnipotent desire.

Late in the day I asked Mike to drive me to Diamond Head. We sat on the cliff above the surf looking out at the vastness of the ocean. There was no sun. The ocean was a deep blue, not the sparkling effervescent aqua blue when the sun hits it. Above the ocean a light gray mist seemed to be dominant. Only way above could you sense any blue sky. You could only sense it. You couldn't see it. It was late in the day now, the sky was darkening.

Then she came to me. I knew it was her. I sensed her presence. She came in the form of a rain squall, straight out of the south, the direction Samoa was in. The cloudlike feisty rainstorm was very compact and was aimed right at Mike and me. It was a shade of heavier gray than the light gray ocean mist around it, yet it's edges seemed to loft away and dissipate into the broader and lighter, all-encompassing gray mist. Her message was, "It's all right. I'm okay. You can go on."

Just like Yvonne. Simplifying everything – no guilt, all innocence. Even in her own death, a creature so devoid of selfishness, moral hang-ups or baggage, that she had already come to terms with her existence and was prepared to go on. Now she was preparing me to go on.

Yvonne's father, John Cotté came to Hawaii a week later. I learned a lot more about her family. John and I got along very well. We drank together- not to excess, just enough to take the edge off, as this was clearly a very difficult situation for both of us. You have a grieving father whose eldest of three daughters had died six thousand miles from home. From my background of traditional southern mores, the fact that she was living the fast lifestyle with, as well as habitating with a Waikiki bartender/physical education major/surfer, would have given John the right to have treated me with (at the very least) disdain. But he didn't. He was nonjudgmental, warm, and engaging, and even hinted an intimation of what Yvonne must have shared with him about me. He said several things that indicated to me that John had been aware of this thing Yvonne and I had going.

At any rate, he only stayed in town a few days. Most of his time was spent handling her affairs at Pan Am and of course picking up all her personal things at my house. It was a very tough time. He came back to Honolulu two weeks later to attend the eulogy service at the church in downtown Honolulu that Pan Am had set up for the crew of Flight 80631. This time Yvonne's two younger sisters, Yvette and Jeannette, were with him. John and the girls stayed with me about a week, and as well as the continued grieving, we also did some healthy bonding.

It was during this time that I became interested in distance running. Ever since the death of the three girls' mother a few years ago, John told me he needed to come up with some healthy activity that the girls could get lost in. Yvette and Jeanette got a tremendous amount of love and support from older sister Yvonne, but John felt they also needed to be active in a physical activity that was very demanding. He chose distance running, and the girls took to it like feathers on a chicken. In and around the San Francisco Bay area (they lived near San Jose) they were quickly developing a reputation as two of the very best female long distance runners in their age bracket. Soon they were being recognized as two of the best in the nation.

I fell in love with them almost as quickly as I had with their older sister. It was a thing of beauty to see them run. John was a very strict coach. They never missed training runs, sleep regimens, diet regimens, etc. Well, almost never. John knew when to ease up on them when the situation called for a less hectic pace. Certainly now was one of those times. During their stay with me, John had entered them in a marathon (26.2) miles) on the island of Maui.

I went with them. The girls only ran about half the race. They had not had enough time to acclimate to the heat, and of course they were burdened with a lot of emotional baggage. John and I were glad they didn't continue. I learned a lot from all three of them. To see these little girls work so hard and be rewarded time and again with their victories really helped me overcome some of the grief and sadness of Yvonne's loss.

Yes, the fast life sure took its toll on me, but from before Yvonne's death and even during that painful period, the sports were about all I had to help keep my sanity. Basketball, swimming, surfing, tennis, volleyball, and other sports activities were my passion until the Cottés introduced me to distance running. From the time I met the girls and watched them, their courage, I have been a runner ever since.

# Chapter Five

The running was going to be the easy part. For now I had more important things to worry about. Supporting Debbie and the boys while I was gone was quickly becoming my main worry. In late February 1986, I received another direct communication from God. Like the night of the airliner that could not have been there but was, God intervened in such a way only the hardest core skeptic could deny His power and control.

I had been on the verge of giving notice to my employer that I was going to request a leave of absence in order to accomplish this run. But I couldn't; I was torn. If I did that, then total commitment to the American Marathon of Help would have been announced. There would be no turning back. The nagging worry of how to pay bills for the duration of the project would be full in my face. This dilemma was tearing me apart. Yes, I wanted to make the run. The Ruskin night gave me a direct communication from God to do it. This never left me. It burned in my heart and drove me. But how could it be done without sacrificing the well-being of my family? This is the age-old dilemma that Christians face every day. It is not easy to give up everything to God's will. For my situation God was going to make it a wee bit easier.

Here is what happened. Somewhere near the end of February, I was driving to work in Nashville early in the morning and felt the need to make a decision, this morning, here and now, about my total commitment to the project. I had stopped off at the Tammy Wynette office several times in the past two weeks. I had worked on some plans for the run and mostly stopped to see about some of the other details Paul said Touchstone was going to help me with. As I drove along, the big question gnawed at me. Is this the day I go all the way? Is this the day I take a leave of absence from work? Or do I continue working at Standard Coffee and continue waiting for things to happen at Touchstone? Shouldn't I march into Paul's office and say, "Let's get this thing fired up. I'm ready to run! Come on Paul, I am ready! Get the PR people moving, the fund-raising people moving, the morning shows moving – all the things you said you'd help me with. Come on, we'll raise the money for Touchstone. Let's go; let's move it out. I'm ready to run! I need to run! I have to run!"

These two choices were swimming around inside my head. Drive on to work, or turn off to Paul's. For the life of me, I could not make the decision. As I drove, I realized I'd better make it quick. There is a split a couple of miles ahead. If I go straight, I go to work today as usual. If I take the off ramp to the right, I go to see Paul at Tammy Wynette's office. What is it going to be? This is where the rubber meets the road. *Oh ye of little faith.* I didn't know what to do. I didn't want to keep my car going straight to work. Yet, I couldn't turn off the freeway to go and see Paul. I eased my grip on the steering wheel. I said a little prayer, "Father, please help me. I don't know what to do."

I eased my grip on the wheel even more. The split was right in front of me. Only in an emergency to avoid an accident would my fingers have tightened on the wheel – my grip was that loose. I felt the wheel turning under my feather-light fingertip touch, not even a grip at this point. The wheel was definitely turning on its own. I had not turned it at all. I was shocked, and for a moment, I was amazed. The wheel had turned the car toward the right, toward Music Row, toward Paul Ritchey.

I knew immediately I was going to run across America. I thought what a tremendous thing. God really is in control of it. All the questions would now be answered, and the sleepless nights of worry would be over. Little did I know, they were just getting started good.

The next four months were an endless series of obstacles other than my employer granting me the leave of absence that was a necessity. The leave of absence wasn't with pay. If it had been with pay, all my worry would have ceased. It was with benefits though, and with the promise that I'd have a job when the run was over. I've always been grateful to them for that.

In order to provide some kind of income while I was training and planning the run, and waiting for Touchstone to get the things they had promised moving, I began soliciting local businesses for contributions to the American Marathon of Help. It was all legal. Touchstone had their IRS charitable organization status all set up. Given the fact that contributions were tax deductible, and the fact that the names of the country music stars were on the contribution forms and the fact that I had some endorsements from several anti-drug organizations, we actually raised some money – very little, in the $2000 range. Most of that was used for expenses I was incurring, not actually replacing my lost income.

My training was improving. By May I was running seventy miles per week, and my weight was less than two hundred pounds, twenty pounds less than where I had started. On my 6 foot 3 ½ inch frame, that was acceptable. Did I say earlier that running was going to be the easy part? All distance runners risk injury when they dramatically increase their mileage. I was no different.

My left knee had not been locking up on me in many years. An old high school football injury, cartilage torn in that knee, had haunted me on and off ever since the original injury in 1963. Now, of all times, it had come back. In the last ten years I had run a full marathon, several half marathons, many 5 and 10K's, and logged thousands of training miles. The knee had never locked up like it was now. When it happens, it "gets stuck" with the knee bent at about a 45 degree angle, and there is no more running. Walking on it for mile after mile is not painful. Running on it when it locks up is impossible. The pain is simply too much. Distance runners are used to pain, but we also know that a knee joint in big time pain is a red flag. If you force the running, you may destroy the joint and never run again.

Needless to say, this could not have come at a worse time for me. I'd been telling the world I was going to run across the country. I had left my job to do so. God had directed me to do so. Now here I am, not even knowing if I can run on a daily basis. If I can, how many miles can I run before the knee might lock up? A trip to the best orthopedic clinic in Nashville was in order.

The doctor confirmed my worst suspicions. "Mr. Baker, you will never put thirty miles a day on this knee. I could not guarantee you that kind of mileage even if I went in and did all I could possibly do for it." Thirty miles a day is what I told the doctor I planned on running when the marathon started.

*Okay, God. I'm getting more than a little frustrated down here. You told me to run across the country for Touchstone. For over four months I've been doing all I know how to do in order to prepare myself. I felt like You had placed Touchstone in my path, not only that I might help them, but also that they might help me pull this thing off. God, I think Paul is a good man, and I know he is trying to help me, but God, other than the use of the office on Music Row, there hasn't been anything else. God, my wife is worried. I'm worried. I've brought no income home for two months now.*

I was ready to reconsider the entire project. Maybe the American Marathon of Help was not to be. Debbie and I talked it over. She never tried to talk me out of it. I never really tried to sell it to her. I only explained to her that I continued to feel that I needed to go on with it, that I didn't understand why doors weren't opening for us, but that I must continue. She always supported me. She was and is amazing. I love her so much and owe her so much.

Touchstone was never able to assist me with the national fund-raising organization, the PR package, the TV exposure, or the support van. I delivered a letter to Paul one day in May. In it I said that the American Marathon of Help was, from this point on, looking for a new sponsor. I began writing letters to a myriad of anti-drug, anti-alcohol organizations, celebrities whose history with drugs and alcohol were well-documented, to politicians, etc. I wrote to anyone I thought might sponsor the run and do the heavy lifting on the national fund-raising effort. Should an organization step up and take on those responsibilities, I still intended to put a healthy share of the fund-raising proceeds into Touchstone.

I was glad that Paul accepted my decision to search for a new sponsor, and I'm sure he was glad I intended to have that sponsor share some of the proceeds with Touchstone. My thinking always was that without Paul and Touchstone, the run never could have been.

For another month I continued searching for new sponsorship, but it wasn't to be. Several organizations and companies nibbled but were not prepared to make the commitment I needed. Finally, about mid-June 1986 I abandoned all hope for the kind of sponsorship I felt I needed. I decided that if I could just run under the banner of MADD (Mothers Against Drunk Driving), Just Say No, The Anti-Drug Coalition … that somehow the other parts of the puzzle would fall into place.

I was now contemplating making the run truly on a shoestring budget. Forget the national exposure, the fund-raising, a support van, expense money. Just run. Just run. Somehow, some way, some good will come out of it. I'll help others in some way. Maybe the simple message of my own drying out and leaving drugs behind will inspire someone along the way to do the same thing.

As this thought entered my mind, I reflected back over the last five months. I recalled the last drink I'd had. It was in Louisville at my brother's house, during the Christmas holiday. Most of our extended family was there. I only drank two beers. A few days later Debbie, the boys, and I were back in Tennessee, and I had no more desire to fall back into my drinking pattern. To most observers that drinking pattern would have seemed harmless. I never missed work because of my drinking. I never woke up in strange places. Never had a DUI. I wasn't loud and obnoxious.

None of the signs you associate with a drinking problem did I possess, yet I knew something wasn't right. I couldn't remember the last time I went twenty-four hours without something to drink. I also noticed that every day I started looking up at the clock to decide when cocktail hour had arrived. Just little things, but they were adding up. Then the night the Nashville police officer let me slide. Now that really got my attention. Then after God got my attention the night of the phantom airliner at Ruskin, well, I just never had another drink. I certainly had no desire to start again. How did this happen? I can only say it was God's will. After all, He certainly wasn't going to instruct a drinker to run across the country while at the same time imploring others to stop drinking. No, I don't think God would do that.

As time went on, the identity I had taken on as a nondrinker fit me like a $1000 tailored Italian suit. I never felt more freedom in my entire life. I had been drinking since I was sixteen. I was now forty, and I was now officially a nondrinker for five months. As for the drugs, I had not used anything in that category for about four or five years. The old days in Hawaii of smoking marijuana nearly every day had long been replaced by the responsibility of making a living and taking care of Debbie and the boys. I attributed this to God also. From that night in Hawaii when I was truly at the bottom of the pit, until now, just look at what God had done. I had said four words that night, "Jesus, please take me", and since then I had been on an unmistakable journey upwards out of the pit.

From an aimless, fast-living bartender on the Waikiki strip to now, I had changed tremendously. I finished my undergraduate degree at the University of Hawaii, came to the mainland, and finished graduate school at Indiana University. I met and married the prettiest and finest girl in the state of Virginia. I taught school five years. I fathered the two best sons in the state of Virginia. I had a good job, and now I had even stopped drinking.

Believe me; Gary Baker was not responsible for any of this. It was all God's doing. He did it because one night a long time ago, I said four words, "Jesus, please take me." If this sounds overly religious, it's not; it has everything to do with a lost soul reaching out for a lifeline and being saved.

Do you know what it's like to be a lost soul? Let me see if I can give you an idea of what it meant to me. Not long before I had met Yvonne in Hawaii, there were two evenings not too far apart that I believe defined me as a lost soul. The exact same thing happened on both of these occasions. I had gone to bed and fallen asleep. Only, I wasn't really asleep. It was that sort of zombie zone. I had complete and total consciousness, yet I wasn't really awake. I was aware of everything around me, all the little noises in and around the house. In fact, it was a very acute awareness and alertness. I then noticed I could not move a muscle. Not a twitch could I muster. I was frozen in pure consciousness but locked up completely in the physical realm. I could only breathe. My eyes were closed, but I didn't need them because I was so totally aware of everything around me. I was not in a dream state or a drug-induced other world. I was right there in my bed, unable to speak out or move.

Then I heard or felt or sensed something stirring in the back of my house. I knew immediately that it wasn't good. I felt it getting closer to my room. It was coming through the dark, quiet house. I wanted to get up, but I wasn't able to move, and now I wasn't even sure I could continue breathing. This thing continued coming toward me. I was able to sense its slow progress all through the house. Then finally it was in my room.

I couldn't sense physical form, but I could certainly sense an aura of evil. Whatever it was, it had no heart. It was a taker, not a giver, and it was checking me out. It came closer; I could feel its breath on my cheek. It seemed like a long time before it went away. While it had been near me, I tried not to think, hoping it might not pick up my vibes and hoping that it would pass on by. But it was hip to this strategy and waited patiently. To this day, I feel the only thing that saved me from this evil spirit was that somewhere, someone was praying for my soul, and I think it was my grandmother.

So, would my seamy history and then my change-over be the cornerstone of the message I should carry across the United States? Would that alone be strong enough to influence others not to make the same mistakes I had made? Or was the country fed up with and tired of folks claiming the moral high road, always it seems after a lifestyle of pure debauchery? Would one more, "Glory, hallelujah! I've seen the light!" just not register with anyone? Wasn't there something hypocritical about celebrities and others making a good living on the lecture and talk show circuit by extolling their good fortune to have made it through the abyss of drugs, alcohol, pornography, overeating, or whatever their evil obsession was?

I've thought about this question many times and always concluded the same thing. If it is truly a God-driven life change, I think the message (individual's story) should be spread.

Who's to say if it is truly God-driven? Only the person telling the story knows. In my case, I know it was God driven. The truth is the truth, and wasn't it Abe Lincoln that said, "The truth is always the best path." Having worked all of that out in my head, it was time to concentrate on a worthy organization to run for. As I already stated, I had given up hope for an organization to do the heavy lifting, financially and otherwise.

Then one day in early June, I was at Tammy Wynette's office and received a phone call from the Just Say No Clubs of America. They were the recipient of one of my earlier letters. They said yes, they were interested in the American Marathon of Help and wanted to know more about my plans.

I had no problem sharing my plans with them. After a few days of more talks, (and I'm sure they were verifying my intent and motivation, and probably a background check) we all agreed that I would run across the United States under their banner. That is to say "for them." They would be direct recipients of any funds raised, of course with the stipulation that Touchstone would receive a cut – eight percent. I immediately changed the name of the project to the Just Say Not Marathon.

Tom Adams was the executive director of the Just Say No organization. He was very helpful and very encouraging.

The First Lady, Nancy Reagan, was instrumental in starting the Just Say No organization. She put some of her own money into it and was highly visible during its early development. The idea was for Just Say No clubs to spring up all across America. These clubs for adolescents and teenagers were designed to be a support base for the youth of America to make a stand against the use of drugs and alcohol in their lives.

The more time I spent learning about the purpose of the organization, I began to realize, yet again, that God was in control. I had begun to think we were on the verge of losing the project because no one was interested in a crazy man running across America to raise money for druggies and alcoholics. But Just Say No was very interested in just such an improbable set of circumstances to come a'knockin on their door. God had done it again. He put me in the right place at the right time and for the right reasons. Hollywood, I don't believe, could have written a script as loaded with God direction as this dream of mine was turning out to be.

I was now a trans-continental marathoner. Now I finally knew it was going to take place. All the doubts and delays were over. They had served a necessary purpose. They tested my resolve. Moreover, they tested the divine intervention that was about to launch me on an adventure of a lifetime. The dream held together. God had brought me this far, and now I was going to run. I was going to run across America.

# Chapter Six

**N**ow it was imperative I find someone to make the trip with me. I needed someone to drive the minivan as my support vehicle. What kind of person would be willing to work for practically nothing and be willing to commit to a life on the road for four months?

I thought about whom I might ask to go with me. Other runners? Friends? Family? Several of the guys at Ruskin Cave came to mind. John Cotté had trained two of his daughters to become star marathoners at the ages of thirteen and eleven. Maybe he would be interested as a tribute to Yvonne's memory.

After a week-long attempt to find a support van driver had failed to turn up any serious candidates for the job, I resorted to running an ad in the help wanted section of the *Nashville Tennessean*. The ad read, "Support van driver for cross-country marathon. Meals and lodging provided. – Gary Baker 767-5535."

I was beginning to get panicky. What if no one answered the ads? The time frame for the start of the run was beginning to look like mid to late July. It was already mid-June. Would I have to run on the self-support system after all? Why not? The self-support system was the original dream. Forrest Gump would later do the ultimate self-support, ultra marathon. Would he not? Sure, but I was not a Forrest Gump. I was too soft. I'd been out of serious training too long. And what about the problems the left knee created? Would I actually be able to run the thirty miles per day I figured would be a target to aim for?

More doubts, more questions, more room for second guessing. I'd best put that to rest. I was going to run! But how was I going to run? Common sense told me I needed a support van driver. Someone who could make sure I had food, water, and a place to sleep. Four weeks to find a driver. If no one can be enticed, enlisted, or coerced to drive for me, then God will find a way, and He will reveal it to me. Surely the *Just Say No* endorsement isn't a fluke. Surely they are serious. Surely they will support me. God will lead the way.

A few responses to my ad started coming in. Most of the applicants were out-of-work truck drivers. When the interviews got as far as the amount of pay my support van driver would receive, the applicant would find a reason to make his exit. I can't say I blamed them. After all, who in their right mind would work for $25 a week for ferrying food and water for a lunatic running across the country?

Then Spencer called.

I was answering applicant phone calls and doing the actual interviews on the second floor of Tammy Wynette's Music Row office in Nashville. The building was a small Cape Cod residence prior to its renovation as a business office and operations base for the "First Lady of Country Music" as Tammy was known. There were plaques and photos on the walls attesting to this. On one photo plaque she was posing with Ronald Reagan at the White House. Of course on many of the walls were gold and platinum albums and singles she was famous for recording. The second-floor office Paul had allowed me to use was overflowing with demo tapes from would-be or wannabe country music writers or singers. There were boxes of tapes all over the entire room. I wasn't a singer; I was a runner, and I was about to receive a phone call from one Spencer Jones.

"This is Gary Baker," I said.

A pleasant, steady, self-assured male voice responded, "I'm calling about the ad in the *Tennessean* for a van driver."

"Right. You've got the correct number. I'm Gary Baker," I repeated. "I ran the ad."

"Well could you tell me what the job entails?"

"Sure. This is what it is: I'm looking for a driver to go with me on a four-month trip across America. I'm running, so I need someone to drive my van that will carry the supplies I will need." Having learned the importance of mentioning the prominent names on the

Touchstone Foundation literature, I added, "The project is being sponsored by the Touchstone Foundation whose board of directors include Tammy Wynette, Johnny Cash ... I will be running under the banner of the Just Say no Clubs of America."  It worked like a charm.  This time I was not going to bring up the subject of pay until the applicant raised the issue.

"Where do I come to talk with you more about the job?"  I gave him directions to the office, and he said he'd be there in about an hour.

"Gary, Spencer Jones is here to see you,"  Donna, the receptionist downstairs, informed me on the intercom.

"Okay, good, would you send him up?"  I stood up from the desk as Spencer Jones approached the open door to the office.  "Hi, I'm Gary Baker," as I extended my hand.

"I'm Spencer Jones."

We shook hands.  Then I motioned him to a chair facing my chair which I pulled away from the desk so we would not have to be impeded by a physical barrier.  "Have a seat."

As he sat, I already had a favorable impression.  Spencer appeared to be in shape and clean cut.  He wore pressed, light blue jeans – fairly new, low cut Nikes, and a non-descript button-up, short-sleeved sport shirt.  I guessed he stood about 5'9", but his medium to slender build made him look taller.  His black hair was trimmed neatly and was cut fairly short.  His shave was clean and close, and in general he presented a very pleasant appearance.  As we talked, though, I detected something in his dark eyes I couldn't quite put my finger on.

"Where are you from?"

"Chicago.  I grew up there and have been traveling a lot ever since."  I assumed that meant he'd been traveling since high school which would have been about ten years ago.  I guessed he was twenty-eight or twenty-nine years old.

"Oh, really?  What kind of traveling do you do?"

"Well, you know, work a job here or there and move on. I guess it's just in my genes. I've never been the type to settle down."

"What kind of jobs have you worked on in the past?"

"A little of everything. Labor mostly, home construction work, some retail. Nothing you would call earth shattering. Just enough to keep me going and keep me out of trouble."

I caught something in the last but didn't pursue it. "Why did you answer my ad?"

"I've just gotten to Nashville recently and I need a job. I wasn't sure what this was about so I thought I'd give you a call."

"Good. I'm glad you did. We haven't hired anyone yet. It's going to take a special person to fill this job. You see, we are on a shoestring budget here. The project has a lot of potential. You could make some decent money, but that's not a guarantee, and it might take some time before the minimum we would start you at would begin to increase."

Good, the bad news was out of the way – sort of. Now to the real salesmanship of my pitch: "What I need in this job, Spencer, is someone who cares about the youth of America, someone who understands the dangers and pitfalls of drug and alcohol abuse. Someone who is willing to share with me the responsibility to go across this country telling kids they can just say "no" to drugs and alcohol. Spencer, I've made mistakes in the past, plenty of them, but none more than abusing drugs and alcohol. I'm lucky though. I made it through the madness without killing anyone, losing my work, or betraying my family. I've been dry now for six months. I haven't done any drugs in several years. I'm committed to make this run. God has taken over my life, Spencer." I was pulling out the heavy ammunition now. "He's going to see this thing through. The Just Say No foundation has allowed me to run under their banner. I expect we will get a lot of publicity. Paul Ritchey has even told me that an appearance on the Today Show is a real possibility."

I explained my relationship to Paul and why I was using this office on Nashville's famous Music Row. I had his attention. "Tell me more about yourself. What are your hobbies? What do you like to do?"

"I like sports. I like movies, and I like to read."

"What kind of reading?"

"Well, most everything: thrillers, science fiction, magazines, and newspapers." He then volunteered. "I guess I'm the articulate drifter. I try to stay up on things, you know, news, current events, stuff like that."

Spencer wondered when it would come out, how long the small talk would continue. What would trigger the truth about his background? Something always did. Oh well, he'd only been in Nashville a few days. If this thing didn't work out, he would keep looking for a quick job. The car washes never ask much about your background, and from what he'd seen so far, Nashville was in the midst of a flourishing construction phase. There was always kitchen work. He recollected he had washed dishes in Atlanta and Memphis more than once in the past two years. But this marathon across the U.S. did sound appealing to him. He thought this Baker guy sure did look the part. He was enthusiastic and he'd obviously been possessed by something. Whether it was God or not, Spencer didn't venture an opinion.

"So, you've only been in Nashville a short time?"

"Right. I got in about five days ago."

"Where are you staying?"

"Well I'm in kind of a temporary place right now. I hope to find something a little more permanent in a few days." He couldn't conceal the wavering in his voice, and he thought *here we go now; he's got me.*

I repeated the question, "Where are you staying?"

"In the downtown area, I believe. I really haven't learned the town well enough yet. You know, everything is still new, and I do well just to barely get around." The attempt to stall off the question was good, but he knew it wasn't good enough. "Look Gary, I'm staying at the mission. I was at a friend's place for several days, but I didn't want to overstay my welcome, and well, I really can't afford a room, you know ... So I've been at the mission for a few days."

"No problem Spencer. I don't care where you're staying. I just want to know as much about each applicant as I can. Let's face it, whoever goes on this trip with me, well, let's just say we'll probably be living in pretty close quarters, and I want to make sure we will be compatible. Tell me what you think about the project so far. Do you see this as something you might want to pursue?"

"Yeah, sure. It sounds good. I've had some problems of my own. I've been in treatment programs myself. I would look on this as an opportunity to stay active on my own recovery and to, you know, maybe give something back to others. You're right about the youth. If there aren't programs for them, it's awfully easy for them to mess up. Drugs are everywhere." He had gone this far; he might as well go all the way now. "That's what happened to me. I started doing recreational drugs when I was a kid, and by the time I was nineteen I had an expensive cocaine habit."

I thought I had ghosts in the closet, and then I ran into a guy like Spencer Jones. How many drug and alcohol related horror stories had I heard in the last seven months or so? It was beginning to be more than I cared to count. What he just said confirmed I was running for the right reason.

"How did you support your habit?"

"I started dealing ... and later robbing."

"Did you get caught?"

He started to hesitate and do another side step, but he didn't. His shoulders slumped a little; his eyes drifted away for a second. "Yeah, I did some time in juvenile detention centers. Then later I got busted for armed robbery. I was hitting Pizza Huts. They were easy. I did six years in a Florida maximum security prison."

My first reaction was "How could this be? Oh no! A seemingly good applicant comes along, and in the first fifteen minutes he tells me he's a convicted felon."

Spencer saw the disappointment in my eyes. He'd seen it before. In fact, it was a permanent condition of his life – not just the last two years since he got out of prison. The dark side of his eyes grew darker. He felt like I would end the interview and say, "I'll be in touch," which meant he had failed again. He thought about the many times he'd been rejected on job interviews immediately after telling the truth about his criminal record. He felt like society might as well brand a swastika on an ex-con's forehead.

I was perplexed. I didn't know what to say. Perhaps I was embarrassed. Perhaps he saw that I was reading his mind and that I was caught doing so, and therefore shared the defeatism and futility that Spencer's life was apparently about. It was awkward for both of us.

He was about to get up and leave, but something wouldn't let him. It was time for me to make a decision. He was the best applicant I'd had so far, and I had interviewed at least eight people. I felt like his appearance and his ability to communicate outweighed his sordid past. Time was running short. I needed a driver.

"Spencer, I think this might just work out. Let me write up a contract and check on a couple of other things. Can you show up back here tomorrow at the same time?"

"Sure. I really appreciate this opportunity. I'll do my best for you." That was the perfect answer, no doubt.

That afternoon I talked with Paul. I wanted to see if Spencer might be able to stay at Ruskin and help out in some way. Paul said yes, so as far as I was concerned, Spencer Jones would be the van driver for the Just Say No Marathon.

Spencer showed up the next day and signed a contract I had drawn up. We gathered up his things. That was easy; they were all in one small bag. That afternoon I took him back home with me to meet Debbie and get him started at Ruskin.

# Chapter Seven

It's mid-June 1986. I've got a project, the Just Say No Marathon. I've got a van driver, Spencer Jones. I've got a minivan for him to drive, my very own 1985 Plymouth Voyager. I've got a runner, me. I've got God involved in a large way. I've got everything I need except plans, a trip itinerary. Dates, routes, logistics, etc. needed to be hammered out. Now I needed the discipline necessary to tie up all the loose ends. Here's what I came up with (see next two pages.)

You'll note from the photo of the minivan that I already had the American Marathon of Help logo on it. After Just Say No got on board, I put a Just Say No box on top which is not shown in this photo. It made a good storage area and afforded some space for our sponsors' names.

Begins:
July 16, 1986
Virginia Beach, VA.

Ends:
November 13, 1986
Los Angeles, CA.

THE
"JUST SAY NO"
MARATHON
IS RUNNING
AND WALKING
ACROSS THE U.S.A.

Gary Baker is a runner, a walker, a father of two young sons, and a concerned citizen. His concern is about the drug and alcohol use of more and more young people across America. Starting on July 16, 1986, Gary will be running and walking across the United States. Gary's support van driver is Spencer Jones. Spencer is also concerned about drug and alcohol use among our nation's youth. The message Gary and Spencer are carrying is a simple one: You can be a strong, independent, and happy person without the use of drugs or alcohol. You can "Just Say No" to drugs and alcohol.

Gary and Spencer challenge your school, group, or town to form a "Just Say No" club, or if you already have a club, the challenge is to form new chapters. Also, Gary and Spencer are challenging all young people to "Just Say No" and to run or walk with Gary for one mile or more to show their commitment to a drug and alcohol free lifestyle.

Your group, or you as an individual can get involved with the "Just Say No" Marathon by taking the following PSA (Public Service Announcement) to your local radio and T.V. stations, and newspapers.

30 Second PSA

This message is for kids from seven to fourteen years old, and to those who care about them. When someone offers drugs or alcohol to you, you don't have to accept. Be smart, "Just Say No". Gary Baker and the "Just Say No" Marathon is running and walking through your town on (fill this space with date from schedule on reverse). Check it out. Walk or run a mile with Gary, and "Just Say No" to drugs and alcohol.

Official schedule of the "Just Say No" Marathon is on reverse side.

Call 1-800-258-2766 for information about the "Just Say No" Marathon, or starting a "Just Say No" club.

| Date | | Town |
|---|---|---|
| July | 16, 17 | VA Beach, Norfolk, VA |
| | 18 | Newport News, Williamsburg, VA |
| | 19 | Providence Forge, Roxbury, VA |
| | 20, 21 | Sandston, Richmond, Short Pump, VA |
| | 22 | Oliville, Gum Spring, VA |
| | 23 | Ferncliff, Zion X-Roads, Charlottesville, VA |
| | 24, 25 | Crozet, Waynesboro, Staunton, VA |
| | 26, 27 | Stuarts Draft, Steels Tavern, Fairfield, Lexington, VA |
| | 28 | Clifton Forge, Covington, VA |
| | 29 | Callaghan VA, White Sulpher Springs, Lewisburg, WV |
| | 30 | Crawley, Rupert, Hines, Charmco, WV |
| | 31 | Rainelle, Lookout. Hico, WV |
| Aug. | 1 | Ansted, Gauley Bridge, Smithers, WV |
| | 2 | Bank, Rand, Malden, WV |
| | 3 | Charleston, Dunbar, St. Albans. Nitro, Hurricane, WV |
| | 4 | Barboursville, Huntington, Kenova, WV |
| | 5 | Cattlesburg, Ashland, Cannonsburg, Grayson, KY |
| | 6 | Olive Hill, Morehead, KY |
| | 7 | Salt Lick, Owingsville, KY |
| | 8 | Mt. Sterling, Winchester, KY |
| | 9, 10 | Lexington, KY |
| | 11, 12 | Frankfort, KY |
| | 13 | Shelbyville, Eastwood, KY |
| | 14, 15, 16 | Louisville, KY |
| | 17 | Valley Station, Ft. Knox, Radcliff, KY |
| | 18 | Elizabethtown, Hodgenville, Sonora, Upton, KY |
| | 19 | Bonnieville, Munfordville, Horse Cave, Cave City, Park City, KY |
| | 20, 21 | Bowling Green, KY |
| | 22 | Franklin, KY, White House, TN |
| | 23, 24 | Goodlettsville, Nashville, TN |
| | 25 | White Bluff TN |
| | 26, 27 | Dickson, Yellow Creek, Ruskin Cave, Edgewood, TN |
| | 28 | Waverly, New Johnsonville, Camden, TN |
| | 29 | Bruceton, Hollow Rock, Huntingdon, Cedar Grove, TN |
| | 30 | Jackson, TN |
| | 31 | Brownsville, Stanton, TN |
| Sept. | 1, 2 | Memphis, TN |
| | 3 | West Memphis, AR |
| | 4 | Forest City, Goodwin, AR |
| | 5 | Brinkley, De Vails Bluff, AR |
| | 6 | Hazen, Carlisle. Lonake, AR |
| | 7, 8 | North Little Rock, Little Rock, AR |
| | 9 | Benton, Malvern, AR |
| | 10 | Donaldson, Midway, Arkadelphia, Gum Springs, AR |
| | 11 | Curtis Gurdon. Prescott, Emmett, AR |
| | 12 | Hope, Homan, Texarkana, AR |
| | 13 | Maud, Corley, TX |
| | 14 | Mt. Pleasant, TX |
| | 15 | Sulphur Springs, TX |

| Date | | Town |
|---|---|---|
| Sept. | 16 | Emory, TX |
| | 17, 18 | Elmo, Mesquite, TX |
| | 19, 20 | Dallas, TX |
| | 21 | Grand Prairie, Arlington, Ft. Worth, TX |
| | 22, 23 | Mineral Wells, Caddo, TX |
| | 24 | Breckenridge, TX |
| | 25 | Albany, Funston, TX |
| | 26 | Anson, Roby, TX |
| | 27 | Snyder, Midway, TX |
| | 28, 29 | Gail, Key, Lamesa, TX |
| | 30 | Sand, TX |
| Oct. | 1, 2 | Seminole. TX, Hobbs, NM |
| | 3, 4 | Loco Hills, NM |
| | 5 | Riverside, Artesia, NM |
| | 6, 7 | Roswell, NM |
| | 8 | Picacho, Hondo, Lincoln, NM |
| | 9, 10 | Carrizozo, Bingham, NM |
| | 11 | San Antonio, Socarro, NM |
| | 12, 13 | Magdalena, Datil, NM |
| | 14 | Pie Town, Quemado, NM |
| | 15 | Red Hill, NM |
| | 16, 17, 18 | Springfield, Show Low, AZ |
| | 19, 20 | Carrizo, AZ |
| | 21 | Globe, Claypool, Miami, AZ |
| | 22, 23 | Florence Junction, Mesa, AZ |
| | 24, 25, 26 | Tempe, Phoenix, Glendale, AZ |
| | 27 | Peoria, Sun City, El Mirage Wittmann, Morristown, AZ |
| | 28 | Wickenburg. AZ |
| | 29 | Aguila, Salome, AZ |
| | 30 | Vicksburg. Bouse, AZ |
| | 31 | Parker, AZ |
| Nov. | 1 | Earp, Vidal Jct., CA |
| | 2-5 | Rice, Twentynine Palms, CA |
| | 6 | Joshua Tree, Yucca Valley, CA |
| | 7 | Palm Springs, CA |
| | 8 | White Water, Banning, Beaumont, CA |
| | 9 | Sunnymeade, Riverside, CA |
| | 10 | Home Gardens, Los Serranos, CA |
| | 11 | La Habra. Whittier, South Whittier, CA |
| | 12 | Pico Rivera, East Los Angeles, CA |
| | 13 | Los Angeles, West Hollywood, Santa Monica, CA |

FOR MORE INFORMATION

CALL 1-800-258-2766

just
say no.

My knee was holding up as long as I walked every time it locked up. You could pretty much count on it locking up between nine and twelve miles. The first time I had a good opportunity to see how it was going to affect the project came in early July. We set up the River to River Run, a seventy mile trek along Highway 70 from the Tennessee River at New Johnsonville to the Cumberland River in downtown Nashville. I planned on this being a test drive. I wanted to see how Spencer and I worked together on the road, how my knee would hold up under serious mileage, and also we challenged Tennesseans to match my run at a dollar a mile. We set it up to do thirty-five miles each of the two days.

The run was a colossal failure. My knee locked up both days after only six or seven miles. I walked the remaining twenty-eight miles each day. The publicity we had hoped to generate in order to saturate the Nashville Metropolitan area with my challenge to match a dollar per mile was also a colossal failure. If that wasn't enough, I also discovered that Spencer's driving skills were sorely lacking. It turned out he had never driven a stick shift. I spent several hours of the next three days teaching him the nuances of driving a stick shift.

So now I knew a little bit better what I did have and what I didn't have. On the have side was God, my family, my willingness to go ahead with the Just Say No Marathon scheduled for a starting date of July 17 in Virginia Beach, Virginia, the backing of the Just Say No organization, some limited sponsorships from the Days Inn motel chain, and from New Balance Running Shoe Company. Days Inn had agreed to provide Spencer and myself with a room at every motel they operated along the route of the marathon. New Balance provided both of us with a full complement of their running gear, including seven pairs of running shoes for me.

On the didn't have side were a solid left knee joint on which I intended to run 2750 miles, a van driver that knew how to drive, and I didn't have any money. Well, you can't have everything.

As the starting date of July 17 drew nearer, I was becoming resigned to the fact that the original goal of actually running 2750 miles was probably not going to happen. I kept telling myself that it would work out the way God wanted it to work out. As for Spencer's driving skills, well, at least he could aim it in the right direction. As for his checkered past, I was beginning to think that it too was all a part of God's plan. If he was sincere in his wish to stay drug and alcohol free, he would be an asset to the Just Say No Marathon. He could sure talk about the horror stories of where addiction can lead. I wasn't sure at this point whether he would want to do that or not. Regardless, how many men would take off on a cross-country adventure that guaranteed $100 a month in pay? That's all I could afford. If we were in fact able to raise any money for Just Say No and Touchstone, then his pay would go up accordingly.

Spencer was probably the perfect individual to accompany me. He was single and only had a brother left from his family in Chicago. In simple terms, he had nothing, repeat, nothing to tie him down. He had nothing to lose might be a better assessment of his situation. In fact, he had everything to gain. What if this Just Say No Marathon was a huge success? He might be able to parlay the exposure, the experience, the connections we might make along the way into a real job, a real future. He eluded this to me in our conversations. I hoped all of that would work out for him in the future. In the meantime, I was fortunate to have him. Yes, I believe God's fingerprints were all over Spencer's selection as my support van driver.

# Chapter Eight

It was July 15, 1986 – two days before the Just Say No Marathon was scheduled to commence in Virginia Beach, Virginia. Around seven in the morning, Spencer and I loaded up the minivan with food, clothes (mostly running gear), maps, a tent, two sleeping bags, a first aid kit and twenty cartons of Gator-Aide. We were ready, at long last, for the big adventure. We drove out of Edgewood, Tennessee, then through Nashville, and turned north on Interstate 65.

At about the Kentucky state line it rained so hard the engine in the minivan started missing. The water from the road was splashing up inside the engine compartment, nearly drowning out everything. For a moment I thought we'd not make another mile. But the rain eased up, and by the time we were east of Lexington, Kentucky on Interstate 64, we had blue skies.

Passing through the Bluegrass region and into the western slope foothills of the Appalachian Mountains, we stopped at Olive Hill, Kentucky, and several other small towns to distribute the Just Say No flyers to schools, police departments, and churches. Our thinking was that because our return trip from Virginia Beach would retrace the exact same route we were now on, that maybe enough interest would be stirred up by the flyers and would energize group leaders to get their kids out for our run through their town. We challenged all kids to run a mile with me, thereby publicly showing their commitment to Just Say No to drugs and alcohol. Some folks I'm sure would have been skeptics as to the depth and sincerity of my belief in and commitment to the Just Say No philosophy. After all, it was only six and a half months ago that Gary Baker was a drinker himself, and everyone knows that once a drinker and a pothead, always a drinker and a pothead.

What gives him the right to go all across America challenging kids not to use drugs and alcohol?  I certainly could understand the reasoning a skeptic might use.  But like I said earlier, if it is a God-led message you are giving, then you need to give it.  In my case, it was God driven and, nearly as important, this first six and a half months of non-drinking proved to be just the start for me.  From late December of 1985 until about September of 2002, I never had the first drop of alcohol.  Nearly seventeen years.  By 2003 my children were grown and raised – my two sons out on their own and my daughter ready to go off to college.  I saw no harm at that point to drink a beer or two occasionally.  As for the drugs, I never picked them up again after around 1981 and never will.

The point I'm trying to make is this.  When the Just Say No Marathon kicked off on July 17, 1986, I don't believe you could have found a more gung-ho anti-drug and anti-alcohol person than me.  I not only talked to kids all across the country about the Just Say No concept from a deeply seeded personal and spiritual conviction at the time, but also continued preaching the message for many years afterward.  In short, I talked  the talk, and more importantly, I walked the walk.

After spending the night in a motel in Ashland, Kentucky, we started out early the next morning for the final push across West Virginia, into Virginia, and finally down to our motel at Virginia Beach, Virginia.

I remember the restaurant we were in.  It had six foot high dividers between the booths, cluttered with all kinds of neat knick-knacks.  There in the midst of all the knick-knacks was a stuffed rag doll dressed in a hobo outfit complete with the red bandana on a long stick over his shoulder, and he was looking right at me.  His head was porcelain and painted bright and shiny in contrast to his ragged body.  Maybe a Bo Jangles with a sort of happy-go-lucky look that he was piercing me with.  There was a sign in his hand that said, "California or Bust."

Now just because we were embarking on a California or bust trip ourselves doesn't mean Mr. Bo Jangles happened to be at that particular spot because of some surreal sixth dimension thing going on, certainly not because God was getting involved in things again. It couldn't be. Bo Jangles' appearance was only coincidence, right? Wrong! You know who was at it again, and I'm sure glad He was.

Runners have a traditional meal the night before any grueling endurance run, spaghetti and meat sauce. That's what Spencer and I had. That night I was very excited and just a little apprehensive about what tomorrow would bring. We were in bed early, and to my surprise, I got a pretty good night's sleep. I was going to need it.

\* \* \*

Finally, the morning of July 17, 1986, the Just Say No Marathon was preparing to launch. I breakfasted on granola, fruit, and all the liquids my gut would hold. In my planning and dreams, I had always seen the run across this great United States of America as being just that – a run from sea to shining sea. I wanted to start at the water's edge and end at the water's edge. So that's what I did.

It was already plenty hot at 10:15 a.m., and I walked down to the surf on the beach at Virginia Beach. I walked in just enough to get soaked to my ankles, then turned westward, walked to a bench along the wide, paved promenade maybe eighty yards from the ocean, sat down, cleaned the sand off my feet with a towel, powdered my socks and running shoes, put them on and laced them up. Next came a handful of sunblock smeared on every skin surface that wasn't covered. Then some lip balm, down the hatch with a Gator-Aide, and I was ready to start.

Spencer had been busy the last few days, and he was starting to relish his role in the Just Say No Marathon. He was not only a van driver; he was also taking over the role of PR man, press secretary,

Just Say No ambassador, and travel coordinator in charge of restaurant and motel lodgings.

This morning as I was ready to start the run, he had lined up a local politician's wife to send us off. She brought with her a TV crew and a couple of reporters. Also on hand was a radio station mobile unit who was going to track my progress on air as I ran northward through Virginia Beach to Norfolk some twenty miles away.

It wasn't a crowd of thousands to send me off. No, it was maybe fifteen people. The crowd didn't mean much to me. Getting started, getting a few miles under my belt meant everything. I had been praying this first morning for a good start, a safe trip, and praying for those this run was for: anyone in the grips of addiction or any young person who was facing the decision of whether to use or not to use drugs and alcohol.

I said to the few people gathered around, "Anyone want to run across America this morning?" and started out from 25th and Atlantic. I ran six blocks down the promenade and turned left on Laskin Road which went all the way to downtown Norfolk.

The first two hours went quickly. Spencer stayed close so that I could get plenty of water and Gator-Aide. Then he went on ahead. He returned to report that the TV people wanted to do an interview at a park at the eighteen mile mark. We were scheduled to meet a Just Say No club there, but if I didn't show up soon, they were going to leave.

I picked up the pace as best I could. It must have been 95 plus degrees. My pre-race training had dropped off significantly the final month before we arrived here at Virginia Beach, and now I was feeling it. There were so many other things that had to be dealt with. Now I wished I had kept my seventy and eighty mile training weeks going. I would just have to run myself into shape the first week of the marathon. I didn't have much of a choice. Already, after only about sixteen miles under my feet, I was beginning to get an inkling of what it was going to take to do thirty miles a day.

I saw a little humor in my predicament. I could see the local 6:00 news – Forty year old ex-druggie, ex-drinker dies first day of cross-country Just Say No Marathon. About then I saw another Bo Jangles-like character, only this one was not a rag doll. He was a cyclist pumping away and going the same direction I was. His contraption was a three-wheeler with all the pots, pans, sleeping gear, water jugs, etc. hanging on it; it reminded me of the pickup truck the Oklahoma family had tied their fortunes to in Steinbeck's *Grapes of Wrath*.

I asked him, "How far you going?"

"Heaven."

A mile away from the park, on the corner of Virginia Beach Boulevard and Route 460, fifteen Just Say No kids were waiting and ran with me into the park. I was a little light-headed and getting chills, the first signs of dehydration. The TV crew had not waited, but the radio unit was there along with some reporters and some Just Say No club leaders and parents.

The radio guys talked with me, Just Say No had a brief ceremony, and at 3:30 p.m. the park was empty. I needed ten more miles before my day would be over.

"Spencer, you know what? I think we should wait til the sun starts going down before I finish the mileage for today. I'm about half-cooked."

"You're running, not me," he said, knowing that waiting until dark meant he wouldn't be getting to bed early that night. We drove back to the motel. I took a cold shower and rested until near sundown, and then we drove back to the park. I started running from there headed for the tunnel under the Hampton Roads.

"Spencer, go on ahead about five miles. I'll need water."

"Alright, man. I'll see you up the road," and he drove off.

The running was much better after the sun went down. The knee threatened to lock solid several times but never did. I was able to walk it off in a mile or less. I should have been seeing Spencer anytime now. I guessed he was still in front of me somewhere. This sure didn't look like the part of Norfolk I remembered visiting about nineteen years ago when my ship was home ported here when I was in the Navy. Nope, the downtown area I ran through was much nicer, much cleaner than the parts of town we used to spend liberty in – another life, another time.

*Where was Spencer?*

Spencer showed up an hour later. He had been lost. My thirty miles for day one completed, we headed back to the motel.

Friday, July 18, day two, was bright and sunny and just as hot as day one. Across the tunnel in Hampton, Virginia, we had a date with another Just Say No club. This group was a little larger than yesterday's group and their kids today really did want to run. They did about two miles with me. There were parents, a few reporters, and again some of the leaders made a brief speech. A few pictures were taken; then Spencer and I were off again. The next stop would be Williamsburg, Virginia, but we wouldn't make it there until 6:00 a.m. on day three. Because of the danger of the extreme heat, I chose to hold off most of day two mileage until the sun went down. I ran and walked all night the second night.

At sunup on day three, I was running through old colonial Williamsburg and really did feel the history behind this town. Debbie and I had honeymooned here eight years ago, and we had been back several times. But I never felt the pride of being an American quite like I was feeling it this morning at sunup. I suppose that part of what I was feeling was the fact that what I was doing was important.

It was very early on day three and already thirty or so young folks had shown up to run with me. Did they really understand that by doing so, they were telling the world that they did not want to use drugs and alcohol? I think most of them understood the stand they were taking, and this sure helped me keep going, and I believe spotlighted the importance of what I was doing.

At 6:30 a.m. on the northwest end of Williamsburg, we camped at a deserted little league baseball park. There were two rabbits in the wet, early morning grass just eyeballing us for all they were worth. Around noon a thunderstorm ran us out of the ball park. We headed for the nearest Shoney's Restaurant and chowed down on spaghetti and meat sauce and a ton of green salad.

Then we got on the road westward, bound for Richmond. I was now stopping about every two miles to soak my feet, pop blisters, hydrogen peroxide them, bandage them up, and change to dry socks. I was finding blisters everywhere, places I never knew you could get blisters. I was thinking they looked like ripe juicy ears of silver queen corn.

That night I ran until about 11:00 p.m. Just after dark Spencer told me to keep an eye out for a hitchhiker up ahead who, in Spencer's judgment, was high and acting crazy. I ran through the area the crazy hitchhiker was spotted in, but I didn't see a sign of him.

When I finally caught up with Spencer there was a Virginia state trooper stopped at the minivan talking with him. The trooper had recently participated in a marathon of police runners who carried a torch from Virginia Beach to Richmond to benefit the Special Olympics. He told us how much he appreciated what we were doing, and he wished us good luck. It was a great ending to a good day. I was able to run a good six miles at the end of the evening, so we were through for the night. We headed for the motel in Richmond about twenty five miles away.

Three days under my belt and I had run and walked a total of eighty miles. My goal was to do thirty miles a day, so at this point in the run I was ten miles behind schedule. This would have to be made up soon, tomorrow if possible. I was dead set on doing the thirty miles per day, not just because of my determination to actually do what I told the world I was going to do, but the trip's itinerary was designed with thirty miles a day in mind. With a map in hand, if you looked at the schedule and plotted the towns I was scheduled to run through each day, you would notice that the towns would average out at thirty miles apart on a daily basis.

Other than painful blisters and the wicked heat, I'd have to say that I had not encountered any serious problems so far. *Thank you Father; thank you Jesus; thank you Holy Spirit for getting me this far. Let me be strong, aim me, guide me, direct me, lead me the way you want me to go.* This was my constant prayer, as well as that the Lord would take care of Debbie and the boys.

Day four. Sunday, July 20, we were in the motel at Richmond, Virginia. I basked in the luxury of sleeping in until 8:00 a.m. I had a huge breakfast; then I walked five miles down Broad Street. The temperature was 93° by the time I got back to the motel. I took a cold shower, worked some more on my blisters, then lazed around waiting for a reporter from the *Richmond Times Dispatch* who was coming at 3:30 p.m. This is what was published: (I have chosen not to correct several errors the reporter made in regards to timing of certain events.)

DRUG FOE USING MARATION TO CARRY MESSAGE ACROSS U.S.
By Olivia Winslow, Times-Dispatch staff writer

When Gary Baker talks about his "mission", he leans forward, his blue eyes taking hold of a visitor.
His walk and run across the country that began five days ago is no longer just for him and his fulfillment of a 10 year old dream. It is, he said, a mission to help prevent young people from trying drugs and alcohol.
The 40 year old Baker, from Dickson, Tn., plans to take his message of "Just Say No" to cities and towns from Virginia Beach, where he began the 2,860 mile trek Wednesday, to Los Angeles.

The slogan takes its name from a program begun in Oakland, Calif., a little more than a year ago in which 7 to 14 year-olds are encouraged to join Just Say No clubs in schools and communities, Baker said.

His goal is to encourage communities to form such clubs or start new chapters where clubs already exist.

Baker says he is not a counselor with the organization and not an expert in its methods to prevent drug and alcohol use. Basically, he said, Just Say No involves "peers helping each other to avoid temptation."

Baker talked about his trip during a stop in a Richmond motel yesterday afternoon – a few hours before he was to resume the run in Providence Forge. It took him back to Richmond just after midnight.

He is scheduled to run through Oilville and Gum Spring tomorrow and arrive in Charlottesville by Wednesday. Other Virginia cities he plans to run in before heading into West Virginia include Waynesboro, Staunton, and Lexington.

Baker's involvement with the Just Say No Foundation came about as he searched for a cause whose banner he could carry on his cross country marathon.

His 6-foot plus frame and long, lanky legs, and slight build point to his avocation. An avid long-distance runner, Baker said he has long been interested in running across the country. But until recently it was a selfish goal.

"But seven months ago that changed. I got a message. I won't go into it because it's personal, but the message was to go ahead with your dreams, but do it for others.

"This spiritual awakening," said Baker, "was the magic turning point." He said he hadn't been able to do anything about his dream of running across the country until he had a purpose.

He took a leave of absence from his job five months ago as a salesman with the Standard Coffee Co. in Tennessee and set out to find an organization that would sponsor his trip so he could raise money for a good cause.

As a father of two sons, 4 and 6, Baker said his concern about alcohol and drug abuse among youngsters has been an "evolutionary" thing. This concern led him to Touchstone, an anti-drug and alcohol abuse organization in his home state. With that group behind him, Baker said 10 to 15 other national organizations were approached to find one to sponsor what had been conceived of as a fund-raising cross country marathon.

"That never worked," Baker said. "So we had to change direction." That direction was to send a message to people. The Just Say No Foundation, one of the organizations that had originally turned down his request of doing a fund-raising event, was reached and agreed to let Baker carry his message nationwide.

In the Hampton Roads area, Baker recalls that children in some of the 26 Just Say No Clubs in that area ran a mile with him. That is the kind of public commitment he hopes to inspire.

He said he has every intention, and now is on target, of arriving in Los Angeles by Nov. 13.

He is accompanied by support van driver Spencer Jones, who also handles public relations duties. Besides Touchstone, Baker is sponsored by New Balance, a running shoe manufacturer, and Days Inn which provides lodging for him and Jones.

"The run has been about what I expected ... pain, blisters, heat," Baker said.

A few months ago, he sustained a knee injury. That has meant that he has to break his stride periodically and walk.

Because of the heat that has gripped the region for two weeks, Baker usually begins to run just before sundown. "It's suicide to try to run in anything over 90°."

But he made an exception when he started the run in Virginia Beach – he was excited, he said. He ran 20 miles in the middle of the day and overextended himself. But he said the effects of that experience have been overcome, and he has met his minimum goal of 30 miles a day on the average. As for his start in the East instead of the West, Baker notes that some runners will be suspicious of this because of the headwinds that will work against him once he is west of the Mississippi River. In fact, he had planned to go from West to East, but changed his mind because he wanted to start in a place with which he was familiar.

Virginia is that place, he said. Baker's wife, Debbie, was born and reared in Emporia, and Baker said he has many friends and relatives here and knows the roads.

* * *

That night I started running and walking westward on Route 250 coming out of Richmond. We stopped and camped alongside the highway sometime after 11:00 p.m. I was still fretting over the fact that I was still ten or so miles behind schedule. That night I did something about it. From our camp I ran about five miles westward and ran most of the five miles back.

Spencer thought I was going nuts. I'm not sure he totally comprehended my commitment to see the thing through all the way. I think the skeptic part of him, the ex-con part of him was probing my dedication and commitment to see when the real me would come out, see when I got tired of this silly adventure, packed it up and went home to my wife and kids.

Nonetheless, Spencer and I got along fairly well. There weren't any serious conflicts. He provided a service without which the run may have been impossible. Yet, there was a slight but constant tension between us just under the surface. Most outsiders would not have detected it, but it was there.

Certainly Abe and Stubby didn't detect the tension. We crossed their path fifteen miles east of Charlottesville, Virginia on July 23. The two-man traveling show, I guessed, worked this heavily touristed section of Virginia every season. I'm not sure what Stubby's role was, but the guy playing Abe Lincoln was a dead-on ringer.

Thomas Jefferson's Monticello was just up the road a few miles. I had taught school here in Albemarle County eight years ago, and I remember that many of the locals ascribed to the two-hundred year-old rumor of Mr. Jefferson's seed having been lavishly spread around in this part of then early America – not just Sally Hennings. No, the locals here felt there was more than one.

Monticello itself was built on a much smaller hill than Brown's Mountain which was abruptly south of it. It was on Brown's Mountain in October, 1977 that I met Debbie Powell who would later marry me. Dan Felton and Rebecca had invited us to dinner at their apartment high atop Brown's Mountain.

Several unique modern apartments were built into a huge old house-barn from which you had a magnificent view of most of the surrounding countryside. I believe that it was considered something of an exclusive residence in the Charlottesville area. Not pretentious or blue-blooded or even very expensive, just a bit unusual and in a gorgeous and historic location.

Debbie had my attention immediately. Although her conversation was mostly with Rebecca, and mine mostly with Dan, I knew I wanted to see her again. Not only was she very pretty, there was something about her, something that was wonderful. I did not have a good set of adjectives to describe her. From the start it was more of the feeling of a consuming mystery. I simply wanted to know more and more about her. To this day I feel the same way.

I still had some friends scattered about these foothills of the Blue Ridge Mountains, so I ventured a call to Shelt and Sharon Root who lived out in the country about seventeen miles west of Charlottesville. Spencer and I spent the night with them on July 24. I had a wonderful time visiting. Shelt and Sharon's two sons, Shelt, five and a half, and Garrett, three and a half were great kids. The next day Shelt ran with me four miles halfway up Afton Mountain; then we said goodbye, and Shelt went home.

I almost got to the top of the mountain, another five miles, before the knee locked up and I had to walk. On top of Afton Mountain you can see a good part of the Shenandoah Valley spread out below to the west. Oh yes, the beautiful Shenandoah Valley. Wonderful memories of Debbie and I raising the boys. We lived way out in the country with the Shenandoah River maybe three-hundred yards from our backyard.

You know, I sometimes think that these strange things I always seem to be seeing just have a way of seeking me out. It could be that I'm one of those people that is a lightning rod to some other dimension or some other reality.

One night somewhere along about 1983, after I was no longer teaching and I was away from home on the road selling coffee, I got a call at my motel from my wife, Debbie. It seems she had just experienced a little other reality of her own. She was a tad shaken and thought maybe it would be good for me to return home as soon as possible.

"Honey, what happened?"

"Oh, I feel silly telling you about this, but I'm just a little freaked out. I was in the living room, and I heard some cattle or horses running behind the house. I didn't know what to think. You know we've never had anything like that here. I looked outside. Of course, it was dark, and I didn't see or hear a thing. There was just something strange, but I didn't see anything. Oh, I shouldn't have called you. I'm sorry. I'll be fine."

"No, honey. I'm glad you did. Look, it's probably nothing to worry about. Maybe some farmer's cattle got out and just happened by our place. I'm sure everything will be all right."

"Well, okay. I guess so. Don't try to get home tonight; I'll see you this weekend." There was still some apprehension in her voice, but I was sure there wasn't anything going on.

"Okay, honey. I love you. Tell the boys I'll be home in a couple of days."

About a month later with no more cattle or horses having been seen or heard, I was home one night sitting in the living room with Debbie. We both heard what sounded like six or seven horses at a pretty good gallop outside just beyond the east end of the house. She looked at me like, "See, I told you so," and I was out the door quickly to see what was going on. I went to the end of the house where the sound had come from. There was nothing. No horses, no sounds, no evidence of anything having galloped through our property. I thought maybe at daylight I would discover hoof prints that were impossible to see in the dark. I went in the house and called my closest neighbor to see if he had heard anything.

"No, not a thing. It could have been deer, you know." He was right. Six or seven deer probably trotted through. But the next morning's light showed no tracks of any kind, no trampled down grass, no droppings, nothing.

A week later I was telling a local old-timer about it. "Aw, ain't nothing all that strange about it. Folks around here been hearin' horses at night for a long time. You know that bottomland 'tween your house and the river?"

"Yeah," I said, getting into whatever he was about to tell me.

"Back in the Civil War a cavalry skirmish was fought there. Your house on that hill is awful close to it. Well, you know what I'm a'sayin'. Folks around here, especially the old-timers, still hear those horses running. What you got is ghost horses from the Civil War."

We had a lot more than that. The old house we lived in was a nesting haven for snakes. We didn't have a clue back before we bought the place. We went out there to take a look at it, and the people that lived there had a little boy about five or six years old. He kept talking about the monsters and snakes around the place. Naturally, we thought he simply had a vivid imagination, so we bought the place and moved in.

We didn't see or hear anything for two or three years. Then, should I even say it? All hell broke loose. About the same time we heard the ghost horses, we started finding snakes in the house. The first time was when Debbie was looking for a belt that had been misplaced. She thought she spotted it under the bed. When she reached for it, it moved! For the next two years, until we sold the place and moved away, we found snakes everywhere: in the closet, under the sink, on the kitchen floor, in the bedrooms, under the house in the crawl space, in the attic, climbing up the side of the house, in the trees, in the shed, and a few of the old-fashioned kind, in the grass.

The locals called them rat snakes or corn snakes. I guessed they were a common variety of black snake. I became very well versed in snake identification. As long as they weren't copperheads, rattlesnakes, or coral snakes, I felt like we could be safe.

We tried to get rid of them with extermination, chemicals, and other things, but apparently the snakes were in the house to stay. We got so used to them that we joked about it and joked about when we would see the next one. However, we were very careful about reaching into dark spaces for things.

As for the monsters the little boy talked about, we never actually saw them, but we sure did hear them. On several occasions we'd be in bed and hear an eerie, high-pitched tone, almost like an electric tone but so close to us it made our skin crawl. On two occasions, again at night while we were in bed but not asleep, we both heard something moving around in the upper part of the wall or even higher in the attic. I thought, *finally something going on that has a plausible explanation. That noise up there must be a critter of some kind, maybe a rat, although we've never seen evidence of any rats. Maybe a bird, or – heaven forbid! – a snake large enough to make that kind of noise.* Whatever it was, we never found out.

Going back to the monsters, one night the high-pitched sound had us frozen in bed. We were literally too scared to move. Finally, I mustered up enough courage or insanity to rise up and look out the window behind the headboard of our bed. I thought I saw a shadow of a person move quickly. *Now this is more like it, an enemy I can deal with.*

"Honey," I whispered, "I think there is somebody out there. I want you to get in the closet and wait until I come back. I'm going to call the sheriff, and then I'm going outside."

Debbie slipped quietly out of bed and delicately (she was seven months pregnant at the time) took a position in the corner of the closet. I kissed her lightly on the forehead, slid the closet door shut, called the sheriff, picked up a baseball bat, and in the best Navy Seal impersonation I could muster up, slipped quietly out of the house and began searching for the Boogie Man. My search was a failure, as was the sheriff's search when he arrived twenty minutes later.

# Chapter Nine

**M**aybe I wasn't a lightning rod to strange sights and events. My experiences may have been nothing more than the average Joe has all the time. This was going through my mind the day after the Just Say No Marathon crossed Afton Mountain. Then two things happened that put a damper on my average Joe theory.

I was running southwest towards Stuart's Draft, Virginia on Route 340, a very narrow, hilly, and winding country road. Running on the left side to see any possible cars coming my way, I had no shoulder to run on. What should have been a shoulder was a drop off to a ditch twenty feet below. I was running on the edge of the road. That's all I had to work with in the event of oncoming traffic, and traffic was oncoming. Only I couldn't see it because I was approaching the hump of a fairly steep hill. In the time it takes a frog to snatch a fly, a car was over the hill and was less than ten feet from me.

The flashback of my lifetime did not exactly happen as you often hear about, but almost. What went through my mind was God, Debbie, and the boys. In an instant that's what I thought about. I guess the reason the God thought came first was because when the car passed me, either the door handle or an area just below it grazed the fabric of my running shorts.

Now let's face it. That's a pretty thin margin between me and the car. I was sort of shook up for a few minutes, mentally I mean, but after a while, I concluded this was more proof of who was really in control of events. I actually gained strength from the near miss.

Then I met the Lightning Man. No, not a rag doll, a cyclist going to Heaven, a phantom airliner, or a reference to this very morning of my wondering about my own manifestation of a lightning-rod-like quality. Nope. This was the real Lightning Man.

I had turned south on Highway 11. The running in the hour since I was almost hit was good. The sun was blocked by impending thunder clouds rolling in from the southwest, and my blisters were a thing of the past. My meticulous care for them had paid off. The once painful, tender layer of swollen pus-filled dermis had turned to rough callous. I was striding out, breathing good, arms pumping. I might have been at the five mile stage of a 10K (6.2mile) run.

It started raining lightly, and the sky was getting darker. I welcomed the rain but wasn't enthusiastic about the rumbling and crackling thunder that was way off to the southwest. The rain was getting harder, and the storm was getting nearer. Then, when I was about two miles north of Fairfield on Route 11, I saw a bolt of lightning touch down straight on, dead ahead of me about a mile away. The sharp earsplitting CRACK!! followed it immediately.

*Hmm, this is no time to be on an open road. I think I better duck into a shelter if I can find one.* Spencer was up the road in Lexington looking for a motel for us tonight. *No help there. Aw. Fiddlesticks, no big deal. Just a little thunder, lightning, and rain.*

In a few minutes I noticed an old tire shop maybe thirty feet off the left of the road and headed straight for it as the storm was now at its peak. There was a man bent over, picking up coins off the concrete pad which a Dr. Pepper cold drink machine was sitting on. The area was under an overhanging roof and protected from most of the rain the storm was throwing at us.

"What happened?" I asked.

He stood and with no surprise in his voice at my sudden appearance said, "Well, a few minutes ago a bolt of lightning hit yonder across the road." I think I knew the very one he was talking about. "Why it rolled across the road in a big old fireball, hit this here Dr. Pepper machine, and it commenced to spittin' out all the change. It burnt all the wiring out of the machine and went on to the back of the shop and burnt out some more equipment I got back there."

I smelled the burned electrical insulation. "This happened seven, eight minutes ago?" I asked.

"Yep. Sure 'nough did."

"You know, I think I saw the same bolt of lightning. I was about a mile back. It looked like it might have hit on or very near the road."

"It did that; I'll tell ya. And that big ole fireball just tore across that wet road and hit the first wiring it came to. I was standin' there in the doorway and seen the whole thing."

"Did it scare you half to death?"

"No, not really. I've seen lots of lightning."

"You've seen it like this? Come across a wet road?"

"No, but you never can tell what it will do. I seen it one time, not too far from here, hit one of them big ole satellite dishes and aim it right back at a house a hundred yards away. It blew half that house to bits."

"You don't say," was all I could counter with.

"Yep. It sure did. Then, I reckon it was 'bout ten year ago, we knew a woman who was rockin' her seven-week old baby. Lightning hit her and killed her, but the baby wasn't hurt at all." He spoke very matter of factly and had an unmistakable tone of expertise and authority on the subject.

I pointed out my observation to him. "Wow, you sure do have some fascinating stories about lightning. I don't think many folks could say the same. What do you think the deal is?"

"Aw, there ain't no deal. You know, just that some folks knows quite a bit about some things, and others know other things. It seems like I've always knowed about lightning. That's all."

I felt like if I kept asking him, he could have told me stories for hours, but the storm was letting up a bit, and I thanked him for his shed's protection and trotted off southbound down Route 11.

An hour later I saw Spencer coming in my direction. He pulled over and told me he had a nice motel lined up in Lexington, and a restaurant was going to feed us tonight. He had some more work to do up ahead, so he turned the minivan around and headed off back to Lexington.

Things were looking pretty good for the evening ahead. I ended up with twenty-seven miles for the day, and I felt like I had finally gotten the Lightning Man off my mind. Before turning in, I wanted to call Debbie to see how everything was at home.

"Hi honey, How are you?"

"Good, good. How are you?"

"Well, pretty tired, as usual, but things seem to be going okay. The blisters that were killing me are a lot better. How are the boys?"

"They're fine. Just fine. That lightning today got our attention though."

"Lightning? What lightning?" The Lighting Man's image flashed across my brain.

"A bolt of lightning hit the maple tree just outside the kitchen this morning."

"You're kidding," I said. "This morning?"

"Yes. I was washing dishes in the kitchen. In fact, I was looking out the window, and BOOM! It hit the tree and split a long branch down the middle. Why?"

"Honey, you're not going to believe this." I told her about the bolt of lightning I had seen that morning and about my conversation with the Lightning Man.

"Okay. Wait a minute," she said. "I think I see where you're going with this. You think there's a connection." Of all the wonderful and inspiring traits my lovely wife has, a sense of the unusual, the unexplained, is not one of them.

"Well maybe. Sure. You've got to admit it sure is one heck of a coincidence." I wanted to say more to build my case, but she cut me off.

"Come on, Gary. Now you know that could have happened anywhere, anytime. There's no weird tie-in between the two events."

*Anytime* she said. "Time.  That's it," it triggered my rebuttal. "Honey, what time did the lightning hit the tree?"

"That's easy.  It was 10:15."

"Are you sure?"

"Yes, the clock is right there on the wall."

*Unbelievable.* "Honey, the lightning I saw hit at 11:15, the exact same time when you consider the time zone difference."

# Chapter Ten

**M**y Average Joe theory was shattered all right, but I still had around 2,600 miles left to run and 110 days left to run them in. What else could be in store for me? I didn't know, but I was ready to find out.

We were deep in the Appalachian Mountains by now. Running through Lexington, Virginia a half-hour before sundown, I was aware of the historical significance of the two schools here – VMI (Virginia Military Institute) and Washington and Lee University. Like the morning at Williamsburg, Virginia, I felt a sense of American history and pride and a sense that I might be adding something to it on the run across this beautiful land.

From July 27 through August 6, we were in western Virginia and West Virginia. Here are my notes (word for word, no editing) of that eleven-day period:

Thursday July 31 – The last five days have gone by like a flash. State trooper escorting me off I-64 fifteen miles west of Lexington. Spencer getting us free motels four nights in a row. Rob Gibson running five miles with me in Covington. Four radio interviews/talk shows. Hating walking on U.S. 60. Knee locking up late at night in Lewisburg, W. Va. Excellent response from people in W. Va. School principal gave us $20 at Rainelle. Young girl, sixteen, and lady asking, "Are you the guy who is running all the way from Lewisburg?" Beautiful room at Hawk's Nest.

Monday Aug. 4 – Spencer got Holiday Inn in Charleston two nights. Nice running on the Levee by the Kanawha River. T.V. interview in Charleston – they said practically nothing about "Just Say No," mostly about my ten year dream.   Yesterday walked in roadside beer joint on 60 east of Hurricane.

"Do you have any sandwiches?" I asked.

"Hot dogs, hamburgers."

"Any milk or juice?"

"Just tomato juice."

"I'll have beer nuts, a milky way, and a glass of water, please." Waitress gave a real "What kind of scoundrel are you" kind of look.   Half drunk farmer at bar next to me telling an uninterested listener that he thinks he'll get good and drunk tonight, stay drunk tomorrow, find a nice shade tree to lie under tomorrow and "see what the old bitch has to say about that!"

Wed. Aug 6 – Spencer complaining of no money.   Tom Adams says telegram from White House arriving in afternoon.   I'm tired of Spencer's sarcasm.   Thunderstorms predicted.   Sky's getting dark already.   I sit down and pray. Then one hour paperwork to sort out Spencer's problems. Telegram arrives – very nice.   Am worried, I've only done four or five miles by five p.m.   Big trouble here.   Meeting with Mayor at six.   Look out!   Later that night I get about ten miles around the city streets of Huntington.   Will still be twenty or so miles behind when we cross over to Ky. tomorrow.   Spencer not in room until 2:30 a.m.   He's out making it with the chick who hosted the meeting.   When I met her she touched my arm with an urgency that communicated promises to come later in the night if I was interested.   I wasn't.   She did the same to Spencer.   He was.

```
   JUUXXI-UUb3b+1218 U0/UU/66
TWX WHITEHOUSE WSH DLY PD
SUSPECTED DUPLICATE
 048 GOVT DLY WHITE HOUSE DC AUG 6
PMS MR. GARY BAKER, (DLR DONT DWR - R-U-S-H)
C/O HOLIDAY INN (C/O ASST MNGR ON DUTY)
1415 FOURTH AVENUE, ROOM 429
HUNTINGTON WV 25701


DEAR MR. BAKER:

I AM DELIGHTED TO LEARN OF YOUR SUCCESS AS YOU RUN ACROSS
AMERICA ON BEHALF OF THE JUST SAY NO CLUBS! DRUG AND ALCOHOL
ABUSE IS A PROBLEM THAT HAS TOUCHED ALL AMERICANS, ESPECIALLY OUR
YOUNG PEOPLE, AND CAN NO LONGER BE IGNORED. THE TIME HAS COME FOR
EACH ONE OF US TO TAKE A MORAL STAND.

THE INITIATIVE YOU HAVE TAKEN TO BRING YOUR MESSAGE INTO THE
TOWNS AND NEIGHBORHOODS ALONG THE WAY IS TRULY INSPIRING, AND ONE
WHICH I KNOW WILL BE VERY EFFECTIVE. KEEP UP THE GOOD WORK!

WITH BEST WISHES FOR CONTINUED SUCCESS,

  SINCERELY,

  NANCY REAGAN

1414 EST

IPM05WV
```

Coming into Kentucky really was a homecoming of sorts for me. I had always had a special place in my heart for the state I was born in. I remember growing up in Louisville. The place my family had lived the longest was a subdivision exactly on the county line. My front yard was in the city, and beyond my backyard was the country, literally. We played in the woods and fields and on the railroad tracks nearby. I believe it was the presence of that railroad so close to us that had some influence on my later tendencies to travel and probably even on the original seeds which grew into my dream of running across the U.S.

Yes, Kentucky was an important part of me. My family, old friends, and others I met in the next couple of weeks were a very much needed respite from the first three weeks of the Just Say No Marathon.

The morning of August 7, 1987 found me running around the elementary school track at Salt Lick, Kentucky with fifteen or twenty people. That evening I was escorted into Owingsville, Kentucky by two cross-country boys from the local high school, Ernie and Jimmy. Owingsville is on the top of a big hill with a gorgeous view of the mountains to the east and the Bluegrass Region to the west.

I spoke to the high school football team, then to scouts, teachers, 4-H leaders, and about fifty kids. All of that was followed by a radio interview. A local farmer named Tom Oldfield had arranged all of these activities and also invited Spencer and me to stay with his family that night.

To say that God's timing for me to spend the night with this family on this night was perfect, would be a huge understatement. It was more than perfect. They made such an impression on me, I haven't forgotten any of it to this day, and I don't think I ever will. I saw a close-knit family that was also the center of a small community of families that were self-sufficient, cared about things – each other, each other's families, the larger community, the country, issues. You name it, they cared.

The openness and warmth they showed Spencer and me was wonderful. They did the same for friends and neighbors that came by for a visit that night. There were several that would come in for a hug, to borrow a tool, just to say "Hi" or maybe snatch a bite. I was surprised there were any bites left after Tom, his family, and Spencer and I had worked our way through the steak from Tom's herd, pizza, fresh garden tomatoes and cole slaw, hot biscuits with homemade strawberry preserves, and fresh cow's milk also from Tom's herd.

After nearly three weeks on the lonely road, being with these fellow Kentuckians on this evening not only recharged my batteries, but also reaffirmed the knowledge that there are good people left on this sad earth, and they are called Kentuckians.

There were more good people to meet me in Lexington, Kentucky. My mother's side of the family, the Harrisons, were there in numbers. That may not have been all that hard to do when you note that my mother was from a family of thirteen. Four of the remaining five of her sisters were there: Aunts Ona, Edna, Alene, and Ethel. Also, two of my cousins, Larry and Kenny, were there with their families. Larry and I ran a 5K (3.1 miles) the night of August 9 in downtown Lexington. There was a big crowd of around 3,000 runners. I had a great time and enjoyed the visit with my family.

Local television did a piece on the Just Say No Marathon that I felt was excellent. The three days in Lexington allowed me to catch up the twenty miles I was behind and get a little rest. I was going to need it. On August 11, I started out on the twenty-six mile trek to the state capital of Frankfort, Kentucky.

It must have been the hottest day of the summer. It was all Spencer could do to keep me supplied with fluids to drink, and on this inferno of a day, I resorted to simply showering numerous times under a gallon of water I slowly poured over my head. I sure did not want a heat breakdown coming into the state capital.

Six miles out, Don Thurmond of the Kentucky Department of Human Resources, Division of Alcohol and Drug Abuse met me and ran with me to Frankfort. In Frankfort I was notified that the Just Say No organization wanted to make the Just Say No Marathon a national fund-raising event. Tom Adams, the Just Say No executive director with whom we were in communication on a regular basis, told me an official press release was prepared and would be made available to the media today. Of course this is what I always wanted – the run to be able to raise money for the fight against drug and alcohol abuse. When we left Virginia Beach, I was content with simply spreading the Just Say No message and did not know if an actual fund-raising effort would ever be mounted.

As for the actual mechanics of how the money would be raised, all I was aware of was a toll-free phone number that a potential donor could call in their financial pledge. I did write up a lengthy press release of my own stating the same thing – that the Just Say No Marathon was now officially a national fund-raising event. I wanted to have a good prepared statement ready for the media when we got to my hometown, Louisville, in three days.

At the end of the press release I stated that I was dedicating the Kentucky portion of the Just Say No Marathon to Mr. Joe Canary. Joe was my Aunt Ona's husband. He had passed on recently and had a big heart. He was liked by everyone and always supported young people.

In Louisville my homecoming continued. Debbie, Jeff, and Conor drove up from Tennessee. We stayed with Mon and Dad, and again I was able to get a little rest and catch up on mileage I owed.

Local TV and newspapers reported the news of the run becoming a fund-raiser, and old friends and family came out to my old high school, Fairdale, to support me (see photo next page). We did a couple of miles on the track around the football field I had played on some twenty-two years ago.

August 17, 1986 – It was time to get back on the road. I started out in Valley Station, Kentucky, ten miles south of Louisville running down U.S.31-W or the "Dixie Highway" as it was and still is known. It's a good thing I got some rest in Louisville. That first day out of there I logged over forty miles, all the way to Elizabethtown, Kentucky.

By the time I reached the courthouse in "E-Town", as locals called it, I was ready to drop. The heat again was merciless. But at least I had put Louisville, Valley Station, Ft. Knox, Radcliff, and E-Town behind me.

GARY BAKER CAUGHT BY NEWSPAPER PHOTOGRAPHER
AS HE PASSED THROUGH ELIZABETHTOWN, KY.

I began at this point in the run to actually start thinking about how it was all going to end. Would I, could I stay on schedule and reach Santa Monica, California by November 13? For now, my short-term goal was set on reaching the Mississippi River in Memphis. There certainly were distractions that threatened any and all of my long and short-term goals. But I was getting pretty good at pushing them aside and focusing, really focusing, on what I knew I had to do – average thirty miles per day on foot. The financial plight of Debbie and the boys was worsening daily, and come mid-March of 1987, it would be Debbie, the boys, and the newest Baker child.

Debbie told me about the third child's conception back in Louisville. I was thrilled and at the same time guilt-ridden with the knowledge that for some nearly five months now, I had provided no income to my growing family.

Like I said though, I was getting good at pushing ever-mounting obstacles aside and focusing on doing the mileage. I was getting *too* good at it. The one problem that was clearly growing to the point of threatening the integrity of what the Just Say No Marathon was about was Spencer. The tension between us was growing. I had reason to believe he had been drinking on several occasions in the last week or so. I think I was able to deal with the drinking itself if that were in fact true. I confronted him on it and did not get the confirmation or denial of my suspicions. What I was more concerned with was of course the image it would project on the integrity of the entire project.

If it were simply one or two beers and it did not affect his performance in the many duties he had taken on, I don't think I would have said a thing. After all, I know good and well that many of the community leaders we had spoken to in the last month were drinkers themselves. Maybe not 'problem drinkers', maybe only 'social drinkers', but were drinkers nonetheless. I was one myself until eight months ago.

No, ordinary drinking that did not affect his responsibilities, I think I could have dealt with. I may not have been happy with it on account of the media focus on us and the fact that we undoubtedly would have lost credibility. But evidently Spencer's commitment to the entire project was beginning to diminish significantly, and the drinking was just part of the drop off in his overall performance. He would be late for things I counted on him getting done on time, primarily being ready to roll each morning at the specified time. This was becoming a chronic problem. It was also becoming difficult to count on him picking me up from a certain place at a certain time. In short, he was getting less and less dependable.

In weighing his value versus his shortcomings, he was far ahead on the value side. He was doing a great job securing us lodging and meals almost every night. For this reason and the fact that I liked him, I took a very low-key approach with the differences we had. I was willing to let a lot of small things slide by, just so long as things didn't get out of control. And what would I do if that line were crossed? It was plenty difficult for me to just barely get my mileage every day. I did not need any additional problems. When I got off the road at the end of the day, we usually went to the motel first before we would go out to eat. I would walk in and collapse on the bed and not move a muscle for maybe an hour or so. Then I would finally get up and shower, put on some sweats, and we'd go out to eat.

I'm not sure you could actually describe what I did to a plate of food as eating. It was more like an ambush. I could eat two or three normal portions of everything, not only at dinner, but also at breakfast the next morning. Believe me; I was not putting on any weight. I simply burned it all up, every day. You ought to try running and walking thirty miles a day for your weight loss program. I can guarantee you will get results.

August 18 – I've been running on the Dixie Highway for two days now. We stopped in Bonnieville, Kentucky to speak to a middle school. The kids were laughing and giggling at something that must have been visible showing through the front of my sweat-soaked running shorts. There's nothing like kids to put an old forty-year-old wannabe athlete in his place.

I remembered when I was a kid myself. My dad and I drove down from Louisville several times to rabbit hunt on farms not far from this little town of Bonnieville, Kentucky. I also remembered hitch hiking the Dixie Highway all the way from Louisville to where I currently live in Tennessee. My friend, Jim Ray, and I had the adventure of a teenager's lifetime on the two hundred mile journey. It took us six rides to get there and five to come back. Mostly farmers were willing to pick us up and a few truckers.

Jim had been a real nemesis of mine from the time I was eight or nine years old up until I was about fourteen. Jim had three brothers and two sisters and a mother who did her best to control them but was facing a mammoth task. Mr. Ray died when Jim was about nine years old.

His brother John (we called him Pete) and I were best friends all the way through high school. His other brothers were Garnie, older than Jim, and Phillip, one year younger than me. In our neighborhood there were about four or five families with at least two boys. Many were the days my brother Steve and I felt like D-Day at Normandy was mild indeed compared to the battles we fought around south Louisville in the 1950's.

For some reason (I would later figure it was simply convenience) Jim Ray would use me as his personal punching bag. Jim would fight anybody, anytime, for any reason, and on some occasions for no reason at all. I wasn't much of a physical specimen at age eleven or twelve, and Jim, it seemed, didn't have a complete day unless he personally destroyed me. Most of it was my own fault for being such a wimp and not fighting back.

Then one day he was chasing me through the woods. I crossed a waist-deep creek on a fallen log. In hot pursuit across the same log, Jim slipped and fell in the creek. I knew that when he came up out of the creek, my life would be over if he could catch me. I decided not to let him out of the creek.

About the only place he could come out was a slippery, muddy bank, so I grabbed a stout tree limb on that bank as my anchor and proceeded to kick him back into the creek every time he mounted an advance up the slippery slope. I kicked him in the head, the mouth, his shoulders, his belly, his arms, and his back. This went on for quite some time, and by the time I finally let him crawl up the muddy bank, he was plumb tuckered out. He never again laid another hand on me.

I always tell people that because I finally stood up to him he ceased his attacks on me. Well maybe, but part of it had to be that

I was so scared of what I just knew he would do to me that day that I kind of lost control of myself for a few moments. In other words, sheer terror was at work, not any long overdue bravery finally awakening. Yep, Jim and I got along pretty well from then on. If ever the great American story about four brothers is told (and I'm doing the telling) then Garnie, Jim, Phillip, and Pete Ray will be who that story is told about.

Dixie Highway is where Jim and I hitchhiked to Tennessee in 1960, and now in 1986 I find myself running its gravelly and sometimes grassy shoulders trying to make Bowling Green, Kentucky, in two more days.

August 20 – Bowling Green, Kentucky. Spencer gets out more radio and newspaper challenges to young folks who would show their commitment to a drug and alcohol free lifestyle by coming out to the Western Kentucky State University track and run with me. A few came out, most notably three of Western's cross-country team and one of Western's football players.

The three cross-country guys really had to slow their pace down so they wouldn't leave me in the dust. Two of these guys were world-class runners from Africa. The football player had only been on campus a couple of weeks. He said he was homesick and was thinking about packing up and going back home to Cincinnati.

I did twenty-two miles that day, fifteen of them on the track. There would be plenty of time to catch up the eight mile deficit because I was scheduled to be back in my hometown of Dickson, Tennessee in six days, and I had built several days off into the schedule.

The next day I walked seventeen miles to Franklin, Kentucky, near the Tennessee state line. I recalled reading that around 140 years ago Kentucky frontiersmen, soon to become Colorado mountain men, cited as one of the primary reasons they sought the wide open spaces of the West was that the dark, overgrown, overcrowded, compressed hills and hollers of Kentucky bound them in too much. "There wasn't room to breathe."

They could not have been referring to the beautiful, open, rolling countryside I walked through that morning. In the Bluegrass State, one must not be overly expectant to actually see blue grass; certainly not where I was this morning. Deep and luxuriant shades of green stretched off in all directions, lightly wafting in a gentle breeze as if they were unbroken surf lines off an island in paradise.

In White House, Tennessee we were warmly greeted by four hundred students and the faculty and staff of a middle school. The kids asked a lot of good questions, and the principal bought me a Coke. From there we drove through Nashville to Dickson. I ran the final fifteen miles to my home Edgewood. Debbie brought the boys to Dickson, and they rode with Spencer as he escorted me first to Ruskin Cave, then the final two miles home.

Paul and the guys at Ruskin gave us a warm welcome. Things were somewhat chaotic at home for the two and a half days I was there. Mom and Pop had come down from Louisville; Spencer and I were having our differences; Debbie was pregnant. In short, everyone was pretty grumpy. There were no solutions in sitting around stewing over the problems. I left on schedule, the 28th of August, ran up Wilson Hollow, turned west on Old Number 1 Highway, a stage route a century ago, and stopped at the McEwen School where I spoke to an assembly of four hundred students and teachers.

I was able to make it over the Tennessee River that day, almost all the way to Huntingdon, Tennessee, a total of well over forty miles. I think it was the most mileage I'd done in one day so far.

Jackson, Tennessee, August 30, 1986 – Tom Adams had planned an appearance for me at a country music Just Say No concert in Jackson. Shelly West and T. G. Sheppard were the headliners. For some reason the details of this event have completely deserted my failing memory, not because I'm getting older. The details of this even had deserted my memory way back then.

Over the years I have tried to go back in my mind and recapture what exactly happened that night, but I have failed every time. I think that the reason I can never recapture what occurred that evening is because maybe nothing happened. Years later I would dream about that night and manufacture things that I'm pretty sure did not happen. What I do know is this:

Tom Adams had made preparations for my stop in Jackson to be a big deal. Appearing at the concert that night was to be the highlight of the Just Say No Marathon up to that point in time. Spencer had been talking about it for days prior to our arrival in Jackson. I was getting excited too. I didn't know what I would say if I were invited on the stage to address the huge audience, but that's what Spencer had told me Tom Adams had in mind. Debbie and the boys had made the short trip from Edgewood and were going to stay with me in the motel that night.

I remember Spencer produced tickets for all of us; we went to the arena, went in and sat near the back. The show started, but from then on, for the life of me, I have never been able to differentiate what actually happened from what my confused dreams had over the years tangled in with reality. Sometimes I see myself having been invited up on the stage and saying a few motivational words about staying drug and alcohol free. Sometimes I see myself backstage but never having been invited out front. Sometimes I feel none of us (Debbie, the boys, Spencer, myself) were ever recognized as having been in the audience.

My notes tell me that I felt like the headliner of the concert, Shelley West, used poor judgment on one of the songs she chose, "Jose Cuervo", and her comment about the tequila drinkers in the audience. I also seem to remember that neither Debbie nor myself particularly enjoyed the music, and I think we left early.

None of what did or did not happen that evening damaged my resolve to see the run all the way through, but it did put some doubts in my mind as to Just Say No's commitment to mount a serious fund-raiser or to follow through on plans they were telling us they had made.

There was one other thing that I'm certain did happen that night. Spencer's late-night carousing, drinking, or whatever, prevented him from showing up at the motel the next morning at 8:00 a.m. He simply was not there, was not ready to go. Finally, around 9:00 a.m., he called and said he was on the way, he had a good excuse, and would I wait for him? He did not have the minivan. He had said last night, "You guys take the van back to the motel. I won't need it. I'll catch a ride back later. See you in the morning."

My response this morning was quick, "No, I don't think so Spencer. I'm going on to Memphis in the van. Look man. I don't know what's going on with you, but if you can't be dependable, then maybe your part in this thing just wasn't to be."

"Aw, look Gary ... you don't understand ... it's just that ... uh, well. Look, it's not what you think. All right, I screwed up last night. It won't happen again."

"Spencer, I'm sorry. I'm going to Memphis. I'll be at the Days Inn we are scheduled to be at. If you still want to be a part of the Just Say No Marathon, I'll see you there in two days."

He sounded pretty much deflated and didn't counter with any more excuses. Debbie and the boys had left to return home to Edgewood early that morning. Spencer's absence changed things. Instead of running the eighty-five miles from Jackson to Memphis, I drove straight on through to Memphis, checked in the motel, and started working on my mileage for the day.

Before I left the motel I received a message to telephone a reporter from the Memphis Commercial Appeal. I called and she wanted an interview. We met in mid-town Memphis, some eight or so miles from my motel. Instead of driving, I ran and walked. Sixteen miles would be out of the way, and only fourteen more to do when I got back from the interview. I showered, rested some, ate what must have been two pounds of granola, apples, bananas, and yogurt, and then went out, and finished up the fourteen miles.

The next day I was up early and ran maybe six to eight miles while it was still cool – meaning it was already near eighty degrees at seven in the morning. I rested for a while, shoveled down a huge breakfast, and studied a Memphis street map. My plan was to get my remaining twenty-two miles for the day accomplished by simultaneously touring the downtown Riverwalk, Mud Island, and Beale Street blues strip. So that's what I did. By the time I ran and walked down to Beale Street, it was already 4:00 or 5:00 p.m. I ran and walked all over downtown Memphis, then returned to Beale Street around 7:30 p.m. A blues band was cranking it out at H. C. Handy Park just off the Beale Street strip itself. I didn't come all this way to happen upon real blues and then just keep on jogging by. Nope, I sat on a bench and got lost in the sound and the unique aromas of Memphis: barbeque, beer, people, cigarette smoke, cigar smoke, horses (mounted police), and the mighty Mississippi itself.

I recalled just a couple of years ago I was here in Memphis selling coffee. I came down to Beale Street that night, walked into one of the many blues clubs, sat at a table, and ordered a beer. The band was good - lead guitar, bass, drums, keyboard, maybe a rhythm guitar – I can't remember for sure – and a horn or two.

What I do remember that night was how many different musicians would simply walk in off the street, step up on the stage, plug in, and wail away for a couple of numbers or for an entire set. Of course I realized there was a whole lot more going on than rank strangers stepping up there and playing so effectively. I'm sure the "guest" musicians were working across town, and this was their night off. Or they were people from the club across the street, and they had a thirty minute break. It was impressive - very talented people seemingly interchangeable.

The music went on and on. I didn't think it could get any better. Then a young wiry white guy walked in carrying a guitar case. The musicians on stage all gave him a knowing nod of the head and continued hammering out whatever classic Memphis blues tune they had in progress. All except the lead guitar man who simply backed away from front center stage, leaned over, and unplugged from the amp. He gave a thankful bow to the audience and a big smile and stepped off the stage.

By the time the lead guitar man got to the bar, the young, wiry, white guest picker was already plugged in and hitting some downright mournful licks that made you want to cry. Here's the thing: once he got settled in, and it didn't take a minute, he knocked that place completely apart. Note by note, chord by chord, lead runs you hoped would never stop. Sultry, slower tempo pieces that had you melting into your chair, this blues picker had Memphis mesmerized.

He did not stop for over an hour. He ran one tune right into another, no breaks. In the meantime the other band members were stepping out routinely when another fabulous musician would sit in for them. But wiry, white lead picker ignored everything around him and simply tore the place up. I had never before, and never have since witnessed such an exhibition of musical nirvana. Only two years ago and only two blocks away, yet another world.

The world I was currently in forced me to my feet. It was getting dark and I had ten miles between me and the motel. I started back towards the motel in a southeasterly direction. After about three or four miles, I realized the return route I was on was different from the route I had come in on earlier today. *Oops.* I had gotten myself lost, but at least I felt sure I was going in the right direction. I noticed that the area I was in could correctly be described as a slum, a ghetto.

Then I noticed a gang of teenage boys just to the right of an overpass I would be running under up ahead of me, maybe two hundred yards. At first they didn't register a blip on my internal screen of things to look out for, but as I got closer, I noticed that they had noticed me. There was something in their body language and something in the audible but unintelligible taunts that changed their screen status from routine to the highest priority.

I thought about turning around and heading back the way I had come. No, they would probably see me as an easy mark. This would be no different than running up on a bad dog's territory. In those instances I had learned to do three things: cross to the other side of the road if possible, pick up a handful of rocks, and pick up the pace. Here there would be no crossing to the other side of the road, and I was way too tired to pick up the pace, but I did pick up a scrap two-by-four about three or four feet long. I thought, *Well, if they want to do something, I would at least be able to crack open one or two of them before they succeeded in taking me down.*

The closer I got, the clearer it became that picking up the two-by-four was a good idea. They were increasing the physical and verbal taunts, but I did not even look their way. I continued at a steady trot and carried the two-by-four snugly under my right arm. I ran on past them and noticed that my pace had indeed increased, and I was thankful that they were not in pursuit. I dropped the two-by-four ten minutes later.

The next morning I was making preparations to drive across the mighty Mississippi into Arkansas where I would begin my assault on the Great American West, the final 1,470 miles of the run.

There was a knock on the door. It was Spencer.

"Hey Spencer, what's up?"

"You said show up if I wanted to be part of the deal. Right?"

"Yes, that's what I said. So tell me, do you understand we have an image, and anything against that image, I won't tolerate?"

"Yeah man, I understand. I want to do a good job. I'm ready to go."

He didn't really convince me. On the other hand, it wasn't a morning I wanted to get started on a sour note, and the truth of the matter was that I needed him. If I were to simply drive on by myself to each motel that Days Inn had a room reserved for us and make up the mileage I owed, we would miss a lot of contact with a lot of small-town America; miss a lot of opportunities to talk with kids, to challenge them. Without Spencer, the contact with the media would disappear. Without the media, our chances of reaching the kids were extremely limited.

"All right, I haven't talked to Tom Adams or anybody else at Just Say No. They don't know a thing about what happened. If we stay cool, I think everything will be okay, as long as it doesn't happen again."

With a little more confidence this time he said, "Don' worry, it won't."

# Chapter Eleven

The Big Muddy, as the Mississippi River is known, was three hundred feet below us. Arkansas was spread out in front of us, flatter than the proverbial pancake. Cotton fields were all across the place, still a couple of months from harvest.

We stayed in Forest City our first night in Arkansas. It was a Friday night and high school football was in the air. I love the smell, the sights and sounds of football games in mid to late autumn, and even though September was a little early, some of those unmistakable signs were floating around the little town we were in.

I was running by a high school stadium around 7:00 p.m., and the parking lot was filling up, the visiting team's student buses were arriving, the band was tuning up, and the drummers getting that rhythmic marching rat tat, rat tat, rat ta tat tat tat thing going. I could smell the grilled hot dogs, hamburgers and onions, and the freshly mowed grass.

Instantly I went back twenty-three years to the night I suited up and was ready to start at defensive tackle in our team's first game of the season. The anticipation, the excitement, the thrill of my first real challenge in football combat was overriding. I had played the game since age eight, mostly sand lot. I was more often than not ineligible to play (academics) in grades 8, 9, and 10. In the 11th grade I had a paper route to take my time.

But finally the summer leading to my senior year, I had made up my mind that I was going to be in shape when practice started in mid-August. For me being in shape meant I would quit smoking two weeks before practice started and maybe do some push-ups. Serious training for high school athletics wasn't the same thing in 1963 it is today.

To my surprise I held my own in pre-season practices and scrimmages, and to my amazement, line coach Joe Goodman started me on opening night. It would turn out to be my first and only shot at football glory.

I never remembered taking a hit that night that would have torn cartilage in my left knee, but the next morning my left knee was locked up tight in the now familiar 45 degree position.

It wasn't locked up this night in Arkansas. I ran back to the motel and was looking forward to our stop in Little Rock in a couple of days.

One of the nights before we made Little Rock, I walked into a small-town restaurant before returning to our motel. Spencer was not with me. The place wasn't fancy, more along the lines of a working class "meat and three" diner. I sat down, ordered my meal from the waitress, and waited. I noticed an older black man, probably close to sixty sitting alone at a table by a wall some twenty feet from me. His hands were clasped together in front of his chest, his head bent forward a little bit, and his eyes were closed. He was praying, saying a silent grace before he ate his meal which was on the table in front of him. There wasn't anything at all that would have diverted his attention away from what he was doing.

I'm sure no one else in the diner even noticed him. There was something so poignant and beautiful about his silent, still, but deep prayer of grace that moved me and penetrated my soul. It was so simple, yet so meaningful. I can still see him today. He would not have had any knowledge of the impression his simple grace prayer had on me then, and truthfully, for the rest of my life.

Spencer was back in form doing the PR work he had done so well early on. He had scheduled a "meeting" with a politician on the steps of the state capital in Little Rock, presumably to be a photo op and to help us get out the message and challenge of Just Say No. This "meeting" was a farce. The politician wanted self-exposure only. Not surprisingly, this happened many times in the course of the Just Say No Marathon.

What alarmed me more was the consistent message I was getting from ordinary people, parents, scout leaders, church leaders. Back behind the scenes when we were not in front of a camera or a microphone, they would tell me that everyone knew who was in on the illegal flow of drugs into their little town. It was always some official – a judge, a district attorney, a politician, and more often than not, a sheriff or chief of police.

The first few times people said these things to me it made little impression on me, but the more stories I heard of local corruption in the supposed illegal drug trafficking enforcement system, the more I knew these people were correct. That is, the very people we count on to stop the illegal flow of drugs into our towns, schools, and jails are the same people who are receiving hush money or kickbacks from criminals and allowing the drug trade to thrive.

Of course, this only deals with the supply side. Unfortunately, the demand side is the most important issue. I've always thought if there were no demand for illegal drugs, then the problems of stopping their supply would go away. There was no question which one of the two elements of supply and demand I was directing my efforts at. I always felt that if somehow my efforts could be a counter to just one kid getting involved in the mostly downward spiral into addiction, then the Just Say No marathon would be a success.

We plowed on through the Arkansas towns of Benton, Malvern, Donaldson, Midway, Arkadelphia, Gum Springs, Curtis Gurdon, Prescott, Emmett, Hope, Aoman, and Texarkana.

We crossed the Texas state line and on September 14, we were warmly greeted in Mt. Pleasant, Texas. A doctor and his family invited Spencer and me into their home for lunch. They were the movers and shakers of Mt. Pleasant's anti-drug efforts, and they had a good group of kids who ran with me around the school track (below).

There was another day at some small Texas town between Mt. Pleasant and Dallas that a group of church ladies brought us to their church for lunch. They were so nice and friendly. They made us feel at home. These experiences always lifted me and helped give me fortitude to continue.

As we approached Dallas, Spencer was telling me that we had been invited to attend a large Just Say No rally at the Capital Building in Austin. Like Jackson, Tennessee we expected to address the crowd.

When the day arrived, we drove down about three hours from Dallas, and things went sour again. But unlike Jackson, Tennessee, this time I was positive. Absolutely nothing happened. The rally was going on; there were several thousand people there, but we were never recognized. I couldn't help but think it was all politics. Maybe the local organizers were Democrats, and of course the Reagans were Republicans.

Whatever the mix-up was, it ruined most of a day in addition to lowering our confidence in Just Say No (the organization, not the message) even more. From this point on Spencer, I believe, was just going through the motions. Up to now I felt like he was hoping something positive would come out of his efforts in the Just Say No Marathon – maybe a decent job, maybe a new direction for his life.

Just the opposite was happening. He was only making a hundred bucks a month. As far as we knew, there was no money being raised by the Just Say No Marathon, therefore no incremental increases of the pay I was just giving him out of my meager resources. He was losing confidence in the Just Say No organization. I was losing confidence also, but not nearly as much as Spencer. I suspected the work was beginning to be boring to him. I also suspected he was not as committed to the Just Say No message and philosophy as I was.

On top of all of this, he had just received news from his home-town of Chicago that his brother was found dead, stuffed in the trunk of a car. It was probably a drug deal gone bad. I realized his staying with me all the way to California was starting to look like a long shot.

Given all the difficult circumstances and bad news of late, we both could have quit, but we didn't. We put Austin, Dallas, Grand Prairie, Arlington, and Ft. Worth behind us and continued following the sun into the vast reaches of west Texas.

Long days, long nights, long roads, and everything is flat. I remember seeing towns on the horizon that were so far away it would take me sometimes six hours to get to on foot. Most of my daily routines out here were just that – routine. I would usually be up shortly after dawn, stretch a few minutes, start putting fluids (including coffee) in me, and leave the motel for a five or six mile run heading out of town in one direction or another. It didn't make any difference which direction I chose because after the five or six miles, I would turn around and retrace my route back to the motel.

I liked these early morning runs. The stifling heat was a few hours away, and it was nice to be out of town all alone. I could look back at the town and think about all the people just waking up, getting ready for work, probably going to the same place they've been to every day for the last five years, probably doing the same thing they've done every day for the last five years.

I felt aloof at these times. I was fortunate indeed. I really did break out of the rat race, if for only a few months. I was living a dream and knew I had better savor the time left before I woke up back in the real world. I thanked God every day for the opportunity He had given me, and I prayed diligently that His strength would see me through to the end. Yes, I enjoyed these early mornings in west Texas, out of town with just God and me.

The other thing I remember about the west Texas towns of Breckenridge, Albany, Funston, Anson, Robey, Snyder, Midway, Gail, Key, Lamesa, Sand, and Seminole was the cultural ways of the people. If I hadn't known we were in west Texas, I could have easily identified the people as Alabamans, Tennesseans, or other southerners. Their speech patterns and their friendliness I felt was identical to the people in the south I was so familiar with. Like rural southerners, folks in west Texas lived life at a slower pace than most of us. My own pace of thirty miles per day finally had taken me approximately five hundred miles across Texas and into New Mexico.

At Hobbs, New Mexico, we got a lot of attention – TV appearances, newspaper coverage, and meetings with community leaders. There was a very strong interest in our message and in what the town needed to do to form up Just Say No clubs.

A few days later, west of Roswell, running on Route 70, we were still in flat prairie country, but not for long. Up ahead, maybe ten miles, I could see mountains. The elevation I'm sure had been increasing from somewhere in west Texas, but you didn't notice as everything was so flat. Now I took notice. Spencer was leading me today. That is, he would park every couple of miles ahead of me until I arrived, see if I needed anything, then drive on a couple of more miles to wait again.

About halfway up the first mountain I suggested he go on over it and check things out in the next town, Carrizozo. We would, of course, like to secure another motel room if at all possible. So far we had only camped out just that one night west of Richmond, Virginia, and I certainly preferred a bed as opposed to a sleeping bag in a tent.

He went on, and I continued running up the mountain. The higher I got, the more the temperature dropped. I loved it! It was the first really cool weather I had been in since the marathon started eighty-three days ago. My knee was holding up today; I had cool weather; we had just left Roswell where we were very successful in our mission; and I was running strong. What better circumstances could I ask for? Well, maybe a jacket would be nice. My very light t-shirt and ultra-light nylon running shorts didn't provide much of a barrier from the now plummeting temperature.

By the time I reached the top of the mountain, I was sure it was below forty degrees. It was about then I noticed, I felt! the wind was picking up, and there were serious looking gray and black clouds closing in on me from the west. I was getting cold. No doubt about it. After eighty-three days of the worst heat of the season, I was now running downhill into a near blizzard. By the time the first icy drop-lets started pelting me by the whipped up wind, I was sure the temperature was closer to thirty-two degrees than it was to forty. Then the bottom fell out; it rained cats and dogs, and I ran harder to try to keep up my body temperature. Spencer showed up at just about the peak of the storm and rescued me, but the damage had already been done. I was chilled to the bone, which these days weren't far at all from my skin. That night I fell into bed weaker physically than I had been on the entire trip. The fact is, I had had no physical illness up to now, other than the knee problem and nearly daily exhaustion. Now I had a real problem.

The next morning I was in no shape to run and walk two miles, forget thirty! I was cold, weak, and felt like somehow a valve to my insides had been opened, and they had all flowed out. Later that day, I attempted a five-mile walk. No go. I got back in bed and rested until around 5:30 or 6:00.

I was hungry, so Spencer and I got in the van, and after a quick search through this tiny Indian village, we picked one of the two small restaurants available. The menu showed two kinds of chili: red and green. I ordered the green, thinking it would be the milder of the two. I assumed that my choice would be heavily fortified with great juicy chunks of beef, along with the red beans, onions, green peppers, mushrooms ... Instead, the bowl placed before me appeared to be a steamy pepper soup. I could not locate any of the tasty ingredients I was hoping for. Well at least it looked hot.

I dropped some crackers into the pepper soup listed on the menu as chili, let them get good and mushy, and then lifted a spoonful of steamy pepper soup to my trembling mouth. MY GOD! MY GOD! Why hast Thou forsaken me? I would have screamed if I could, but I couldn't. All I could do was gag, try to catch my breath, and locate the water glass as quickly as possible.

If I wasn't half starved, I would have gotten up and walked out right then. But there wasn't much of an option. We had little money to waste on a non-eaten meal, even if it was a volcanic eruption of hot peppers. I forced down several spoonsful of the volcano chili with no meat in it. We went back to the motel where I continued dousing the fire with glass after glass of water.

The next morning I felt not a hundred percent, but well enough to do a regular day's mileage. Years later I would experiment with the same principle I believe was responsible for my miraculous overnight recovery. Cayenne powder was the magic elixir I would use a few years later to treat just about any ailment that came along. I ordered twenty pounds of it, and for about six months, consumed more cayenne powder than an army of Mexicans. I don't know how much cayenne powder was in the volcano pepper soup-chili that night in New Mexico, but it was enough.

The next town of any size we came to was Socorro, New Mexico. Spencer's efforts to secure lodging failed to find a motel, but did produce a private residence. We were welcomed by several bachelors that lived there. With my mileage for the day completed and a meal under our belts, Spencer and I arrived at the private residence where I promptly crashed in a small bedroom which had a water bed.

Spencer, being the night-owl in our two-man team, stayed up with our hosts. It was a small house and the walls must have been thin because I could hear the talk and commotion going on in the kitchen. The bachelors and Spencer had hit it off, and a rip-roaring party was underway. The booze had been broken out, and I figure it was just a matter of time before I would smell the marijuana. That never happened, but there was still a shock waiting for me.

The boisterous laughter and talk had turned toward the subject of homosexuality. It didn't take me long to figure out that some of the four men in that kitchen were gay. I didn't think Spencer was, but as for the other three men, at least a couple of them certainly were.

I was thinking, "How can this be? I'm running across this nation, trying to be a model of clean living and abstinence from vices of all kinds, yet I find myself trying but failing to get some sleep because of a drunken, homosexual party going on in the kitchen down the hall."

I got very little sleep that night, and when daybreak finally arrived, I saw Spencer sitting on a chair, his head slumped over in his hands. He would occasionally make a low guttural whine. Hangover or no hangover, it was time for a confrontation. My patience was running out, but I couldn't get angry enough to lay the law down.

The next two days Spencer was a total wreck. He was physically ill as well as being an emotional junk heap. By the time we reached Springerville, Arizona, on October 17, he had come clean and told me about all of his drinking the last thirty days. The worst night he had was at the homosexuals' home in Socarro. He said he drank a quart of whiskey and thirty beers. My suspicions had been correct all along. He had been drinking consistently for most of the Just Say No Marathon.

All of my common sense was telling me that I was jeopardizing the entire project each day Spencer stayed with the Just Say No Marathon. I was certain that whatever credibility we had would vanish if word got out about Spencer's drinking. After all, it would have been a natural progression to link me up to drinking also.

What really bothered me was the fact that Spencer, like myself, was being interviewed by media and was talking to kids about their commitment to stay drug and alcohol free. He was a phony. He was saying one thing and doing the exact opposite. The good folks running Just Say No would have every right to disassociate themselves from the run I was making.

Despite all of this, I liked him and found it difficult to drop the ax on him. Maybe I was being the quintessential co-dependent, ignoring the obvious problem because I didn't want to face the reality. I knew the only real help for Spencer Jones in the long run, not just the next twenty-nine days the Just Say No Marathon was scheduled for was God. I said that to him and then listed the three rules which he had to follow from here on out in order to stay with the Just Say No Marathon: no more lying, no more drinking, and an 11:00 p.m. curfew. Then I asked him to take my hand. I suppose he was reluctant but in the condition he was in right now, he probably thought it would be the easiest way out.

"Dear Father in heaven, please hear our prayer this morning. Father, I lift up Spencer to You. Please give him strength, Father. Help him keep his head up and not stumble again. Take care of him, Father. Let him know that only through Jesus can he come through this fog and not let Satan trap him with alcohol or drugs. See us through our mission Father, and be with all those who are fighting against addiction. Lead us, guide us, teach us to do Your will. In Jesus name we pray. Amen."

That morning I headed for the mountains outside of Springerville trying to forget the last three days. Running and walking, being alone with God, always helped and always did and still does give me solace, peace, and hope.

Oct. 22 – Our first night in the Phoenix area we got in late and checked into our room at the very nice Days Inn in Scotsdale, a high-dollar, affluent residential and tourist area to say the least. We both watched a little TV then went to sleep. Spencer was edgy. Something was going on, but I didn't know what.

The next day I aimed my weary feet towards a soccer field a few miles away where I met a reporter from the *Scotsdale Progress*. That went off without a hitch. On my way back I was duly impressed by the very well-kept city. It looked like every blade of grass was manicured.

Nearing our motel, I was thinking about a cold shower and a snack before heading back out to do more mileage. I was walking through the beautiful, open-aired lobby and glanced over into the open patio bar, and I noticed Spencer at the bar. I walked over to him.

"What's going on? Do you want to talk about it?"

He shrugged his shoulders; he didn't say anything to me but ordered another screwdriver. I turned and went on up to our room. I showered, rested, and made a couple of phone calls.

Spencer came into the room a little later. He noticed I had gathered my stuff into a neat little bundle.

"What are you doing?" he asked.

"I've got another motel room on the other side of town. I've checked with Days Inn. You'll be able to keep this room for a couple more days. I'm sorry it didn't work out."

"Aw man. I don't know what I'm going to do."

I felt pretty bad, but I meant what I was about to say. "Spencer, I'd like to help you any way I can, but I am not going to take anybody who is drinking into California with me to finish this thing up. We had rules. You knew what they were. I'll try to help you. Let's stay in touch."

He surprised me with what he said next: "Where's the love? You're a man of God aren't you? Where's the love?"

"Spencer, love is a two-way street."

I have thought about what I said to him many times over the years. I'm not sure it conveyed my exact feelings, but it was pretty close. At any rate, just like I told him, I wasn't about to finish this thing up with a drunk at my side. We expected a lot of press coverage in L.A. There was even talk of a grand finale at the Rose Bowl in Pasadena. I would run into the Rose Bowl with Just Say No kids to the cheers of thousands of supporters. This wasn't a rumor. The Just Say No people had been talking about it for the last thirty days. Given their track record on these kinds of events, I'd believe it when I saw it. In my eyes Spencer was now a serious liability, a huge risk that could negate the credibility of the Just Say No Marathon.

I left the Scotsdale Days Inn and Spencer behind and drove across Phoenix to the Black Canyon Days Inn. I stayed there eight days. I was out early every day to get my thirty miles per day. I was building up a reserve of completed mileage so I wouldn't have to fight those miles in the worst part of the desert between Phoenix and L. A.

Phoenix is a nice looking city. It's big and noisy, but it's clean. The air is very dry. The average humidity is something like seventeen percent. I could walk and run for six hours and my t-shirt was mostly dry.

Several days in Phoenix I purposely walked through middle-class neighborhoods to shop for souvenirs I might find at garage sales. Most of the items I bought were cowboy and western stuff for the boys.

Two days after I had split up with Spencer he called me, and we talked at least a half hour. He called two additional times before I left Phoenix. All the conversations centered on what he may or may not be able to do with the rest of his life.

He wasn't blaming me for his predicament. He said he was trying to get into a program. I suggested he try God's program. That is, that he ask Jesus to take him. We talked a lot about my own "Jesus night" back in 1976.  He asked me if I read the Bible.  I told him no. Back then I didn't read the Bible.  I do now.  We talked about what it means to will your life to do good, not evil.

He said he had been under a lot of pressure when we were coming into Phoenix a few days ago.  He had just received a message from an old friend.  His friend talked about the divorce with his wife that Spencer had not known about before now.  Spencer had slept with his friend's wife, and he was feeling guilty, especially since the couple had two children.

Also, he told me that he had felt bad the first day in Phoenix because a newspaper did not want to run a story on the Just Say No Marathon.  That's when he sat down at the bar, and I walked in on him.

Oct. 31, 1986 – I'm driving west on Interstate 10.  I am eighty miles west of Phoenix, and it's all desert with mountains only in the far distance.  There are 334 miles to go to the ocean.  I'm listening to a call-in talk show on the radio.  They're talking about Halloween.  One man says, "What about the evil in the night?"

I knew a little something about evil in the night, but I am so thankful that now it doesn't seem nearly the threat it used to be.  I also thought about the day in New Mexico, just about a month ago. I was walking towards a little Indian shanty-town and noticed the largest black crow I'd ever seen flutter up from the sandy front yard of a tiny, dilapidated house.  It flew right at me but veered a little, then flew several tight circles around my head, all the while squawking like crazy.

No, it can't be!  Carlos Castenada's famous anthropological series on Native American/Southwest Indian cultures, primarily the Yaqui, was coming to life before my eyes.  In his books Castenada describes the crow as a creature laden with occult powers.  Castaneda claims that certain enlightened and highly skilled Indian medicine men, or sorcerers, can in fact transform themselves into crows.

Is this just a coincidence? There had been no crows flying around my head before now. What was this one doing? Was he trying to tell me something? After all that was about to happen with Spencer, I suppose I should have listened. No, I'm not going to lapse back into 'what-ifs' or what I could have or should have done.

The California state line is only three hours ahead. I've run and walked well over 2,450 miles. The past is behind me. I'm now on my own. Spencer helped immeasurably, but his completing the trip must have been doomed from the start. I look off to the horizons on the north and the south and wonder at the beauty of the distant mountains now bedazzling me with burnt reds, purples, crimsons, browns, and misty blues.

Nov. 2, Banning, California – I was staying at the Banning Inn, a very nice and clean motel. I walked eight miles up to the top of Cabazon Mountain and eight miles back down, then walked eleven around Banning for a total of twenty-seven miles for the day.

It was not the forty miles I had wanted. My thinking was to start knocking off forty a day so I would be able to cut the Just Say No Marathon short a few days and insure I would be home to see the last game of the season for my son Jeff's soccer team. The game was scheduled for the 15th of November.

I was also starting to think about cheating a little on mileage. Who would know? It seemed like the closer I got to the end, the harder it was to keep going. Also, my running was getting less, and my walking was getting more. As hard as I tried, I didn't seem able to increase my daily average beyond thirty miles.

Today on Cabazon Mountain I picked up some fool's gold for the boys, and while I was up there, I noticed the constant flow of air traffic coming from the east on final approach to LAX. I was getting close.

That night as I finished off the twenty-seven miles for the day, the Banning Police were checking me out. A squad car kept me in sight for over an hour. They would cruise by me in one direction, and then a few minutes later come back and do it again.

Their methods of checking me out were not unlike what I had experienced from teenage boys all along the way. I thought about all the small towns I'd been through and the pattern that the young studs took in every town. When they first saw me, they would be very vocal and aggressive. Whether in a car or on foot they would go by and check me out aggressively several times. Then they would lose interest. I never showed any signs of return aggression. I always walked or ran straight ahead, not looking at them. It was simply turf protection, and I had enough sense not to pose a threat. After all, it was their turf.

Nov. 4, Corona, CA – This is my second day in Corona. The Just Say No people have told me that a rally is planned for November 11th at Hamilton school in Pasadena, California. That will be the culmination of the marathon. No mention of the Rose Bowl and my grand entrance to the cheers of thousands. I had dreamed of such an ending but never really expected it.

I should feel elated that at least Just Say No is planning something to recognize my efforts. I don't. I'm in a blue funk for a variety of reasons. Without Spencer the message I am supposed to be carrying is dying. It is dying for two reasons: One, without him I am not getting the audience I had before; two, the fact that Spencer himself succumbed to one of his old addictions spoke volumes. It's almost as if I'm a shadow out here. Walking and running thirty miles a day for what? The only people I talk to are waitresses and motel clerks.

The other thing getting under my skin is the moral decay I'm seeing here. The difference in small-town, rural America and what I've seen here in the greater L.A. basin in only my second day here is almost unbelievable. All the talk around here is gay this or gay that. Then it drifts into prostitution, the amateur variety. Record numbers of young girls breaking into the business. Police are in a quandary because when they arrest the pimps, the girls will not testify against them. Some things I've seen right here in this motel around the noon hour get me further depressed.

"Father, I'm no saint, and I certainly have plenty of skeletons in my own closet, but to see all of this going on around me is tearing me down. It's no wonder people turn to drugs and alcohol," was my internal conversation with God this morning. I needed some help.

I noticed the gorgeous Santa Anna Mountains looming over the southwest rim of Corona and asked a lady on the street, "How do you get to the top of those mountains?"

She didn't hesitate for even a moment, "You go down there and turn right on Lincoln to Chase and turn right.  Go past the orange trees and cross the drain ditch by the canyon and turn left. St. Angeles National Park and Skyline Drive are on top.  You just follow the trail on up."

I thanked God. I knew this was His way of settling me down – getting me up on that mountaintop, alone with Him. I felt better already. It really was nice up there. I had time to collect my thoughts and reflect on who I was and why I was doing this. And I prayed.

I went up there two days in a row. The first day up there I carried my lunch with me – two bananas, three tangerines, one granny white apple, one pear, one lemon, and one canteen of water.

It took six hours to get on top and of course another six hours coming down. I walked the entire distance both days. I had hurt the knee on a twelve-mile run back in Banning. I couldn't run pain free so I walked.

The second day up there I got a late start in the morning, so by the time I came back down, it was close to midnight. It was very cool on top of the mountain that night, and the stars were twinkling brightly. I was above the smog but started choking on it when the elevation decreased as I stumbled down the mountain in the dark. These two days of walking and talking with God did me a lot of good.

The next morning I was preparing to leave Corona and drive on into L.A. on the Riverside Freeway. At the restaurant where I was having breakfast I was uplifted again. My waitress said, "Just one person can make a difference. We thank you for what you've done." My spirits were restored, and full of confidence I aimed the van towards L.A. I knew I could meet any challenge the next six days had in store for me.

I got settled into the Days Inn motel just east of LAX. I was in my room studying street maps of L.A. With only six days left I wanted to maximize my walking. That is, I wanted to see as much of the city as I could. Careful planning would be important. The knee was in such bad shape I did not want to risk further injury to it by running. So it came down to this: my glorious dream of running from coast to coast was never to be. Of course, I'd known this since before we started back on July 17th. I would walk around L.A. the final six days, but at least I would complete every inch of the marathon on foot. Or would I? The notion of cheating on my daily mileage continued to tempt me.

The phone rang in my room. A lady introduced herself and explained that she was a local Just Say No leader and that she was helping with the planning of the Just Say No rally on November 11th in Pasadena. Could we get together and go over a few things?

I thought *how strange*. I had been running and walking under the Just Say No banner for almost four months now, and I never had a higher-up in the Just Say No chain of command want to get with me personally one on one. Spencer had handled all of the communications and liaisons with Just Say No, so maybe this was perfectly innocent and not out of the ordinary. But still, something just didn't sound or feel right about this lady's call. I told her I was sorry, but I was behind on my mileage and that today I needed to get out there and put miles behind me. I *was* behind on my mileage. Cheating a little was starting to look better every minute. I finished my map study and headed out onto the streets of infamous South Central L.A.

My plans were to walk to the USC campus. Armed with my map, notes, a couple of small water bottles in my fanny pack, and some snacks for lunch, I started out. The weather was near perfect. Some of the notorious L.A. smog had been blown out. I was looking forward to seeing a few sights today. The Great Western Forum was on my way to USC, but I didn't stop to take a close look at it. I was trying to make miles.

I was about two miles south of the USC campus and saw him about a block away. The black dope pusher was working this black neighborhood for all it was worth. An almost steady stream of cars would pull over to the curb; he went to the window, an exchange was made, and then he quickly scanned both sides of the street.

On the same side of the street he was on, his quick scan revealed a tall, skinny, white guy walking toward him. The guy was wearing skimpy green running shorts, almost new running shoes, a Vietnam style brown bush hat, a fanny pack, and WHOA! - a green t-shirt with a large white Just Say No insignia on it. The pusher had spotted me spotting him, and we both knew it.

*Think quickly Gary! What are you going to do now?* My gut instincts told me to do the same thing I had always done in these situations. *Don't, I repeat, DON'T make eye contact. Just keep on walking past him as if you never saw him.* Yes, we had visually made contact, but not the eye to eye, 'looking inside' contact that he would have interpreted as a threat. That would have been impossible from a block away.

I shouldn't have been so worried. He was making an exchange with a customer as I walked by less than twenty-five feet away. He probably had never heard of Just Say No, or if he had, it wasn't about to slow down his free market enterprises this afternoon. I walked by and never looked back.

Over the years and after a great deal of reflection on my involvement in the Just Say No movement of the late eighties, I would come to look back at my 'look the other way' that day in Los Angeles as one of the reasons why we fail so completely as a society at winning the war on drugs.

Not confronting that pusher on that street corner in L.A. that day made me just another big mouth saying all the things we ought to do but not willing personally to get my hands dirty. I've tried to do better since then. I've tried over and over again to get the attention of officials here in middle Tennessee and share some of the insight I gained from the Just Say No Marathon, and I've been involved in other ways, but I think I'll always regret not confronting that pusher back in L.A.

The USC campus was smaller than I had expected. I found the student bulletin board and posted a note on it that I was looking for a co-driver to go back east with me on November 11. If there was any way to speed up my trip back to Tennessee I was going to use it.

I walked back toward my motel, stopped to eat at a Bob's Big Boy on Century Boulevard, and then went to the motel to check for messages. The lady from Just Say No had called again. I still had miles to do. I didn't call her back. Instead I headed out toward the airport. I was awfully lonely, and at least at the airport I would be around a lot of people.

November 7 – I drove from the motel to the UCLA campus, parked the van, and continued my walking tour. Today I went to Santa Monica, then north toward Malibu. Tomorrow I would again park at UCLA, but from there I would walk to Sunset Boulevard, Bellaire, and Pacific Palisades where I would watch youngsters playing soccer.

I got more anxious for the marathon to be completed. I wanted very badly to see Jeff play soccer about a week from now back in Tennessee.

I got back to the motel; then I went to the same Bob's Big Boy where I had been eating for several days. There were two waitresses there that I enjoyed talking with. One was a twenty-eight year old from the Virgin Islands, and the other girl was from Mexico. We talked about family and God.

They both told me that back in their old countries a girl's family had to approve of the man she would marry. Also, they both believed in God, but not always in the church. In my mind I was thinking about my own belief in God and where it had led me thus far and where would it lead me in the future?

November 9 – With the exception of ten miles that I ran, the rest of my mileage for the day was spent walking two circles around the outside perimeter of LAX which I would guess was around ten miles each trip. On my first trip around I spotted a drunk sitting on a curb and then three hours later on my second trip around, he was still sitting in the same spot. He didn't look like he had moved an inch. I asked him if he wanted to talk.

"No. I take care of myself."

November 10 – I walked the now-familiar ten miles around LAX, went back to the motel for a quick map study, and then started out walking in the direction of Hollywood. Before leaving the motel, my messages indicated that the Just Say No Lady had called again. Apparently she had given up on wanting to get together with me to "go over a few things." She simply gave me the address of the Hamilton School in Pasadena and the time for the event to start – tomorrow at 1:00 p.m.

I walked as far as I could in the direction of Hollywood. The route I was using was easier than the route I took to the USC campus several days ago because the roads stayed out of blatant dope dealing turf. It was maybe an hour before sunset when I decided to turn back south toward the motel. I didn't make it all the way to Hollywood, but I figured I would need a good night's rest before the final day's activities tomorrow.

On my way back I was reviewing in my mind the mileage records that I kept, usually scribbled down on the worn edges of my maps. I realized that because the Just Say No Marathon was ending two days earlier than I planned, that there was no way I was going to be able to finish up the actual mileage I owed by tomorrow's Just Say No event at 1:00 p.m.

I finally got back to my room after midnight and looked hard at all of my mileage records. I went over the records several times. I was going to be thirty-three miles short of the promise I had made to average thirty miles a day. I was dead tired. There would be no running or walking tonight or tomorrow before the 1:00 Just Say No event.

I felt like I would be viewed as a fraud, a nut case who talked a mean game, but just could not completely pull it off. I could not sleep. At 2:00 in the morning, I started praying and continued for some time. I needed help on what I would say to the students at the Hamilton School tomorrow, and I needed answers on what to do about the thirty-three mile deficit I would have.

# Chapter Twelve

November 11, 1986 – The final day of the just Say No Marathon. I didn't sleep last night. I stayed in my room until 8:00 a.m. I felt remarkably well. Something was pushing me on. I had another huge breakfast then drove to Pasadena. I located the Hamilton School but didn't stay as it was only 11:00 a.m.

I parked near Colorado Boulevard and walked three miles, then drove back to the Hamilton School. The thirty-three miles I owed was now down to thirty. All night long I had worried over what I was going to do, and the answer finally came. I would finish the mileage after the ceremony. What else could I do?

The Hamilton School was an average size elementary school. An assembly was arranged in the auditorium. There were to be five or six speakers. Jim Brown, the nationally recognized sports anchor was the announcer. He introduced each speaker. The list included school officials, politicians, Just Say No officials, and me.

I don't recall the exact order of the speakers, but I remember I was either the next to last or the last speaker. Before the ceremony I was told I'd have about five minutes. I probably finished under the allotted time.

God's answer to my prayer last night was to tell the truth. So that's what I did. I looked out at the throng of young children and told them I didn't sleep last night, and that I started praying and asking God to help me with what I should say today. I told them that God's answer was for me to tell the truth.

"You'll never achieve your dreams with drugs. I know, because I couldn't. You are in control of your own life. You can be popular without drugs. It's a lie when others turn you on to drugs, or when your parents allow you to use drugs and alcohol. In Los Angeles I've seen two things that help explain this."

I told them about the conversations I had with the waitress from the Virgin Islands a couple of days ago. The girl told me that in her country they believed that parents know best. I said that's fine as long as the parents don't lie about drugs and alcohol.

I told the children, "I know some of your parents abuse drugs and alcohol and that some of them abuse the drugs and alcohol with you. If that's the case with you, you must not only just say no, you must also try to help educate your parents to just say no."

I looked around at the adults, the important people, the dignitaries, and noticed that some of them were visibly uneasy. They avoided my eyes. Jim Brown was getting fidgety. He was ready to conclude this thing.

"The other thing I've seen here is the tremendous success George McKenna has had turning around an inner city school program from failure to success. His secret was educating the parents as well as the students.

"Your responsibility is two-fold: If your parents tell you the truth and live the truth, you should spread the word to just say no. If your parents lie, you must educate them first.

"A runner carries a message. I've come nearly three thousand miles on foot to bring you a simple message. Just say no to drugs and alcohol and help us educate those who are weaker to say the same thing – JUST SAY NO! Thank you."

I thought I heard a collective sigh of relief that I didn't continue in the direction I was going. Sorry – that's the way I felt about it. And don't forget, God did tell me to speak the truth.

Jim Brown wrapped up the proceedings inside, and then we all went outside for the flag-raising ceremony. The White House had sent a special Just Say No flag to be raised for the event today. The kids and I recited the Just Say No pledge, and a couple of songs were sung, a few pictures were taken, and it was over.

My celebrity status faded quickly. There would be no more TV, radio, and press coverage. No more women calling to "go over a few things." On the plus side, there would also be no more lonely motels, no more bottles thrown at me on the outskirts of some dusty western hamlet, and no more worrying about Debbie, the boys, and my still unborn third child.

It was over. Well it was almost over. I still had thirty miles to do. In order for me to be able to live with myself for the rest of my life, I intended to do them.

It would have been easy to pack it up right then and drive east to Tennessee, and I was very, very close to doing just that. Instead, I drove back to the same parking lot I was in earlier today, off Colorado Boulevard. I counted the buck and a half of change I had left and inventoried what little food was left in the van, ate most of it, greased up with sunblock, and started walking.

"This is for the kids," I told myself. "No, I don't have to do it. Nobody would ever know." But as I told the crowd just a half hour ago, we lie to the kids too much. No, nobody would ever know that I cheated at the very end – nobody but me. "I'm not going to lie to them."

Having thus bolstered my resolve, I continued walking. Nearing a large church, I noticed ten or fifteen homeless souls, some on the steps to the entrance. Others sprawled out in the large, grassy, almost a park area, between the sidewalk and the entrance.

One lady, I guessed around sixty-five or seventy, caught my attention. I stopped and we started talking. She was a charmer, and I could see her forty years ago as a real California beauty. All of her belongings were in the plastic bag at her side. In just a few minutes she recounted much of her life story, including her Spanish ancestry and her husband's death which resulted in her receiving a monthly check for $69 from social security because of his veteran status.

Her name was Isadora Mata. I felt Isadora and I had some things in common. She was on a very limited income. I was on no income at all. She was alone. I was alone. Her glory days of beauty and status were behind her. My recent grasp at fame was flowing away even as we talked. I thought it fitting that we met and talked for a few minutes.

The afternoon wore on. I walked out to the Rose Bowl and was able to get a good look at it inside and out. Then I turned back toward downtown Pasadena, and by the time I made it back, night was closing in quickly.

I estimated that I had about nine or ten miles more to do. There was no doubt in my mind that I would finish off those ten miles. You might think I was starting to celebrate and rejoice in being so close to completing the journey, but I wasn't.

I was walking along in a middle class residential neighborhood some ways south of downtown. I could see the lights in the homes, a TV set flickering, a car pulling in or out of a driveway, a dog barking – all the normal mundane things of America at home in the evening with family. I felt pretty low. I wouldn't see my family for a couple more days.

I thought about today's ceremony, the words I had said, and the real truth about our country's so-called 'War on Drugs.' Yes, the Just Say No organization was focusing their efforts in the right direction, our youth. More correctly stated, they were focusing their efforts in one of the right directions. All the other things that could and should be done – not necessarily by Just Say No, but by the government and the people – for the most part, have been relegated to the "it would be good if we did launch a frontal assault type of war on drugs, but we have bigger fish to fry" school of thought. When it comes right down to it, each one of us will wrestle with the choices we have, to put unhealthy stuff into our bodies or not. You know the adage, "If there were no demand, the supply would dry up."

It was around 9:00 p.m. My knee was the worst it had been on the entire trip, and I wasn't even running. My right hip was hurting a great deal. It was a good thing I only had three or four miles to go. I turned north back toward Colorado Boulevard, spotted a coffee shop, and walked in. With my last buck and a half, I purchased a cup of coffee and drank it as I slowly made my way to Colorado Boulevard and turned left, heading back toward the minivan. I was thinking about the Bo Jangles rag doll back in Virginia Beach the night before I started the Just Say No Marathon, and I thought about the sign he had, "California or Bust." About thirty seconds later I was at a side street intersecting Colorado Boulevard. I looked up to read the street sign. It said Virginia Avenue.

My spirits were lifted. God's little personal message to me confirmed that the 1986 Just Say No Marathon had nearly come full circle. I had less than a mile to go.

As I approached the minivan, a perfect feeling of peace and calm overcame me. I felt as though fifty tons were being removed from my body. No one was around. The city was quiet. I said the Lord's Prayer and got in the van, fumbled around for my keys, and then started the motor. My spirits were definitely picking up now. Tape recorder rolling, this is what came out of my mouth:

"Old buddy, I'm here to tell you, she's fired up. Ya hear that? Got her shifted into 1st. You hear that? And by gosh, the Lord willing and the moon keep shining, I'm coming home. It's over. Okay here we go. The time is 11:30 here in Pasadena, California, the Rose Bowl City. The marathon has been completed as of five minutes ago. Now I'm in the car, the nose is in the wind. I'm heading east, and I'm Dickson bound. Yellow Creek, here I come. Edgewood, I'll never leave you again."

I drove east, deep into the desert that night, slept three or four hours, then drove to eastern New Mexico the next day, into Arkansas the next day, and finally arrived home well before noon on the third day. The next day was Saturday, and I was at the soccer field watching my son, Jeff, play soccer.

THE WHITE HOUSE
WASHINGTON

December 24, 1986

Dear Mr. Baker:

Congratulations!  Your cross-country run is yet another
heartwarming sign of an American determination to pull
together and support the national crusade against drug
abuse.

Wherever Nancy and I go, we have been encouraged by the
growing resolve among young people to say no to illegal
drugs.  To reach our goal of a drug-free America, we need
the commitment of every citizen.  Your courageous display
of public concern has been an encouragement to us and
especially to those you met along the way.  You can be
proud of your accomplishment and the tremendous consensus
you are helping to build with the "Just Say No" clubs.
The dedication of concerned and public-spirited individuals
like yourself make me more confident than ever that we will
stand together in this battle -- and that we will win.

Nancy joins me in sending you our heartfelt appreciation
and best wishes.

Sincerely,

Ronald Reagan

Mr. Gary Baker
Rural Route 3
Dickson, Tennessee  37055

## *Postscript*

Nothing God does surprises me anymore. That may be the supreme lesson I learned, not only from the Just Say No Marathon, but also the following twenty years. I could tell you lots of miraculous things that have happened to me since 1986. I have simply come to expect that truly "With God all things are possible." I know it so deeply, so profoundly, and I've known it for so long now, that I wear it very comfortably – probably too comfortably. That is, sometimes I feel like I should be more vocal about my certainty of the knowledge I possess about how God can take over one's life. But in His way and in His timing, He always provides me an outlet to witness His workings.

All of this is about a few very simple things:
1) God is alive and works in our lives every day.
2) To get America where it should be, we have to do things for others. We have to give more of ourselves to those who need help.
3) We must have huge dreams, and we must allow individuals and organizations of all sizes the opportunity to pursue those dreams.

All I did was to pursue my dream, and as soon as I put it in God's hands everything worked out. I simply encourage everyone to put their lives in God's hands and to seek ways to help others, and I believe their dreams will come true.

Gary H. Baker grew up in Louisville, Kentucky and is proud to claim his status as an "original baby boomer". The class of '46 was just that, and it marched off into the 60s as a force to be reckoned with. While some protested, and some sought peace and love, Gary did a four year enlistment in the Navy and pulled a tour of duty off the coast of Vietnam. He later earned an undergraduate degree from the University of Hawaii and a master's degree in alternative education from Indiana University. Along the way Gary worked as a bouncer, bartender, teacher, coach, coffee salesman, insurance salesman, financial services broker, lawn care business owner, and truck driver. Gary currently calls himself a novelist.

In 1986, Gary ran two thousand seven hundred miles in four months to promote the Just Say No clubs, the forerunner to DARE (drug abuse resistance education). Gary sees his writing as an attempt to follow God. Jesus is his Savior, and Gary will tell you quickly that he falls short most of the time, but that won't keep him from trying again.

# THE TRUCK DRIVER SERIES

Rookie Truck Driver
West Bound, Hammer Down, Trouble in Montana
Truck Dreams
If My People …

Information on these books is available at the author's website:
*www.garyhbaker.com*